Fitz-Greene Halleck, Joseph Rodman Drake

The Poetical Writings of Fitz-Greene Halleck

With extracts from those of Joseph Rodman Drake

Fitz-Greene Halleck, Joseph Rodman Drake

The Poetical Writings of Fitz-Greene Halleck
With extracts from those of Joseph Rodman Drake

ISBN/EAN: 9783337105440

Printed in Europe, USA, Canada, Australia, Japan

Cover: Foto ©Andreas Hilbeck / pixelio.de

More available books at **www.hansebooks.com**

Yours truly,
Fitz-Greene Halleck

O F

FITZ-GREENE HALLECK

THE

POETICAL WRITINGS

OF

FITZ-GREENE HALLECK,

WITH EXTRACTS FROM THOSE OF

JOSEPH RODMAN DRAKE.

EDITED BY

JAMES GRANT WILSON.

NEW YORK:
D. APPLETON AND COMPANY,
1, 3, AND 5 BOND STREET.
1882.

PREFACE.

IN this volume will be found all the poetical writings of the late FITZ-GREENE HALLECK included in previous editions, together with a score of poems which the editor has succeeded in recovering from various sources, and which are marked by the characteristic grace and melody of his most admired compositions; also several translations from the French, German, and Italian, that now appear in print for the first time. Among the pieces never before published, are a number of juvenile productions, which may be recognized by the dates appended to them. Between the earliest poem contained in this collection and the latest, a period of threescore and three years intervened. "The Tempest" was written by the handsome and happy schoolboy of fourteen, in the

fourth year of the present century , a translation from the German was made by the
gray - haired veteran who had passed, by
seven summers, the allotted period of man's
life; while **Mr.** Halleck's latest original poem
—" Young **America** "—was written **near** the
close **of the year** 1863, **beneath the shadows**
of the same grand old Guilford **elms** under
which the poet was born and buried.

" THE CROAKERS," that now appear for **the**
first time with Halleck's poetical writings, are
the joint production **of** the attached friends
Fitz - Greene Halleck and Joseph Rodman
Drake. The origin **of these** sprightly *jeux
d'esprit*, as eagerly looked for each evening
as were the war-bulletins of a later day, may
not be without interest to the authors' troops
of admirers. Halleck and Drake were spend-
ing a Sunday morning with Dr. William Langstaff, an eccentric apothecary **and** an accomplished mineralogist, **with** whom they were
both intimate (the **two** last mentioned were
previously fellow-students in the study of
medicine with Drs. Bruce and Romayne),
when **Drake,** for his **own and** his friends'

amusement, wrote several burlesque stanzas
"To Ennui," Halleck answering them in some
lines on the same subject. The young poets
decided to send their productions, with others
of the same character, to William Coleman, the
editor of the *Evening Post.* If he published
them, they would write more; if not, they
would offer them to Major M. M. Noah, of the
National Advocate ; and if he declined their
poetical progeny, they would light their pipes
with them. Drake accordingly sent Coleman
three pieces of his own, signed " CROAKER,"
a signature adopted from an amusing character in Goldsmith's comedy of "The Good-
natured Man." To their astonishment, a paragraph appeared in the *Post* the day following,
acknowledging their receipt, promising the
insertion of the poems, pronouncing them to
be the productions of superior taste and genius,
and begging the honor of a personal acquaintance with the author. The lines "To Ennui"
appeared March 10, 1819, and the others in
almost daily succession ; those written by Mr.
Halleck being usually signed " Croaker Junior,"
while those which were their joint composition

generally bore the signature **of** "Croaker and Co."

The remark made **by** Coleman had excited **public attention, and "THE** CROAKERS" soon **became a subject of** conversation in drawing-**rooms,** book-stores, coffee-houses, on **Broad-**way, and throughout the **city; they were, in** short, a town topic. The two friends contrib-uted other pieces; and when the editor **again** expressed great anxiety to be acquainted with **the** writer, and used **a** style so mysterious as **to excite their** curiosity, the literary partners **decided to call upon him.** Halleck and Drake accordingly, **one** evening, went together, to Coleman's residence in Hudson Street, **and** requested an interview. They were ushered **into** the parlor, the editor soon entered, the young poets expressed a desire for a few min-utes' strictly private conversation with him, and the door being closed and locked, Dr. Drake **said—"I am** Croaker, **and this** gentleman, sir, is Croaker **Junior."** Coleman stared **at the young men** with indescribable and unaffected astonishment,—at length exclaiming: "My God, **I had no idea** that **we had** such talents in America!" Halleck, with his characteristic modesty, was disposed to give to Drake all the credit; but as it chanced that Coleman alluded in particularly glowing terms to one of the Croakers that was wholly his, he was forced to be silent, and the delighted editor continued in a strain of compliment and eulogy that put them both to the blush. Before taking their leave, the poets bound Coleman over to the most profound secrecy, and arranged a plan of sending him the MS., and of receiving the proofs, in a manner that would avoid the least possibility of the secret of their connection with "THE CROAKERS" being discovered. The poems were copied from the originals by Langstaff, that their handwriting should not divulge the secret, and were either sent through the mail, or taken to the *Evening-Post* office by Benjamin R. Winthrop, then a fellow-clerk with Mr. Halleck, in the counting-house of the well-known banker and merchant Jacob Barker, in Wall Street.

Hundreds of imitations of "THE CROAK-ERS" were daily received by the different editors of New York, to all of which they gave publicly

one general answer, that **they** lacked the
genius, spirit, and beauty of the originals.   On
one occasion Coleman showed Halleck fifteen
he had received **in a** single morning, **all**
of which, with a solitary exception, **were con-**
signed to the waste-basket.   **The friends con-**
tinued for several months to keep the city in a
blaze of excitement ; and it **was observed by**
one of the editors, "that **so great was the**
wincing and shrinking at 'THE CROAKERS,'
that every person was on tenter-hooks ; neither
knavery **nor** folly **has** slept quietly since our
first commencement."   **Of** this series of satiri-
cal and quaint chronicles of New-York life half
a century ago, Halleck, in 1866, said **"that**
they were good-natured verses contributed
anonymously to the columns of the New-York
Evening Post, from March to June, 1819, **and**
occasionally afterward.   The writers **con-**
tinued, like the author of Junius, **the sole de-**
positaries of **their own secret, and** apparently
wished, with the Minstrel **in Leyden's** "Scenes
of Infancy," **to**

> "Save others' names, but leave their own unsung."

Among "THE CROAKERS" will be found three

hitherto unpublished pieces from the pen of Mr. Halleck, and, in lieu of the original signatures, the author of each poem is now for the first time made known by the letters H and D; when both letters occur, they indicate the joint authorship of the literary partners, or, to quote Halleck's familiar words to a friend, "that we each had a finger in the pie."

FITZ-GREENE, a descendant of PETER HALLECK or HALLOCK, one of thirteen Pilgrim Fathers who landed at New Haven, Connecticut, in 1640, and of the Rev. John Eliot, the "Apostle to the Indians," who arrived at Boston, Massachusetts, in 1631, was one of the earliest, as he was among the most eminent, of American poets. He left no son to wear his honors, or to perpetuate his name, but, unlike his favorite *Roi d' Yvetot*, there is little danger of his being "*peu connu dans l'histoire.*" When all those whose privilege it was to know the genial poet, and to have been honored by his friendship, shall have passed away, and when the enduring granite obelisk which now marks his grave shall have crumbled to dust, the name and fame of the sweet singer who celebrated in im-

mortal song the glories of the modern Epami-
nondas, will remain fresh and green, not only
in the country of his birth, but in the land of
Bozzaris.   In England, his "Alnwick Castle,"

"Home of the Percy's high-born race,"

will long preserve his name from oblivion;
while in Scotland, the song he sang in praise
of Burns will forever connect him with her
greatest poet.   "Nothing finer has been
written about Robert than Mr. Halleck's
poem," said Isabella, the youngest sister of
the Ayrshire bard, as she gave the writer, in
the summer of 1855, some rose-buds from her
garden, and leaves of ivy plucked from her
cottage door, near the banks of the bonny
Doon, to carry back to his gifted friend.
Neither will those exquisitely beautiful and
tender lines, so familiar to all, in which the early death of his chosen companion and literary
partner, Dr. Drake, was mourned by Mr. Halleck, be soon forgotten.   They are, and will
continue to be, an enduring monument to both
the poets, wherever the English language is
read or spoken.   Like Thomas Campbell,

whose poetical writings he so much admired, Fitz-Greene Halleck gave to the world but few poems — " heirlooms forever " to be prized and cherished by his countrymen through the coming ages and generations, with

> " Earth's and sea's rich gems,
> With April's first-born flowers,
> And all things rare."

The arrangement of the poems, as made by the poet in the last edition of 1858, has been closely followed in this volume, without reference to their chronological order; and in other particulars the present publication has been made to conform to Mr. Halleck's wishes, as expressed to the writer at their last interview, but a few weeks before

> " He gave his honors to the world again,
> His blessed part to heaven, and slept in peace."

The share of the editor in this volume can scarcely be regarded too slightly. He cannot even claim the credit for the notes, as a portion of them were prepared by the poet himself. Among the notes to the Miscellaneous Poems, the first nine will be recognized as

having appeared in all previous editions, while
the notes to "Fanny" and "The Recorder"
are, with a few slight alterations and additions,
substantially Mr. Halleck's; and to him, therefore, the editor trusts will be awarded the
credit for whatever may be found among
them worthy of praise.

51 St. Mark's Place,
New York, *August,* 1868

CONTENTS.

MISCELLANEOUS POEMS.

MARCO BOZZARIS.[1]

A T midnight, in his guarded tent,
  The Turk was dreaming of the hour
When Greece, her knee in suppliance bent,
  Should tremble at his power:
In dreams, through camp and court, he bore
The trophies of a conqueror;
  In dreams his song of triumph heard;
Then wore his monarch's signet ring:
Then pressed that monarch's throne—a king;
As wild his thoughts, and gay of wing,
  As Eden's garden bird.

At midnight, in the forest shades,
  Bozzaris ranged his Suliote band,
True as the steel of their tried blades,
  Heroes in heart and hand.
There had the Persian's thousands stood,

There had the glad earth drunk their blood
  On old Platæa's day;
And now there breathed that haunted air
The sons of sires who conquered there,
With arm to strike and soul to dare,
  As quick, as far as they. .

An hour passed on—the Turk awoke;
  That bright dream was his last;
He woke—to hear his sentries shriek,
"To arms! they come! the Greek! the Greek!"
He woke—to die midst flame, and smoke,
And shout, and groan, and sabre-stroke,
  And death-shots falling thick and fast
As lightnings from the mountain-cloud;
And heard, with voice as trumpet loud,
  Bozzaris cheer his band:
"Strike—till the last armed foe expires;
Strike—for your altars and your fires;
Strike—for the green graves of your sires;
  God—and your native land!"

They fought—like brave men, long and well;
  They piled that ground with Moslem slain,
They conquered—but Bozzaris fell,
  Bleeding at every vein.
His few surviving comrades saw
His smile when rang their proud hurrah,
  And the red field was won;

Then saw in death his eyelids close
Calmly, as to a night's repose,
  Like flowers at set of sun.

Come to the bridal-chamber, Death !
  Come to the mother's, when she feels.
For the first time, her first-born's breath ;
  Come when the blessed seals
That close the pestilence are broke,
And crowded cities wail its stroke ;
Come in consumption's ghastly form,
The earthquake shock, the ocean-storm ;
Come when the heart beats high and warm,
  With banquet-song, and dance and wine ;
And thou art terrible—the tear,
The groan, the knell, the pall, the bier ;
And all we know, or dream, or fear
  Of agony, are thine.

But to the hero, when his sword
  Has won the battle for the free,
Thy voice sounds like a prophet's word ;
And in its hollow tones are heard
  The thanks of millions yet to be.
Come, when his task of fame is wrought—
Come, with her laurel-leaf, blood bought—
  Come in her crowning hour—and then
Thy sunken eye's unearthly light
To him is welcome as the sight

Of sky and stars to **prisoned men :**
Thy grasp is welcome as the hand
Of brother in a foreign land ;
Thy summons welcome as the cry
That told the Indian isles were nigh
   To the world-seeking Genoese.
When the land wind, from woods of palm,
And orange-groves, and fields of balm,
   Blew o'er the Haytian seas.

Bozzaris ! with the storied brave
   Greece nurtured in her glory's time,
Rest thee—there is no prouder grave,
   Even in her own proud clime.
She wore no funeral-weeds for thee,
   Nor bade the dark hearse wave its plume
Like torn branch from **death's leafless tree**
In sorrow's pomp and pageantry,
   The heartless luxury of the tomb :
But she remembers thee as one
Long loved and for a season gone ;
For thee her poet's lyre is wreathed,
Her marble wrought, her music breathed ;
For thee she rings the birthday bells ;
Of thee her babes' first lisping tells ;
For thine her evening prayer is said
At palace-couch and cottage-bed ;
Her soldier, closing with **the** foe,
Gives for thy sake a deadlier **blow ;**

His plighted maiden, when she fears
For him the joy of her young years,
Thinks of thy fate, and checks her tears:
   And she, the mother of thy boys,
Though in her eye and faded cheek
Is read the grief she will not speak,
   The memory of her buried joys,
And even she who gave thee birth,
Will, by their pilgrim-circled hearth,
   Talk of thy doom without a sigh:
For thou art Freedom's now, and Fame's;
One of the few, the immortal names,
   That were not born to die.

ALNWICK CASTLE.[1]

OME of the Percy's high-born race,
  Home of their beautiful and brave,
Alike their birth and burial-place,
  Their cradle and their grave !
Still sternly o'er the castle gate
Their house's Lion stands in state,
· As in his proud departed hours ;
And warriors frown in stone on high,
And feudal banners "flout the sky"
  Above his princely towers.

A gentle hill its side inclines,
  Lovely in England's fadeless green,
To meet the quiet stream which winds
  Through this romantic scene
As silently and sweetly still,
As when, at evening, on that hill,
  While summer's wind blew soft and low,
Seated by gallant Hotspur's side,
His Katherine was a happy bride,
  A thousand years ago.

Gaze on the Abbey's ruined **pile :**
  Does not the succoring **ivy,** keeping
Her watch around it, **seem to** smile,
  As o'er a loved one sleeping?
One solitary turret gray
  Still tells, in melancholy glory,
The legend of the Cheviot day,
  The Percy's proudest border story.
That day its roof was triumph's arch ;
  Then rang, **from** aisle to **pictured dome,**
The light step **of the soldier's march,**
  The music of the trump and drum ;
And babe, and sire, the old, **the** young,
And **the monk's** hymn, and minstrel's song,
And woman's pure kiss, sweet and long,
  Welcomed her warrior home.

Wild roses by the Abbey **towers**
  Are gay in their young bud and **bloom :**
They were born of **a race of** funeral-flowers
That garlanded, in long-gone hours,
  A templar's knightly tomb.
He died, the sword in his mailed hand,
On **the** holiest spot of the Blessed land,
  Where the Cross was damped with his dying **breath,**
When blood ran free as festal wine,
And the sainted air of Palestine
  Was thick with the darts of death.

2

Wise with the lore of centuries,
What tales, if there be " tongues in trees,'
  Those giant oaks could tell,
Of beings born and buried here ;
Tales of the peasant and the peer,
Tales of the bridal and the bier,
  The welcome and farewell,
Since on their boughs the startled bird
First, in her twilight slumbers, heard
  The Norman's curfew-bell !

I wandered through the lofty halls
  Trod by the Percys of old fame,
And traced upon the chapel walls
  Each high, heroic name,
From him[3] who once his standard set
Where now, o'er mosque and minaret,
  Glitter the Sultan's crescent moons ;
To him who, when a younger son,
Fought for King George at Lexington,[4]
  A major of dragoons.

That last half stanza—it has dashed
  From my warm lip the sparkling cup ;
The light that o'er my eyebeam flashed,
  The power that bore my spirit up
Above this bank-note world—is gone ;
And Alnwick's but a market town,
And this, alas ! its market day.

And beasts and borderers throng the way;
Oxen and bleating lambs in lots,
Northumbrian boors and plaided Scots,
   Men in the coal and cattle line;
From Teviot's bard and hero land,
From royal Berwick's[5] beach of sand,
From Wooller, Morpeth, Hexham, and
   Newcastle-upon-Tyne.

These are not the romantic times
So beautiful in Spenser's rhymes,
   So dazzling to the dreaming boy:
Ours are the days of fact, not fable, ·
Of knights, but not of the round table,
   Cf Bailie Jarvie, not Rob Roy:
'Tis what "our President," Monroe,
   Has called "the era of good feeling:"
The Highlander, the bitterest foe
To modern laws, has felt their blow,
Consented to be taxed, and vote,
And put on pantaloons and coat,
   And leave off cattle-stealing:
Lord Stafford mines for coal and salt,
The Duke of Norfolk deals in malt,
   The Douglass in red herrings;
And noble name and cultured land,
Palace, and park, and vassal-band,
Are powerless to the notes of hand
   Of Rothschild or the Barings.

The age of bargaining, said Burke,
Has come: to-day the turbaned Turk
(Sleep, Richard of the lion heart !
Sleep on, nor from your cerements start)
   Is England's friend and fast ally ;
The Moslem tramples on the Greek,
   And on the Cross and altar-stone,
   And Christendom looks tamely on,
And hears the Christian maiden shriek,
   And sees the Christian father die ;
And not a sabre-blow is given
For Greece and fame, for faith and heaven,
   By Europe's craven chivalry.

You'll ask if yet the Percy lives
   In the armed pomp of feudal state ?
The present representatives
   Of Hotspur and his " gentle Kate,"
Are some half-dozen serving-men
In the drab coat of William Penn ;
   A chambermaid, whose lip and eye,
And cheek, and brown hair, bright and curling,
   Spoke Nature's aristocracy ;
And one, half groom, half seneschal,
Who bowed me through court, bower, and hall,
From donjon-keep to turret wall,
   For ten-and-sixpence sterling.

BURNS.

TO A ROSE, BROUGHT FROM NEAR ALLOWAY KIRK, IN AYRSHIRE, IN THE AUTUMN OF 1822.

WILD Rose of Alloway! my thanks;
   Thou 'mindst me of that autumn noon
When first we met upon "the banks
   And braes o' bonny Doon."

Like thine, beneath the thorn-tree's bough,
   My sunny hour was glad and brief,
We've crossed the winter sea, and thou
   Art withered—flower and leaf.

And will not thy death-doom be mine—
   The doom of all things wrought of clay—
And withered my life's leaf like thine,
   Wild rose of Alloway?

Not so his memory, for whose sake
   My bosom bore thee far and long,
His—who a humbler flower could make
   Immortal as his song,

The memory of Burns—a name
That calls, when brimmed her festal **cup,**
A nation's glory and her shame,
In silent sadness up.

A nation's glory—be the rest
Forgot—she's canonized his min**d;**
And it is joy to speak the **best**
We may of human kind.

I've stood beside the cottage-bed
Where the Bard-peasant first drew breath;
A straw-thatched roof above his head,
A straw-wrought couch beneath.

And I have stood beside **the pile,**
His monument—that tells to Heaven
The homage of earth's proudest isle
To that Bard-peasant given!

Bid thy thoughts hover **o'er that spot,**
Boy-minstrel, in thy dreaming **hour;**
And know, however low his lot,
A **Poet's pride** and power:

The pride that lifted Burns **from earth,**
The power that gave **a child of song**
Ascendency o'er rank and **birth,**
The rich, the brave, the strong;

And if despondency weigh down
  Thy spirit's fluttering pinions then,
Despair—thy name is written on
  The roll of common men.

There have been loftier themes than his,
  And longer scrolls, and louder lyres,
And lays lit up with Poesy's
  Purer and holier fires:

Yet read the names that know not death;
  Few nobler ones than Burns are there;
And few have won a greener wreath
  Than that which binds his hair.

His is that language of the heart,
  In which the answering heart would speak,
Thought, word, that bids the warm tear start,
  Or the smile light the cheek;

And his that music, to whose tone
  The common pulse of man keeps time,
In cot or castle's mirth or moan,
  In cold or sunny clime.

And who hath heard his song, nor knelt
  Before its spell with willing knee,
And listened, and believed, and felt
  The Poet's mastery

O'er the mind's sea, in calm and storm,
  O'er the heart's sunshine and its showers,
O'er Passion's moments bright and warm,
  O'er Reason's dark, cold hours;

On fields where brave men "die or do,"
  In halls where rings the banquet's mirth,
Where mourners weep, where lovers woo,
  From throne to cottage-hearth?

What sweet tears dim the eye unshed,
  What wild vows falter on the tongue,
When "Scots wha hae wi' Wallace bled,"
  Or "Auld Lang Syne" is sung!

Pure hopes, that lift the soul above,
  Come with his Cotter's hymn of praise,
And dreams of youth, and truth, and love,
  With "Logan's" banks and braes.

And when he breathes his master-lay
  Of Alloway's witch-haunted wall,
All passions in our frames of clay
  Come thronging at his call.

Imagination's world of air,
  And our own world, its gloom and glee,
Wit, pathos, poetry, are there,
  And death's sublimity.

And Burns—though brief the race he ran,
  Though rough and dark the path he trod,
Lived—died—in form and soul a Man,
  The image of his God.

Through care, and pain, and want, and woe,
  With wounds that only death could heal,
Tortures—the poor alone can know,
  The proud alone can feel;

He kept his honesty and truth,
  His independent tongue and pen,
And moved, in manhood as in youth,
  Pride of his fellow-men.

Strong sense, deep feeling, passions strong,
  A hate of tyrant and of knave,
A love of right, a scorn of wrong,
  Of coward and of slave;

A kind, true heart, a spirit high,
  That could not fear and would not bow,
Were written in his manly eye
  And on his manly brow.

Praise to the bard! his words are driven,
  Like flower-seeds by the far winds sown,
Where'er, beneath the sky of heaven,
  The birds of fame have flown.

Praise to the man ! a nation **stood**
  Beside his coffin with wet eyes,
Her brave, her beautiful, her good,
  · **As when a** loved one dies.

And still, as on his funeral-day,
  Men stand his cold earth-couch **around,**
With the mute homage that we pay
  To consecrated ground.

And consecrated ground it is,
  The last, the hallowed home of one
Who lives upon all memories,
  Though with the buried gone.

Such graves as his are pilgrim-shrines,
  Shrines to no code or creed confined—
The Delphian vales, the Palestines,
  The Meccas of the mind.

Sages, with wisdom's garland wreathed,
  Crowned kings, and mitred priests of power,
And warriors with their bright swords sheathed,
  The mightiest of the hour;

And lowlier names, whose humble home
  Is lit by fortune's dimmer star,
Are there—o'er wave and mountain **come,**
  From countries near and far;

Pilgrims whose wandering feet have pressed
  The Switzer's snow, the Arab's sand,
Or trod the piled leaves of the West,
  My own green forest-land.

All ask the cottage of his birth,
  Gaze on the scenes he loved and sung,
And gather feelings not of earth
  His fields and streams among.

They linger by the Doon's low trees,
  And pastoral Nith, and wooded Ayr,
And round thy sepulchres, Dumfries!
  The poet's tomb is there.

But what to them the sculptor's art,
  His funeral columns, wreaths and urns?
Wear they not graven on the heart
  The name of Robert Burns?

"Dites si la Nature n'a pas fait ce beau pays pour une Julie, pour une Claire, et pour un St. Preux, mais ne les y cherchez pas."

ROUSSEAU.

I.

HOU com'st, iñ beauty, on my gaze at last,
  " On Susquehanna's side, fair Wyoming ! "
Image of many a dream, in hours long past,
When life was in its bud and blossoming,
And waters, gushing from the fountain-spring
Of pure enthusiast thought, dimmed my young eyes,
As by the poet borne, on unseen wing,
I breathed, in fancy, 'neath thy cloudless skies,
The summer's air, and heard her echoed harmonies.

II.

I then but dreamed: thou art before me now,
In life, a vision of the brain no more.
I've stood upon the wooded mountain's brow,
That beetles high thy lovely valley o'er;
And now, where winds thy river's greenest shore,
Within a bower of sycamores am laid;
And winds, as soft and sweet as ever bore
The fragrance of wild flowers through sun and shade,
Are singing in the trees, whose low boughs press my head.

III.

Nature hath made thee lovelier than the power
Even of Campbell's pen hath pictured: he
Had woven, had he gazed one sunny hour
Upon thy smiling vale, its scenery
With more of truth, and made each rock and tree
Known like old friends, and greeted from afar:
And there are tales of sad reality,
In the dark legends of thy border war,
With woes of deeper tint than his own Gertrude's are.

IV.

But where are they, the beings of the mind,
The bard's creations, moulded not of clay,
Hearts to strange bliss and suffering assigned—
Young Gertrude, Albert, Waldegrave — where are
    they?
We need not ask. The people of to-day
Appear good, honest, quiet men enough,
And hospitable too—for ready pay;
With manners like their roads, a little rough,
And hands whose grasp is warm and welcoming, though
    tough.

V.

Judge Hallenbach, who keeps the toll-bridge gate,
And the town records, is the Albert now
Of Wyoming: like him, in church and state,
Her Doric column; and upon his brow

The thin hairs, white with seventy winters' snow,
Look patriarchal. Waldegrave 'twere in vain
To point out here, unless in yon scare-crow,
That stands full-uniformed upon the plain,
To frighten flocks of crows and blackbirds from the
     grain.

VI.

For he would look particularly droll
In his "Iberian boot" and "Spanish plume,"
And be the wonder of each Christian soul
As of the birds that scare-crow and his broom.
But Gertrude, in her loveliness and bloom,
Hath many a model here; for woman's eye,
In court or cottage, wheresoe'er her home,
Hath a heart-spell too holy and too high
To be o'erpraised even by her worshipper—Poesy.

VII.

There's one in the next field—of sweet sixteen—
Singing and summoning thoughts of beauty born
In heaven—with her jacket of light green,
"Love-darting eyes, and tresses like the morn,"
Without a shoe or stocking—hoeing corn.
Whether, like Gertrude, she oft wanders there,
With Shakespeare's volume in her bosom borne,
I think is doubtful. Of the poet-player
The maiden knows no more than Cobbett or Voltaire.

VIII.

There is a woman, widowed, gray, and old,
Who tells you where the foot of Battle stepped
Upon their day of massacre.   She told
Its tale, and pointed to the spot, and wept,
Whereon her father and five brothers slept
Shroudless, the bright-dreamed slumbers of the brave,
When all the land a funeral mourning kept.
And there, wild laurels planted on the grave
By Nature's hand, in air their pale-red blossoms wave.

IX.

And on the margin of yon orchard hill
Are marks where timeworn battlements have been,
And in the tall grass traces linger still
Of "arrowy frieze and wedgèd ravelin."
Five hundred of her brave that valley green
Trod on the morn in soldier-spirit gay;
But twenty lived to tell the noonday scene—
And where are now the twenty? Passed away.
Has Death no triumph hours, save on the battle-day?

JOSEPH RODMAN DRAKE,

OF NEW YORK, SEPT., 1820.

"The good die first,
And they, whose hearts are dry as summer dust,
Burn to the socket."

WORDSWORTH.

GREEN be the turf above thee,
   Friend of my better days!
None knew thee but to love thee,
   Nor named thee but to praise.

Tears fell when thou wert dying,
   From eyes unused to weep,
And long, where thou art lying,
   Will tears the cold turf steep.

When hearts, whose truth was proven,
   Like thine, are laid in earth,
There should a wreath be woven
   To tell the world their worth;

And I who woke each morrow
   To clasp thy hand in mine,

Who shared thy joy and sorrow,
  Whose weal and woe were thine:

It should be mine to braid it
  Around thy faded brow,
But I've in vain essayed it,
  And feel I cannot now.

While memory bids me weep thee,
  Nor thoughts nor words are free,
The grief is fixed too deeply
  That mourns a man like thee.

TWILIGHT.

THERE is an evening twilight of the heart,
   When its wild passion-waves are lulled to rest,
And the eye sees life's fairy scenes depart,
   As fades the daybeam in the rosy west.
'Tis with a nameless feeling of regret
   We gaze upon them as they melt away,
And fondly would we bid them linger yet,
   But Hope is round us with her angel lay,
Hailing afar some happier moonlight hour;
Dear are her whispers still, though lost their early
     power.

In youth her cheek was crimsoned with her glow;
   Her smile was loveliest then; her matin song
Was heaven's own music, and the note of woe
   Was all unheard her sunny bowers among.
Life's little world of bliss was newly born;
   We knew not, cared not, it was born to die,
Flushed with the cool breeze and the dews of morn,
   With dancing heart we gazed on the pure sky,
And mocked the passing clouds that dimmed its blue,
Like our own sorrows then—as fleeting and as few.

And manhood felt her sway too—on the eye,
   Half realized, her early dreams burst bright,
Her promised bower of happiness seemed nigh,
   Its days of joy, its vigils of delight;
And though at times might lower the thunder-storm,
   And the red lightnings threaten, still the air
Was balmy with her breath and her loved form,
   The rainbow of the heart was hovering there.
'Tis in life's noontide she is nearest seen,
Her wreath the summer flower, her robe of summer
    green.

But though less dazzling in her twilight dress,
   There's more of heaven's pure beam about her now;
That angel-smile of tranquil loveliness,
   Which the heart worships, glowing on her brow;
That smile shall brighten the dim evening star
   That points our destined tomb, nor e'er depart
Till the faint light of life is fled afar,
   And hushed the last deep beating of the heart:
The meteor-bearer of our parting breath,
A moonbeam in the midnight cloud of death.

PSALM CXXXVII.

"By the rivers of Babylon."

WE sat us down and wept,
    Where Babel's waters slept,
And we thought of home and Zion as a long-gone,
    happy dream;
    We hung our harps in air
    On the willow-boughs, which there,
Gloomy as round a sepulchre, were drooping o'er the
    stream.

    The foes whose chain we wore,
    Were with us on that shore,
Exulting in our tears that told the bitterness of woe.
    "Sing us," they cried aloud,
    "Ye once so high and proud,
The songs ye sang in Zion ere we laid her glory low."

    And shall the harp of heaven
    To Judah's monarch given
Be touched by captive fingers, or grace a fettered
    hand?

No! sooner be my tongue
Mute, powerless, and unstrung,
Than its words of holy music make glad a stranger
    land.

May this right hand, whose skill
Can wake the harp at will,
And bid the listener's joys or griefs in light or darkness
    come,
Forget its godlike power,
If for one brief, dark hour,
My heart forgets Jerusalem, fallen city of my home!

Daughter of Babylon!
Blessed be that chosen one,
Whom God shall send to smite thee when there is none
    to save:
He from the mother's breast,
Shall pluck the babe at rest,
And lay it in the sleep of death beside its father's grave.

TO ****.

THE world is bright before thee,
    Its summer flowers are thine,
Its calm blue sky is o'er thee,
    Thy bosom Pleasure's shrine ;
And thine the sunbeam given
    To Nature's morning hour,
Pure, warm, as when from heaven
    It burst on Eden's bower.

There is a song of sorrow,
    The death-dirge of the gay,
That tells, ere dawn of morrow,
    These charms may melt away,
That sun's bright beam be shaded,
    That sky be blue no more,
The summer flowers be faded,
    And youth's warm promise o'er.

Believe it not—though lonely
    Thy evening home may be ;
Though Beauty's bark can only
    Float on a summer sea ;
Though Time thy bloom is stealing,
    There's still beyond his art
The wild-flower wreath of feeling,
    The sunbeam of the heart.

THE FIELD OF THE GROUNDED ARMS.

STRANGERS! your eyes are on that valley fixed
   Intently, as we gaze on vacancy,
     When the mind's wings o'erspread
     The spirit-world of dreams.

True, 'tis a scene of loveliness—the bright
Green dwelling of the summer's first-born Hours,
     Whose wakened leaf and bud
     Are welcoming the morn.

And morn returns the welcome, sun and cloud
Smile on the green earth from their home in heaven,
     Even as a mother smiles
     Above her cradled boy,

And wreath their light and shade o'er plain and moun-
     tain,
O'er sleepless seas of grass, whose waves are flowers,
     The river's golden shores,
     The forest of dark pines.

The song of the wild bird is on the wind,
The hum of the wild bee, the music wild
.   Of waves upon the bank,
   Of leaves upon the bough.

But all is song and beauty in the land,
Beneath her skies of June; then journey on,
   A thousand scenes like this
   Will greet you ere the eve.

Ye linger yet—ye see not, hear not now,
The sunny smile, the music of to-day,
   Your thoughts are wandering up,
   Far up the stream of time;

And boyhood's lore and fireside-listened tales
Are rushing on your memories, as ye breathe
   That valley's storied name,
   FIELD OF THE GROUNDED ARMS.

Strangers no more, a kindred "pride of place,"
Pride in the gift of country and of name,
   Speaks in your eye and step—
   Ye tread your native land.

And your high thoughts are on her glory's day,
The solemn sabbath of the week of battle,
   Whose tempests bowed to earth
   Her foeman's banner here.

The forest-leaves lay scattered cold and dead,
Upon the withered grass that autumn morn,
    When, with as widowed hearts
    And hopes as dead and cold,

A gallant army formed their last array
Upon that field, in silence and deep gloom,
    And at their conqueror's feet
    Laid their war-weapons down.

Sullen and stern, disarmed but not dishonored;
Brave men, but brave in vain, they yielded there:
    The soldier's trial-task
    Is not alone "to die."

Honor to chivalry! the conqueror's breath
Stains not the ermine of his foeman's fame,
    Nor mocks his captive's doom—
    The bitterest cup of war.

But be that bitterest cup the doom of all
Whose swords are lightning-flashes in the cloud
    Of the Invader's wrath,
    Threatening a gallant land!

His armies' trumpet-tones wake not alone
Her slumbering echoes; from a thousand hills
    Her answering voices shout,
    And her bells ring to arms!

3

Then danger hovers o'er the Invader's march,
On raven wings, hushing the song of fame,
    And glory's hues of beauty .
    Fade from the cheek of death.

A foe is heard in every rustling leaf,
A fortress seen in every rock and tree,
    The eagle eye of art
    Is dim and powerless then,

And war becomes a people's joy, the drum
Man's merriest music, and the field of death
    His couch of happy dreams,
    After life's harvest-home.

He battles heart and arm, his own blue sky
Above him, and his own green land around,
    Land of his father's grave,
    His blessing and his prayers :

Land where he learned to lisp a mother's name,
The first beloved in life, the last forgot,
    Land of his frolic youth,
    Land of his bridal eve—

Land of his children—vain your columned strength,
Invaders ! vain your battles' steel and fire !
    Choose ye the morrow's doom—
    A prison or a grave.

And such were Saratoga's victors—such
The Yeomen-Brave, whose deeds and death have given
    A glory to her skies,
    A music to her name.

In honorable life her fields they trod,
In honorable death they sleep below ;
    Their sons' proud feelings here
    Their noblest monuments.

RED JACKET.[1]

A Chief of the Indian Tribes, the Tuscaroras.

ON LOOKING AT HIS PORTRAIT BY WEIR.

COOPER, whose name is with his country's woven,
First in her files, her PIONEER of mind—
A wanderer now in other climes, has proven
   His love for the young land he left behind;

And throned her in the senate-hall of nations,
   Robed like the deluge rainbow, heaven-wrought:
Magnificent as his own mind's creations,
   And beautiful as its green world of thought:

And faithful to the Act of Congress, quoted
   As law authority, it passed nem. con. :
He writes that we are, as ourselves have voted,
   The most enlightened people ever known:

That all our week is happy as a Sunday
   In Paris, full of song, and dance, and laugh ;
And that, from Orleans to the Bay of Fundy,
   There's not a bailiff or an epitaph :

And furthermore—in fifty years, or sooner,
  We shall export our poetry and wine; ·
And our brave fleet, eight frigates and a schooner,
  Will sweep the seas from Zembla to the Line.

If he were with me, King of Tuscarora!
  Gazing, as I, upon thy portrait now,
In all its medalled, fringed, and beaded glory,
  Its eye's dark beauty, and its thoughtful brow—

Its brow, half martial and half diplomatic,
  Its eye, upsoaring like an eagle's wings;
Well might he boast that we, the Democratic,
  Outrival Europe, even in our Kings!

For thou wast monarch born. Tradition's pages
  Tell not the planting of thy parent tree,
But that the forest tribes have bent for ages
  To thee, and to thy sires, the subject knee.

Thy name is princely—if no poet's magic
  Could make RED JACKET grace an English rhyme,
Though some one with a genius for the tragic
  Hath introduced it in a pantomime—

Yet it is music in the language spoken
  Of thine own land, and on her herald-roll;
As bravely fought for, and as proud a token
  As Cœur de Lion's of a warrior's soul.

Thy garb—though Austria's bosom-star would **frighten**
That medal pale, as diamonds the dark **mine,**
And George the Fourth wore, at his court at Brighton
A **more** becoming evening dress than thine ;

Yet 'tis a brave one, scorning wind and weather,
And fitted for thy couch, on field and flood,
As Rob Roy's tartan for the Highland heather,
Or forest green for England's Robin Hood.

Is strength a monarch's merit, like a whaler's?
Thou art as tall, as sinewy, and as strong
As earth's first kings—the Argo's gallant sailors,
Heroes in history and gods in song.

Is beauty?—Thine has with thy youth departed;
But the love-legends of thy manhood's years,
And she who perished, young and broken-hearted,
Are—but I rhyme for smiles and not for tears.

Is eloquence?—Her spell is thine that reaches
The heart, and makes the wisest head its sport ;
And there's one rare, strange virtue in thy speeches,
The secret of their mastery—they are short.

The monarch mind, the mystery of commanding,
The birth-hour gift, the art Napoleon,
Of winning, fettering, moulding, wielding, banding
The hearts of millions till they move as one:

Thou hast it.   At thy bidding men have crowded
  The road to death as to a festival;
And minstrels, at their sepulchres, have shrouded
  With banner-folds of glory the dark pall.

Who will believe?   Not I—for in deceiving
  Lies the dear charm of life's delightful dream;
I cannot spare the luxury of believing
  That all things beautiful are what they seem;

Who will believe that, with a smile whose blessing
  Would, like the Patriarch's, soothe a dying hour,
With voice as low, as gentle, and caressing,
  As e'er won maiden's lip in moonlit bower:

With look like patient Job's eschewing evil;
  With motions graceful as a bird's in air;
Thou art, in sober truth, the veriest devil
  That e'er clinched fingers in a captive's hair!

That in thy breast there springs a poison fountain,
  Deadlier than that where bathes the Upas-tree;
And in thy wrath a nursing cat-o'-mountain
  Is calm as her babe's sleep compared with thee!

And underneath that face, like summer ocean's,
  Its lip as moveless, and its cheek as clear,
Slumbers a whirlwind of the heart's emotions,
  Love, hatred, pride, hope, sorrow—all save fear:

Love—for thy land, as if she were thy daughter,
  Her pipe in peace, her tomahawk in wars;
Hatred—of missionaries and cold water;
  Pride—in thy rifle-trophies and thy scars;

Hope—that thy wrongs may be, by the Great Spirit,
  Remembered and revenged when thou art gone;
Sorrow—that none are left thee to inherit
  Thy name, thy fame, thy passions, and thy throne!

LOVE.

. . . . The imperial votaress passed on
In maiden meditation, fancy free.
                        MIDSUMMER NIGHT'S DREAM.

Shall I never see a bachelor of threescore again?
        BENEDICT, IN MUCH ADO ABOUT NOTHING.

WHEN the tree of Love is·budding first,
   Ere yet its leaves are green,
Ere yet, by shower and sunbeam nursed
   Its infant life has been;
The wild bee's slightest touch might wring
   The buds from off the tree,
As the gentle dip of the swallow's wing
   Breaks the bubbles on the sea.

But when its open leaves have found
   A home in the free air,
Pluck them, and there remains a wound
   That ever rankles there.
The blight of hope and happiness
   Is felt when fond ones part,
And the bitter tear that follows is
   The life-blood of the heart.

When the flame of love is kindled first,
  'Tis the fire-fly's light at even,
'Tis dim as the wandering stars that burst
  In the blue of the summer heaven.
A breath can bid it burn no more,
  Or if, at times, its beams
Come on the memory, they pass o'er
  Like shadows in our dreams.

But when that flame has blazed into
  A being and a power,
And smiled in scorn upon the dew
  That fell in its first warm hour,
'Tis the flame that curls round the martyr's head,
  Whose task is to destroy;
'Tis the lamp on the altars of the dead,
  Whose light but darkens joy.

Then crush, even in their hour of birth,
  The infant buds of Love,
And tread his glowing fire to earth,
  Ere 'tis dark in clouds above;
Cherish no more a cypress-tree
  To shade thy future years,
Nor nurse a heart-flame that may be
  Quenched only with thy tears.

A SKETCH.

HER Leghorn hat was of the bright gold tint
     The setting sunbeams give to autumn clouds;
The ribbon that encircled it as blue
As spots of sky upon a moonless night,
When stars are keeping revelry in heaven;
A single ringlet of her clustering hair
Fell gracefully beneath her hat, in curls
As dark as down upon the raven's wing;
The kerchief, partly o'er her shoulders flung,
And partly waving in the wind, was woven
Of every color the first rainbow wore,
When it came smiling in its hues of beauty
A promise from on high to a lost world,
Her robe seemed of the snow just fallen to earth,
Pure from its home in the far winter clouds,
As white, as stainless; and around her waist
(You might have spanned it with your thumb and fin-
     ger),
A girdle of the hue of Indian pearls
Was twined, resembling the faint line of water
That follows the swift bark o'er quiet seas.
Her face I saw not: but her shape, her form,
Was one of those with which creating bards

People a world of their own fashioning,
Forms for the heart to love and cherish ever,
The visiting angels of our twilight dreams.
Her foot was loveliest of remembered things,
Small as a fairy's on a moonlit leaf
Listening the wind-harp's song, and watching by
The wild-thyme pillow of her sleeping queen,
When proud Titania shuns her Oberon.
But 'twas that foot which broke the spell—alas!
Its stocking had a deep, deep tinge of blue—
I turned away in sadness, and passed on.

DOMESTIC HAPPINESS.

. . . . . . The only bliss
Of Paradise that has survived the fall.

I.

" BESIDE the nuptial curtain bright,"
   The bard of Eden sings,
" Young Love his constant lamp will light,
   And wave his purple wings."
But rain-drops from the clouds of care
   May bid that lamp be dim,
And the boy Love will pout and swear
   'Tis then no place for him.

II.

So mused the lovely Mrs. Dash
   ('Tis wrong to mention names)
When for her surly husband's cash
   She urged in vain her claims.
" I want a little money, dear,
   For Vandervoort and Flandin,
Their bill, which now has run a year,
   To-morrow mean to hand in."

III.

" More ? " cried the husband, half asleep,
   " You'll drive me to despair ; "
The lady was too proud to weep,
   And too polite to swear.
She bit her lip for very spite,
   He felt a storm was brewing,
And dreamed of nothing else all night,
   But brokers, banks, and ruin.

IV.

He thought her pretty once, but dreams
   Have sure a wondrous power,
For to his eye the lady seems
   Quite altered since that hour ;
And Love, who on their bridal eve
   Had promised long to stay,
Forgot his promise, took French leave,
   And bore his lamp away.

MAGDALEN.[*]

I.

SWORD, whose blade has ne'er been wet
  With blood, except of freedom's foes;
That hope which, though its sun be set,
  Still with a starlight beauty glows;
A heart that worshipped in Romance
  The Spirit of the buried Time,
And dreams of knight, and steed, and lance,
  And ladye-love, and minstrel-rhyme;
These had been, and I deemed would be
My joy, whate'er my destiny.

II.

Born in a camp, its watch-fires bright
  Alone illumed my cradle-bed;
And I had borne with wild delight
  My banner where Bolivar led,
Ere manhood's hue was on my cheek,
  Or manhood's pride was on my brow.
Its foes' are furled—the war-bird's beak
  Is thirsty on the Andes now;
I longed, like her, for other skies
Clouded by Glory's sacrifice.

III.

In Greece, the brave heart's Holy Land,
   Its soldier-song the bugle sings;
And I have buckled on my brand,
   And waited but the sea-wind's wings,
To bear me where, or lost or won
   Her battle, in its frown or smile,
Men live with those of Marathon,
   Or die with those of Scio's isle;
And find in Valor's tent or tomb,
In life or death, a glorious home.

IV.

I could have left but yesterday
   The scene of my boy-years behind,
And floated on my careless way
   Wherever willed the breathing wind.
I could have bade adieu to aught
   I've sought, or met, or welcomed here,
Without an hour of shaded thought,
   A sigh, a murmur, or a tear.
Such was I yesterday—but then
I had not known thee, Magdalen.

V.

To-day there is a change within me,
   There is a weight upon my brow,
And Fame, whose whispers once could win me
   From all I loved, is powerless now.

There ever is a form, a face
  Of maiden beauty in my dreams,
Speeding before me, like the race
  To ocean of the mountain-streams—
With dancing hair, and laughing eyes,
That seem to mock me as it flies.

VI.

My sword—it slumbers in its sheath;
  My hopes—their starry light is gone;
My heart—the fabled clock of death
  Beats with the same low, lingering tone:
And this, the land of Magdalen,
  Seems now the only spot on earth
Where skies are blue and flowers are green;
  And here I build my household hearth,
And breathe my song of joy, and twine
A lovely being's name with mine.

VII.

In vain! in vain! the sail is spread;
  To sea! to sea! my task is there;
But when among the unmourned dead
  They lay me, and the ocean air
Brings tidings of my day of doom,
  Mayst thou be then, as now thou art,
The load-star of a happy home;
  In smile and voice, in eye and heart
The same as thou hast ever been,
The loved, the lovely Magdalen.

EYES with the same blue witchery as those
    Of Psyche, which caught Love in his own wiles;
Lips of the breath and hue of the red rose,
That move but with kind words and sweetest smiles;
A power of motion and of look, whose art
Throws, silently, around the wildest heart
The net it would not break ; a form which vies
With that the Grecian imaged in his mind,
And gazed upon in dreams, and sighed to find
His breathing marble could not realize.
Know ye this picture ? There is one alone
Can call its pencilled lineaments her own.
She whom, at morning, when the summer air
Wanders, delighted, o'er her face of flowers,
And lingers in the ringlets of her hair,
We deem the Hebe of Jove's banquet-hours;
She who, at evening, when her fingers press
The harp, and wake its harmonies divine,
Seems sweetest-voiced and loveliest of the Nine,
The minstrel of the bowers of happiness,
She whom the Graces nurtured—at her birth,
The sea-born Goddess and the Huntress maid,

Beings whose beauty is not of the earth,
Came from their myrtle home and forest shade,
Blending immortal joy with mortal mirth
And Dian said, " Fair sister, be she mine
In her heart's purity, in beauty thine."
The smiling infant listened and obeyed.

TRANSLATION.

FROM THE GERMAN OF GOETHE.

GAIN ye come, again ye throng around me,
    Dim, shadowy beings of my boyhood's dream !
Still shall I bless, as then, your spell that bound me?
    Still bend to mists and vapors as ye seem ?
Nearer ye come : I yield me as ye found me
    In youth your worshipper; and as the stream
Of air that folds you in its magic wreaths,
Flows by my lips, youth's joy my bosom breathes.

Lost forms and loved ones ye are with you bringing,
    And dearest images of happier days,
First-love and friendship in your path upspringing,
    Like old tradition's half-remembered lays,
And long-slept sorrows waked, whose dirge-like singing
    Recalls my life's strange labyrinthine maze,
And names the heart-mourned many a stern doom,
Ere their year's summer, summoned to the tomb.

They hear not these my last songs, they whose greet-
        ing
    Gladdened my first; my spring-time friends have
        gone,

And gone, fast journeying from that place of meeting,
  The echoes of their welcome, one by one.
Though stranger crowds, my listeners since, are beating
    Time to my music, their applauding tone
More grieves than glads me, while the tried and true,
If yet on earth, are wandering far and few.

A longing long unfelt, a deep-drawn sighing
  For the far Spirit-World o'erpowers me now;
My song's faint voice sinks fainter, like the dying
    Tones of the wind-harp swinging from the bough,
And my changed heart throbs warm, no more denying
    Tears to my eyes or sadness to my brow;
The near afar off seems, the distant nigh,
The now a dream, the past reality.

WOMAN.

WRITTEN IN THE ALBUM OF AN UNKNOWN LADY.

LADY, although we have not met,
  And may not meet, beneath the sky;
And whether thine are eyes of jet,
Gray, or dark blue, or violet,
  Or hazel—Heaven knows, not I;

Whether around thy cheek of rose
  A maiden's glowing locks are curled.
And to some thousand kneeling beaux
Thy frown is cold as winter's snows,
  Thy smile is worth a world;

Or whether, past youth's joyous strife,
  The calm of thought is on thy brow,
And thou art in thy noon of life,
Loving and loved, a happy wife,
  And happier mother now—

I know not: but, whate'er thou art,
  Whoe'er thou art, were mine the spell,
To call Fate's joys or blunt his dart,
There should not be one hand or heart
  But served or wished thee well.

For thou art woman—with that word
  Life's dearest hopes and memories come,
Truth, Beauty, Love—in her adored,
And earth's lost Paradise restored
  In the green bower of home.

What is man's love?　His vows are broke,
  Even while his parting kiss is warm;
But woman's love all change will mock,
And, like the ivy round the oak,
  Cling closest in the storm.

And well the Poet at her shrine
  May bend, and worship while he woos;
To him she is a thing divine,
The inspiration of his line,
  His Sweetheart and his Muse.

If to his song the echo rings
  Of Fame—'tis woman's voice he hears;
If ever from his lyre's proud strings
Flow sounds like rush of angel-wings,
'Tis that she listens while he sings,
  With blended smiles and tears:

Smiles—tears—whose blessed and blessing power,
  Like sun and dew o'er summer's tree,
Alone keeps green through Time's long hour,
That frailer thing than leaf or flower,
  A poet's immortality.

A POET'S DAUGHTER.

FOR THE ALBUM OF MISS ˙ ˙ ˙, AT THE REQUEST OF HER FATHER

" **A** LADY asks the Minstrel's rhyme."
 A Lady **asks?**   There was a time
When musical as play-bell's chime
   To wearied boy,
That sound would summon dreams sublime
   Of pride and joy.

But now the spell hath lost its sway,
Life's first-born fancies first decay,
Gone are the plumes and pennons gay
   Of young Romance;
There linger but her ruins gray,
   And broken lance.

'Tis a new world—no more to maid,
Warrior, or bard, is homage paid;
The bay-tree's, laurel's, myrtle's shade,
   Men's thoughts resign;
Heaven placed us here to vote and trade,
   Twin tasks divine!

" Tis youth, 'tis beauty asks; the green
And growing leaves of seventeen
Are round her; and, half hid, half seen,
  A violet flower,
Nursed by the virtues she hath been
  From childhood's hour."

Blind passion's picture—yet for this
We woo the life-long bridal kiss,
And blend our every hope of bliss
  With hers we **love;**
Unmindful of the serpent's hiss
  In Eden's grove.

Beauty—the fading rainbow's pride,
Youth—'twas the charm of her who died
At dawn, and by her coffin's **side**
  A grandsire stands,
Age-strengthened, like the oak storm-tried
  Of mountain-lands.

Youth's coffin—hush the tale it tells !
Be silent, memory's funeral bells !
Lone in one heart, her home, it dwells
  Untold till death,
And where the grave-mound greenly swells
  O'er buried faith.

4

"But what if hers are rank and power,
Armies her train, a throne her bower,
A kingdom's gold her marriage-dower,
    Broad seas and lands?
What if from bannered hall and tower
    A queen commands?"

A queen?   Earth's regal moons have set.
Where perished Marie Antoinette?
Where's Bordeaux's mother?   Where the jet-
    Black Haytian dame?
And Lusitania's coronet?
    And Angoulême?

Empires to-day are upside down,
The castle kneels before the town,
The monarch fears a printer's frown
    A brickbat's range;
Give me, in preference to a crown,
    Five shillings change.

"But she who asks, though first among
The good, the beautiful, the young,
The birthright of a spell more strong
    Than these hath brought her;
She is your kinswoman in song,
    A Poet's daughter."

A Poet's daughter?   Could I claim
The consanguinity of fame,
Veins of my intellectual frame !
   Your blood would glow
Proudly to sing that gentlest name
   Of aught below.

A Poet's daughter—dearer word
Lip hath not spoken nor listener heard,
Fit theme for song of bee and bird
   From morn till even,
And wind-harp by the breathing stirred
   Of starlit heaven.

My spirit's wings are weak, the fire
Poetic comes but to expire,
Her name needs not my humble lyre
   To bid it live ;
She hath already from her sire
   All bard can give.

CONNECTICUT.

FROM AN UNPUBLISHED POEM.

"The woods in which we had dwelt pleasantly rustled their green leaves in the song, and our streams were there with the sound of all their waters."   MONTROSE.

I.

STILL her gray rocks tower above the sea
   That crouches at their feet, a conquered wave;
'Tis a rough land of earth, and stone, and tree,
   Where breathes no castled lord or cabined slave;
Where thoughts, and tongues, and hands are bold and
      free,
   And friends will find a welcome, foes a grave;
And where none kneel, save when to Heaven they pray,
Nor even then, unless in their own way.

II.

Theirs is a pure republic, wild, yet strong,
   A " fierce democracie," where all are true
To what themselves have voted—right or wrong—
   And to their laws denominated blue;
(If red, they might to Draco's code belong;)
   A vestal state, which power could not subdue,
Nor promise win—like her own eagle's nest,
Sacred—the San Marino of the West.

III.

A justice of the peace, for the time being,
  They bow to, but may turn him out next year;
They reverence their priest, but disagreeing
  In price or creed, dismiss him without fear;
They have a natural talent for foreseeing
  And knowing all things; and should Park appear
From his long tour in Africa, to show
The Niger's source, they'd meet him with—"we know."

IV

They love their land, because it is their own,
  And scorn to give aught other reason why;
Would shake hands with a king upon his throne,
  And think it kindness to his majesty;
A stubborn race, fearing and flattering none.
  Such are they nurtured, such they live and die;
All—but a few apostates, who are meddling
With merchandise, pounds, shillings, pence, and ped-
    dling;

V.

Or wandering through the Southern countries teaching
  The A B C from Webster's spelling-book;
Gallant and godly, making love and preaching,
  And gaining by what they call " hook and crook,"
And what the moralists call overreaching,
  A decent living.   The Virginians look

Upon them with as favorable eyes
As Gabriel on the devil in paradise.

VI.

But these are but their outcasts.   View them near
  At home, where all their worth and pride is placed;
And there their hospitable fires burn clear,
  And there the lowliest farmhouse hearth is graced
With manly hearts, in piety sincere,
  Faithful in love, in honor stern and chaste,
In friendship warm and true, in danger brave,
Beloved in life, and sainted in the grave.

VII.

And minds have there been nurtured, whose control
  Is felt even in their nation's destiny;
Men who swayed senates with a statesman's soul,
  And looked on armies with a leader's eye;
Names that adorn and dignify the scroll,
  Whose leaves contain their country's history,
And tales of love and war—listen to one
Of the Green-Mountaineer—the Stark of Bennington.

VIII.

When on that field his band the Hessians fought,
  Briefly he spoke before the fight began:
" Soldiers ! those German gentlemen are bought
  For four pounds eight and sevenpence per man,

By England's king; a bargain, as is thought.

    Are we worth more? Let's prove it now we can;

For we must beat them, boys, ere set of sun,

OR MARY STARK'S A WIDOW." It was done.

IX.

Hers are not Tempe's nor Arcadia's spring,

   Nor the long summer of Cathayan vales,

The vines, the flowers, the air, the skies, that fling

    Such wild enchantment o'er Boccaccio's tales

Of Florence and the Arno; yet the wing

    Of life's best angel, Health, is on her gales

Through sun and snow; and in the autumn-time

Earth has no purer and no lovelier clime.

X.

Her clear, warm heaven at noon—the mist that shrouds

   Her twilight hills—her cool and starry eves,

The glorious splendor of her sunset clouds,

    The rainbow beauty of her forest-leaves,

Come o'er the eye, in solitude and crowds,

    Where'er his web of song her poet weaves;

And his mind's brightest vision but displays

The autumn scenery of his boyhood's days.

XI.

And when you dream of woman, and her love;

   Her truth, her tenderness, her gentle power;

The maiden listening in the moonlight grove,
   The mother smiling in her infant's bower;
Forms, features, worshipped while we breathe or move,
   Be by some spirit of your dreaming hour
Borne, like Loretto's chapel, through the air
To the green land I sing, then wake, you'll find them
     there.

XII.

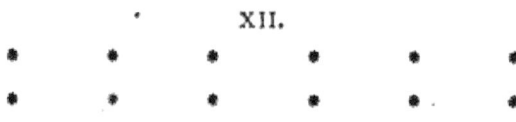

XIII.

They burnt their last witch in CONNECTICUT
   About a century and a half ago;
They made a school-house of her forfeit hut,
   And gave a pitying sweet-brier leave to grow
Above her thankless ashes; and they put
   A certified description of the show
Between two weeping-willows, craped with black,
On the last page of that year's almanac.

XIV.

Some warning and well-meant remarks were made
   Upon the subject by the weekly printers;
The people murmured at the taxes laid
   To pay for jurymen and pitch-pine splinters,
And the sad story made the rose-leaf fade
   Upon young listeners' cheeks for several winters,

When told at fire-side eves by those who saw
Executed—the lady and **the law.**

XV.

She and the law found rest: years rose and set;
    That generation, cottagers and kings,
Slept with their fathers, and the violet
    Has mourned above their **graves a hundred springs:**
Few persons keep a file **of the Gazette,**
    And almanacs **are sublunary things,**
So that her fame **is almost lost to earth,**
As if she ne'er had breathed; and of her birth,

XVI.

And death, and lonely life's mysterious matters,
    And how she played, in our forefathers' **times,**
The very **devil with** their **sons and daughters;**
    And how those " delicate **Ariels** " of her crimes,
The spirits **of the rocks, and woods,** and waters,
    Obeyed **her bidding when in charmèd rhymes,**
She muttered, at deep midnight, **spells whose power**
Woke from brief dream **of dew the sleeping summer**
        flower,

XVII.

And hushed the night-bird's solitary hymn,
    And spoke in whispers to the forest-tree,

Till his awed branches trembled, **leaf and limb,**
  And grouped her churchyard shapes of fan**tasie**
Round merry moonlight's meadow-fountain's **brim,**
  And mocking for a space the dread decree,
Brought back to dead, cold lips the parted breath,
And changed to banquet-board the bier of death,

XVIII.

None knew—except a patient, **precious few,**
  Who've read the folios of one COTTON **MATHER,**
A chronicler of tales more strange than true,
  New-England's chaplain, and her history's **father;**
A second Monmouth's GEOFFREY, a new
  HERODOTUS, **their laurelled victor rather,** .
For in one art he soars above **them** high :
The Greek or Welshman **does not always lie.**

XIX.

Know ye the venerable COTTON ?   He
  Was the first publisher's tourist on this station ;
The first who **made, by** labelling earth and sea,
  A huge book, and a **handsome** speculation :
And ours was then a land of mystery,
  Fit theme for poetry's exaggeration,
The wildest wonder of the month ; and there
He wandered freely, like a bird or **bear,**

XX.

And wove his forest dreams into quaint prose,
  Our sires his heroes, where, in holy strife,
They treacherously war with friends and foes;
  Where meek religion wears the assassin's knife,
And "bids the desert blossom like the rose,"
  By sprinkling earth with blood of Indian life,
And rears her altars o'er the indignant bones
Of murdered maidens, wives, and little ones.

XXI.

HEROD of Galilee's babe-butchering deed
  Lives not on history's blushing page alone;
Our skies, it seems, have seen like victims bleed,
  And our own Ramahs echoed groan for groan:
The fiends of France, whose cruelties decreed
  Those dextrous drownings in the Loire and Rhone,
Were at their worst, but copyists second-hand
Of our shrined, sainted sires, the Plymouth pilgrim-
        band,

XXII.

Or else fibs MATHER. Kindred wolves have bayed
  Truth's moon in chorus, but believe them not!
Beneath the dark trees that the Lethe shade,
  Be he, his folios, followers, facts, forgot;
And let his perishing monument·be made
  Of his own unsold volumes: 'tis the lot

Of many, may be mine; and be it MATHER'S,
That slanderer of the memory of our fathers.

XXIII.

And who were they, our fathers?   In their veins
    Ran the best blood of England's gentlemen;
Her bravest in the strife on battle-plains,
    Her wisest in the strife of voice and pen;
Her holiest, teaching, in her holiest fanes,
    The lore that led to martyrdom; and when
On this side ocean slept their wearied sails,
And their toil-bells woke up our thousand hills and
    dales,

XXIV.

Shamed they their fathers?   Ask the village-spires
    Above their Sabbath-homes of praise and prayer;
Ask of their children's happy household-fires,
    And happier harvest noons; ask summer's air,
Made merry by young voices, when the wires
    Of their school-cages are unloosed, and dare
Their slanderers' breath to blight the memory
That o'er their graves is " growing green to see ! "

XXV.

If he has " writ their annals true ; " if they,
    The Christian-sponsored and the Christian-nursed,

Clouded with crime the sunset of their day
 And warmed their winter's hearths with fires accursed;
And if the stain that time wears not away
 Of guilt was on the pilgrim axe that first
Our wood-paths' roses blest with smiles from heaven,
In charity forget, and hope to be forgiven.

XXVI.

Forget their story's cruelty and wrong;
 Forget their story-teller; or but deem
His facts the fictions of a minstrel's song,
 The myths and marvels of a poet's dream.
And are they not such? Suddenly among
 My mind's dark thoughts its boyhood's sunrise beam
Breathes in spring balm and beauty o'er my page—
Joy! joy! my patriot wrath hath wronged the reverend
  sage.

XXVII.

Welcome! young boyhood, welcome! Of thy lore,
 Thy morning-gathered wealth of prose and rhyme,
Of fruit the flower, of gold the infant ore,
 The roughest shuns not manhood's stormy clime,
But loves wild ocean's winds and breakers' roar;
 While, of the blossoms of the sweet spring-time,
The bonniest, and most bountiful of joy,
Shrink from the man, and cling around the boy.

XXVIII.

But now, like doves " with healing on their wings,"
   Blossom and fruit with gladdening kindness come,
Charming to sleep my murmuring song, that sings
   Unworthy dirges over MATHER'S tomb :
Welcome the olive-branch their message brings !
   It bids me wish him not the mouldering doom
Of nameless scribes of " *mémoires pour servir,*"
Dishonest " chroniclers of time's small-beer."

XXIX.

No : a born Poet, at his cradle-fire
   The muses nursed him as their bud unblown,
And gave him as his mind grew high and higher,
   Their ducal strawberry-leaf's enwreathed renown.
Alas ! that mightiest masters of the lyre,
   Whose pens above an eagle's heart have grown,
In all the proud nobility of wing,
Should stoop to dip their points in passion's poison-
     spring !

XXX.

Yet MILTON, weary of his youth's young wife,
   To her, to king, to church, to law untrue,
Warred for divorce and discord to the knife,
   And proudest wore his plume of darkest hue :
And DANTE, when his FLORENCE, in her strife,
   Robbed him of office and his temper, threw

'Mongst friends and foes a bomb-shell of fierce rhymes,
Shivering their names and fames to all succeeding
  times.

XXXI.

And our own MATHER'S fire-and-fagot tale
  Of Conquest, with her " garments rolled in blood,"
And banners blackening, like a pirate's sail,
  The Mayflower's memories of the brave and good,
Though but a brain-born dream of rain and hail,
  And in his epic but an episode,
Proves mournfully the strange and sad admission
Of much sour grape-juice in his disposition.

XXXII.

O Genius ! powerful with thy praise or blame,
  When art thou feigning ? when art thou sincere ?
MATHER, who banned his living friends with shame,
  In funeral-sermons blessed them on their bier,
And made their death-beds beautiful with fame—
  Fame true and gracious as a widow's tear
To her departed darling husband given ;
Him whom she scolded up from earth to heaven.

XXXIII.

Thanks for his funeral-sermons ; they recall
  The sunshine smiling through his folio's leaves,
That makes his readers' hours in bower or hall
  Joyous as plighted hearts on bridal eves ;

Chasing, like music from the soul of Saul,
  The doubt that darkens, and the ill that grieves;
And honoring the author's heart and mind,
. **That** beats to bless, and toils to ennoble human kind.

XXXIV.

His chaplain-mantle worthily to wear,
  He fringed its sober gray with poet-bays,
And versed the.Psalms of David to the air
  Of YANKEE-DOODLE, **for** Thanksgiving-days;
Thus hallowing with the earnestness of prayer,
  And patriotic purity of praise,
Unconscious of irreverence or wrong,
Our manliest battle-tune and merriest bridal song.

XXXV.

The good the Rhine-song does to German hearts,
  Or thine, Marseilles! to France's fiery blood;
The good thy anthemed **harmony imparts,**
  " GOD save the Queen!" to England's field and flooᴊ
A home-born blessing, Nature's boon, not Art's;
  The same heart-cheering, **spirit-warming good,**
To us and ours, where'er we war or woo,
Thy words and music, YANKEE-DOODLE!—do.

XXXVI.

Beneath thy **Star, as one** of the THIRTEEN,
  Land of my lay! through many a battle's night

Thy gallant men stepped steady and serene,
  To that war-music's stern and strong delight.
Where bayonets clinched above the trampled green,
  Where sabres grappled in the ocean-fight ;
In siege, in storm, on deck or rampart, there
They hunted the wolf Danger to his lair,
And sought and won sweet Peace, and wreaths for
    Honor's hair !

XXXVII.

And with thy smiles, sweet Peace, came woman's,
    bringing
  The Eden-sunshine of her welcome kiss,
And lovers' flutes, and children's voices singing
  The maiden's promised, matron's perfect bliss,
And heart and home-bells blending with their ringing
  Thank-offerings borne to holier worlds than this,
And the proud green of Glory's laurel-leaves,
And gold, the gift to Peace, of Plenty's summer sheaves.

MUSIC.

TO A BOY OF FOUR YEARS OLD, ON HEARING HIM PLAY
ON THE HARP.

SWEET boy ! before thy lips can learn
 In speech thy wishes to make known,
Are " thoughts that breathe and words that burn,"
 Heard in thy music's tone.

Were Genius tasked to prove the might,
 The magic of her hidden spell,
She well might name thee with delight
 As her own miracle.

Who that hath heard, from summer trees,
 The sweet wild song of summer birds,
When morning to the far-off breeze
 Whispers her bidding words;

Or listened to the bird of night,
 The minstrel of the starlight hours,
Companion of the firefly's flight,
 Cool dews, and closèd flowers;

But deemed that spirits of the air
  Had left their native homes in heaven,
And that the music warbled there
  To earth a while was given?

For with that music came the thought
  That life's young purity was theirs,
And love, all artless and untaught,
  Breathed in their woodland airs.

And when, sweet boy! thy baby fingers
  Wake sounds of heaven's own harmony,
How welcome is the thought that lingers
  Upon thy lyre and thee!

It calls up visions of past days,
  When life was infancy and song
To us; and old remembered lays,
  Unheard, unheeded long,

Revive in joy or grief within us,
  Like lost friends wakened from their sleep,
With all their early power to win us
  Alike to smile or weep.

And when we gaze upon that face,
  Blooming in innocence and truth,
And mark its dimpled artlessness,
  Its beauty and its youth;

We think of better worlds than this,
  Of other beings pure as thou,
Who breathe, on winds of Paradise,
  Music as thine is now.

And know the only emblem meet
  Of that pure Faith the heart adores,
To be a child like thee, whose feet
  Are strangers on Life's shores.

LIEUT. WILLIAM HOWARD ALLEN,

OF THE AMERICAN NAVY.

HE hath been mourned as brave men mourn the
    brave,
And wept as nations weep their cherished dead,
With bitter, but proud tears, and o'er his head
The eternal flowers whose root is in the grave,
The flowers of Fame, are beautiful and green;
And by his grave's side pilgrim feet have been,
And blessings, pure as men to martyrs give,
Have there been breathed by those he died to save.
—Pride of his country's banded chivalry,
His fame their hope, his name their battle-cry;
He lived as mothers wish their sons to live,
He died as fathers wish their sons to die.

  If on the grief-worn cheek the hues of bliss,
Which fade when all we love is in the tomb,
Could ever know on earth a second bloom,
The memory of a gallant death like his
Would call them into being; but the few,
Who as their friend, their brother, or their son,
His kind warm heart and gentle spirit knew,

Had long lived, hoped, and feared for him alone;
His voice their morning music, and his eye
The only starlight of their evening sky,
Till even the sun of happiness seemed dim,
And life's best joys were sorrows but with him;
And when, the burning bullet in his breast,
He dropped, like summer fruit from off the bough,
There was one heart that knew and loved him best—
It was a mother's—and is broken now.

TO WALTER BOWNE, ESQ., [10]

MEMBER OF THE COUNCIL OF APPOINTMENT OF THE STATE OF
NEW YORK, AT ALBANY, 1821.

> " Stand not upon the order of your going,
>   But go at once."
>
> " I cannot but remember such things were,
>   And were most precious to me."
>   MACBETH.

WE do not blame you, Walter Bowne,
    For a variety of reasons;
You're now the talk of half the town,
A man of talent and renown,
    And will be for perhaps two seasons.
That face of yours has magic in it;
Its smile transports us in a minute
    To wealth and pleasure's sunny bowers;
And there is terror in its frown,
Which, like a mower's scythe, cuts down
    Our city's loveliest flowers.

We therefore do not blame you, sir,
    Whate'er our cause of grief may be;
And cause enough we have to " stir
    The very stones to mutiny."

You've driven from the cash and cares
Of office, heedless of our prayers,
Men who have been for many a year
To us and to our purses dear,
 And will be to our heirs forever.
Our tears, thanks to the snow and rain,
Have swelled the brook in Maiden Lane
 Into a mountain river ;
And when you visit us again,
Leaning at Tammany on your cane,
Like warrior on his battle-blade,
You'll mourn the havoc you have made.

There is a silence and a sadness
 Within the marble mansion now ;
Some have wild eyes that threaten madness,
 Some think of " kicking up a row."
Judge Miller will not yet believe
That you have ventured to bereave
 The city and its hall of him :
He has in his own fine way stated,
 " The fact must be substantiated,"
 Before he'll move a single limb.
He deems it cursed hard to yield
The laurel won in every field
 Through sixteen years of party war,
And to be seen at noon no more,
Enjoying at his office door
 The luxury of a tenth segar.

Judge Warner says that, when he's gone,
  You'll miss the true Dogberry breed;
And Christian swears that you have done
  A most UN-Christian deed.

How could you have the heart to strike
From place the peerless Pierre Van Wyck?
And the twin colonels, Haines and Pell,
Squire Fessenden, and Sheriff Bell;
Morrell, a justice and a wise one,
And Ned McLaughlin the exciseman;
The two health-officers, believers
In Clinton and contagious fevers;
The keeper of the city's treasures,
The scaler of her weights and measures,
The harbor-master, her best bower
Cable in party's stormy hour;
Ten auctioneers, three bank directors,
And Mott and Duffy, the inspectors
  Of whiskey and of flour!

It was but yesterday they stood
All (ex-officio) great and good.
But by the tomahawk struck down
Of party and of Walter Bowne,
Where are they now? With shapes of air,
The caravan of things that were,
Journeying to their nameless home,
Like Mecca's pilgrims from her tomb;

  5

With the lost Pleiad ; with the wars
Of Agamemnon's ancestors ;
With their own years of joy and grief,
Spring's bud, and autumn's faded leaf;
With birds that round their cradles flew ;
With winds that in their boyhood blew ;
With last night's dream and last night's dew.

Yes, they are gone ; alas ! each one of them ;
Departed—every mother's son of them.
Yet often, at the close of day,
When thoughts are winged and wandering, they
Come with the memory of the past,
   Like sunset clouds along the mind,
Reflecting, as they're flitting fast
In their wild hues of shade and light,
All that was beautiful and bright
   In golden moments left behind.

THE IRON GRAYS.[11]

WE twine the wreath of honor
   Around the warrior's brow,
Who, at his country's altar, breathes
   The life-devoting vow,
And shall we to the Iron Grays
   The meed of praise deny,
Who freely swore, in danger's days,
   For their native land to die?

For o'er our bleeding country
   Ne'er lowered a darker storm,
Than bade them round their gallant chief
   The iron phalanx form.
When first their banner waved in air,
   Invasion's bands were nigh,
And the battle-drum beat long and loud,
   And the torch of war blazed high !

Though still bright gleam their bayonets,
   Unstained with hostile gore,
Far distant yet is England's host,
   Unheard her cannon's roar.
Yet not in vain they flew to arms ;
   It made the foeman know

That many a gallant heart must-bleed
Ere freedom's star be low.

Guards of a nation's destiny !
  High is that nation's claim,
For not unknown your spirit proud,
  Nor your daring chieftain's name.
'Tis yours to shield the dearest ties
  That bind to life the heart,
That mingle with the earliest breath,
  And with our last depart.

The angel-smile of beauty
  What heart but bounds to feel ?
Her fingers buckled on the belt,
  That sheathes your gleaming steel
And if the soldier's honored death
  In battle be your doom,
Her tears shall bid the flowers be green
  That blossom round your tomb.

Tread on the path of duty,
  Band of the patriot brave,
Prepared to rush, at honor's call,
  " To glory or the grave."
Nor bid your flag again be furled
  Till proud its eagles soar,
Till the battle-drum has ceased to beat,
  And the war-torch burns no more.

AN EPISTLE TO * * * *.

DEAR * * * *, I am writing not *to* you, but *at* you,
    For the feet of you tourists have no resting-
      place ;
But wherever with this the mail-pigeon may catch you,
  * May she find you with gayety's smile on your face ;
Whether chasing a snipe at the Falls of Cohoes,
Or chased by the snakes upon Anthony's Nose ;
Whether wandering, at Catskill, from Hotel to Clove,
Making sketches, or speeches, puns, poems, or love
Or in old Saratoga's unknown fountain-land,
Threading groves of enchantment, half bushes, half
      sand ;
Whether dancing on Sundays at Lebanon Springs,
   With those Madame Hutins of Religion, the Shakers ;
Or, on Tuesdays, with maidens who seek wedding-rings
   At Ballston, as taught by mammas and match-
     makers ;
Whether sailing St. Lawrence, with unbroken neck,
From her thousand green isles to her castled Quebec ;
Or sketching Niagara, pencil on knee
   (The giant of waters, our country's pet lion),
Or dipped at Long Branch, in the real salt sea,

With a cork for a dolphin, a Cockney Arion;
Whether roaming earth, ocean, or even the air,
Like Dan O'Rourke's eagle—good luck to you there.

For myself, as you'll see by the date of my letter,
I'm in town, but of that fact the least said the better ;
For 'tis vain to deny (though the city o'erflows
With well-dressed men and women, whom nobody
    knows)
That one rarely sees persons whose nod is an honor,
A lady with fashion's own impress upon her ;
Or a gentleman blessed with the courage to say,
Like Morris (the Prince Regent's friend, in his day),
" Let others in sweet shady solitudes dwell,
Oh ! give me the sweet shady side of Pall Mall."

Apropos—our friend A. chanced this morning to meet
    The accomplished Miss B. as he passed Contoit's
        Garden,[12]
Both in town in July !—he crossed over the street,
    And she entered the rouge-shop of Mrs. St. Martin.[13]
Resolved not to look at another known face,
Through Leonard and Church Streets she walked to
        Park Place,
And he turned from Broadway into Catharine Lane,
    And coursed, to avoid her, through alley and by-street,
Till they met, as the devil would have it, again,
    Face to face, near the pump at the corner of Dey
        Street.

Yet, as most of " The Fashion " are journeying now,
With the brown hues of summer on cheek and on **brow,**
The few *"gens comme il faut"* who are lingering here,
Are, like fruits out of season, more welcome and dear,
Like " **the** last rose of summer, left blooming alone,"
Or the last snows of winter, pure ice **of** *haut ton,*
Unmelted, undimmed by the sun's brightest ray,
And, like diamonds, making night's darkness seem day.
One meets them **in** groups, that **Canova** might fancy,
At our new lounge at evening, the *Opera Français.*[14]
In nines like the Muses, **in threes like the Graces,**
Green spots **in a** desert **of commonplace faces.**
The Queen, Mrs. Adams, goes there sweetly dressed
   In a beautiful bonnet, all golden and flowery;
While the King, Mr. Bonaparte, smiles on Celeste,
   Heloise, and Hutin, from his box at the Bowery.

For news, Parry still the North Sea is exploring,
   And the Grand Turk has taken, they say, the **Acrop-**
      olis,
And we, in Swamp Place,[15] **have discovered, in boring,**
   A mineral spring to refine the metropolis.
The day we discovered **it was, by-the-way,**
In the life of the Cockneys, **a** glorious day.
For we all had been taught, by tradition and reading,
   That to gain what admits us to levees of kings,
The gentleness, courtesy, grace of high breeding,
   The only sure way was to " visit the Springs."
So the whole city visited Swamp Spring *en masse,*

From attorney to sweep, from physician to pavior,
To drink of cold water at sixpence a glass,
    And learn true politeness and genteel behavior.
Though the crowd was immense till the hour of de-
        parture,
    No gentleman's feelings were hurt in the rush,   •
Save a grocer's, who lost his proof-glass and bung-starter,
    And a chimney-sweep's, robbed of his scraper and
        brush.   ·
They lingered till sunset and twilight had come,
    When, wearied in limb, but much polished in man-
        ners,
The sovereign people moved gracefully home,
    In the beauty and pride of "an army with banners."
As to politics—Adams [16] and Clinton yet live,
    And reign, we presume, as we never have missed 'em,
And woollens and Webster continue to thrive
    Under something they call the American System,
If you're anxious to know what the country is doing,
Whether ruined already or going to ruin,
    And who her next President will be, please Heaven,
Read the letters of Jackson, the speeches of Clay,
All the party newspapers, three columns a day,
    And Blunt's Annual Register, [17] year 'twenty-seven.

FANNY.

> "A fairy vision
> Of some gay creatures of the element,
> That in the colors of the rainbow live,
> And play in the plighted clouds."
>
> MILTON.

FANNY.

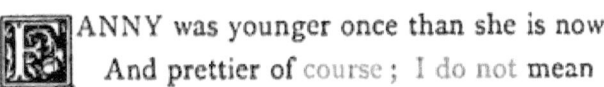

I.

FANNY was younger once than she is now,
  And prettier of course ; I do not mean
To say that there are wrinkles on her brow ;
  Yet, to be candid, she is past eighteen—
Perhaps past twenty—but the girl is shy
About her age, and Heaven forbid that I

II.

Should get myself in trouble by revealing
  A secret of this sort ; I have too long
Loved pretty women with a poet's feeling,
  And when a boy, in day-dream and in song,
Have knelt me down and worshipped them : alas !
They never thanked me for't—but let that pass.

III.

I've felt full many a heartache in my day,
    At the mere rustling of a muslin gown,
And caught some dreadful colds, I blush to say,
    While shivering in the shade of beauty's frown.
They say her smiles are sunbeams—it may be—
But never a sunbeam would she throw on me.

IV.

But Fanny's is an eye that you may gaze on
    For half an hour, without the slightest harm ;
E'en when she wore her smiling summer face on
    There was but little danger, and the charm
That youth and wealth once gave, has bade farewell :
Hers is a sad, sad tale—'tis mine its woes to tell.

V.

Her father kept, some fifteen years ago,
    A retail dry-goods shop in Chatham Street,
And nursed his little earnings, sure though slow,
    Till, having mustered wherewithal to meet
The gaze of the great world, he breathed the air
Of Pearl Street—and "set up" in Hanover Square.

VI.

Money is power, 'tis said—I never tried ;
    I'm but a poet—and bank-notes to me

Are curiosities, as closely eyed,
　　Whene'er I get them, as a stone would be,
Tossed from the moon on Doctor Mitchill's table,
Or classic brickbat from the tower of Babel.

VII.

But he I sing of well has known and felt
　　That money hath a power and a dominion ;
For when in Chatham Street the good man dwelt,
　　No one would give a *sous* for his opinion.
And though his neighbors were extremely civil,
Yet, on the whole, they thought him—a poor devil.

VIII.

A decent kind of person ; one whose head
　　Was not of brains particularly full ;
It was not known that he had ever said
　　Any thing worth repeating—'twas a dull,
Good, honest man—what Paulding's muse would call
A " cabbage-head "—but he excelled them all

IX.

In that most noble of the sciences,
　　The art of making money ; and he found
The zeal for quizzing him grew less and less,
　　· As he grew richer ; till upon the ground
Of Pearl Street, treading proudly in the might
And majesty of wealth, a sudden light

X.

Flashed like the midnight lightning on the eyes
  Of all who knew him : brilliant traits of mind,
And genius, clear, and countless as the dyes
  Upon the peacock's plumage ; taste refined,
Wisdom and wit, were his—perhaps much more—
'Twas strange they had not found it out before.

XI.

In this quick transformation, it is true
  That cash had no small share ; but there were still
Some other causes, which then gave a new
  Impulse to head and heart, and joined to fill
His brain with knowledge ; for there first he met
The editor of the New York Gazette—

XII.

The sapient Mr. LANG. The world of him
  Knows much, yet not one-half so much as he
Knows of the world. Up to its very brim
  The goblet of his mind is sparkling free
With lore and learning. Had proud Sheba's queen,
In all her bloom and beauty, but have seen

XIII.

This modern Solomon, the Israelite,
  Earth's monarch as he was, had never won her.

He would have hanged himself for very spite,
   And she, blessed woman, might have had the honor
Of some neat " paragraphs "—worth all the lays
That Judah's minstrel warbled in her praise.

XIV.

Her star arose too soon ; but that which swayed
   Th' ascendant at our merchant's natal hour
Was bright with better destiny—its aid
   Led him to pluck within the classic bower
Of bulletins, the blossoms of true knowledge,
And LANG supplied the loss of school and college.

XV.

For there he learned the news some minutes sooner
   Than others could ; and to distinguish well
The different signals, whether ship or schooner,
   Hoisted at Staten Island ; and to tell
The change of wind, and of his neighbor's fortunes,
And, best of all—he there learned self-importance.

XVI.

Nor were these all the advantages derived
   From change of scene ; for near his domicil
HE of the pair of polished lamps then lived,
   And in my hero's promenades, at will,
Could he behold them burning—and their flame
Kindled within his breast the love of fame—

XVII.

And politics, and country; the pure glow
  Of patriot ardor, and the consciousness
That talents such as his might well bestow
  A lustre on the city; she would bless
His name; and that some service should be done her,
He pledged " life, fortune, and his sacred honor."

XVIII.

And when the sounds of music and of mirth,
  Bursting from Fashion's groups assembled there,
Were heard, as round their lone plebeian hearth
  Fanny and he were seated—he would dare
To whisper fondly that the time might come
When he and his could give as brilliant routs at home

XIX.

And oft would Fanny near that mansion linger,
  When the cold winter moon was high in heaven,
And trace out, by the aid of Fancy's finger,
  Cards for some future party, to be given
When she in turn should be a *belle*, and they
Had lived their little hour, and passed away.

XX.

There are some happy moments in this lone
  And desolate world of ours, that well repay

The toil of struggling through it, and atone
  For many a long, sad night and weary day.
They come upon the mind like some wild air
Of distant music, when we know not where,

XXI.

Or whence, the sounds are brought from, and their
    power,
  Though brief, is boundless. That far, future home,
Oft dreamed of, beckons near — its rose - wreathed
    bower,
  And cloudless skies before us : we become
Changed on the instant—all gold leaf and gilding ;
This is, in vulgar phrase, called " castle-building."

XXII.

But these, like sunset clouds, fade soon ; 'tis vain
  To bid them linger longer, or to ask
On what day they intend to call again ;
  And, surely, 'twere a philosophic task,
Worthy a Mitchill, in his hours of leisure,
To find some means to summon them at pleasure.

XXIII.

There certainly are powers of doing this,
  In some degree at least—for instance, drinking.
Champagne will bathe the heart a while in bliss,
  And keep the head a little time from thinking

Of cares or creditors—the best wine in town
You'll get from Lynch—the cash must be paid down.

XXIV.

But if you are a bachelor, like me,
    And spurn all chains, even though made of roses,
I'd recommend cigars—there is a free
    And happy spirit, that, unseen, reposes
On the dim shadowy clouds that hover o'er you,
When smoking quietly with a warm fire before you.

. XXV.

Dear to the exile is his native land,
    In memory's twilight beauty seen afar :
Dear to the broker is a note of hand,
    Collaterally secured—the polar star
Is dear at midnight to the sailor's eyes,
And dear are Bristed's volumes at "half price ; "

XXVI.

But dearer far to me each fairy minute
    Spent in that fond forgetfulness of grief;
There is an airy web of magic in it,
    As in Othello's pocket-handkerchief,
Veiling the wrinkles on the brow of Sorrow,
The gathering gloom to-day, the thunder-cloud to-
    morrow.

XXVII.

And these are innocent thoughts—a man may sit
   Upon a bright throne of his own creation :
Untortured by the ghastly sprites that flit
   Around the many, whose exalted station
Has been attained by means 'twere pain to hint on,
Just for the rhyme's sake—instance Mr. Clinton.

XXVIII.

He struggled hard, but not in vain, and breathes
   The mountain-air at last ; but there are others   ·
Who strove, like him, to win the glittering wreaths
   Of power, his early partisans and brothers,
That linger yet in dust from whence they sprung,
Unhonored and unpaid, though, luckily, unhung.

XXIX.

'Twas theirs to fill with gas the huge balloon
   Of party ; and they hoped, when it arose,
To soar like eagles in the blaze of noon,
   Above the gaping crowd of friends and foes.
Alas ! like Guillé's car, it soared without them,
And left them with a mob to jeer and flout them.

XXX.

Though Fanny's moonlight dreams were sweet as those
   I've dwelt so long upon—they were more stable ;

Hers were not "castles in the air" that rose
　Based upon nothing; for her sire was able,
As well she knew, to "buy out" the one-half
Of Fashion's glittering train, that nightly quaff

XXXI.

Wine, wit, and wisdom, at a midnight rout,
　From dandy coachmen, whose "exquisite" grin
And "ruffian" lounge flash brilliantly without,
　Down to their brother dandies ranged within,
Gay as the Brussels carpeting they tread on,
And sapient as the oysters they are fed on.

XXXII.

And Rumor (she's a famous liar, yet
　'Tis wonderful how easy we believe her)
Had whispered he was rich, and all he met
　In Wall Street, nodded, smiled, and "tipped the
　　beaver;"
All,—from Mr. Gelston, the collector,
Down to the broker, and the bank director.

XXXIII.

A few brief years passed over, and his rank
　Among the worthies of that street was fixed;
He had become director of a bank,
　And six insurance offices, and mixed

Familiarly, as one among his peers,
With grocers, dry-goods merchants, auctioneers,

XXXIV.

Brokers of all grades—stock and pawn—and Jews
 Of all religions, who at noonday form,
On 'Change, that brotherhood the moral muse
 Delights in, where the heart is pure and warm,
And each exerts his intellectual force
To cheat his neighbor—legally, of course.

XXXV.

And there he shone a planetary star,
 Circled around by lesser orbs, whose beams
From his were borrowed. The simile is not far
 From truth—for many bosom friends, it seems,
Did borrow of him, and sometimes forget
To pay—indeed, they have not paid him yet.

XXXVI.

But these he deemed as trifles, when each mouth
 Was open in his praise, and plaudits rose
Upon his willing ear, "like the sweet south
 Upon a bank of violets," from those
Who knew his talents, virtues, and so forth ;
That is—knew how much money he was worth.

XXXVII.

Alas! poor human nature ; had he been
  But satisfied with this, his golden days
Their setting hour of darkness had not seen,
  And he might still (in the mercantile phrase)
Be living "in good order and condition ; "
But he was ruined by that jade Ambition,

XXXVIII.

"That last infirmity of noble minds,"
  Whose spell, like whiskey, your true patriot liquor,
To politics the lofty heart inclines
  Of all, from Clinton down to the bill-sticker
Of a ward-meeting.   She came slyly creeping
To his bedside, where he lay snug and sleeping.

XXXIX.

Her brow was turbaned with a bucktail wreath,
  A brooch of terrapin her bosom wore,
Tompkins's letter was just seen beneath
  Her arm, and in her hand on high she bore
A National Advocate—Pell's polite Review
Lay at her feet—'twas pommelled black and blue.

XL.

She was in fashion's elegant undress,
  Muffled from throat to ankle ; and her hair

Was all "*en papillotes*," each auburn tress
   Prettily pinned apart. You well might swear
She was no beauty; yet, when "made up" ready
For visitors, 'twas quite another lady.

XLI.

Since that wise pedant, Johnson, was in fashion,
   Manners have changed as well as moons; and he
Would fret himself once more into a passion,
   Should he return (which Heaven forbid!) and see
How strangely from his standard dictionary
The meaning of some words is made to vary.

XLII.

For instance, an *undress* at present means
   The wearing a pelisse, a shawl, or so;
Or any thing you please, in short, that screens
   The face, and hides the form from top to toe;
Of power to brave a quizzing-glass, or storm—
'Tis worn in summer, when the weather's warm.

XLIII.

But a full dress is for a winter's night.
   The most genteel is made of "woven air;"
That kind of classic cobweb, soft and light,
   Which Lady Morgan's Ida used to wear.
And ladies, this aërial manner dressed in,
Look Eve-like, angel-like, and interesting.

XLIV.

But, Miss Ambition was, as I was saying,
  "*Déshabillée*"—his bedside tripping near,
And, gently on his nose her fingers laying,
  She roared out " Tammany ! " in his frighted ear.
The potent word awoke him from his nap,
And then she vanished, whispering *verbum sap.*

XLV.

The last words were beyond his comprehension,
  For he had left off schooling, ere the Greek
Or Latin classics claimed his mind's attention:
  Besides, he often had been heard to speak
Contemptuously of all that sort of knowledge,   .
Taught so profoundly in Columbia College.

XLVI.

We owe the ancients something.   You have read
  Their works, no doubt—at least in a translation ;
Yet there was argument in what he said,
  I scorn equivocation or evasion,
And own it must, in candor, be confessed
They were an ignorant set of men at best.

XLVII.

'Twas their misfortune to be born too soon
  By centuries, and in the wrong place too ;

They never saw a steamboat, or balloon,
   Velocipede, or Quarterly Review;
Or wore a pair of Baehr's black satin breeches,
Or read an Almanac, or Clinton's Speeches.

XLVIII.

In short, in every thing we far outshine them,—
   Art, science, taste, and talent; and a stroll
Through this enlightened city would refine them
   More than ten years' hard study of the whole
Their genius has produced of rich and rare—
God bless the Corporation and the Mayor!

XLIX.

In sculpture, we've a grace the Grecian master,
   Blushing, had owned his purest model lacks;
We've Mr. Bogart in the best of plaster,
   The Witch of Endor in the best of wax,
Besides the head of Franklin on the roof
Of Mr. Lang, both jest and weather-proof.

L.

And on our City Hall a Justice stands;
   A neater form was never made of board,
Holding majestically in her hands
   A pair of steelyards and a wooden sword;
And looking down with complaisant civility—
Emblem of dignity and durability.

6

LI.

In painting, we have Trumbull's proud *chef d'œuvre*,
   Blending in one the funny and the fine :
His " Independence " will endure forever,
   And so will Mr. Allen's lottery-sign ;
And all that grace the Academy of Arts,
From Dr. Hosack's face to Bonaparte's.

LII.

In architecture, our unrivalled skill
   Cullen's magnesian shop has loudly spoken
To an admiring world ; and better still
   Is Gautier's fairy palace at Hoboken.
In music, we've the Euterpian Society,
And amateurs, a wonderful variety.

LIII.

In physic, we have Francis and McNeven,
   Famed for long heads, short lectures, and long bills ;
And Quackenboss and others, who from heaven
   Were rained upon us in a shower of pills ;
They'd beat the deathless Æsculapius hollow,
And make a starveling druggist of Apollo.

LIV.

And who, that ever slumbered at the Forum,
   But owns the first of orators we claim :

Cicero would have bowed the knee before 'em—
    And for law eloquence, we've Doctor Graham.
Compared with him, their Justins and Quintilians
Had dwindled into second-rate civilians.

LV.

For purity and chastity of style,
    There's Pell's preface, and puffs by Horne and Waite.
For penetration deep, and learned toil,
    And all that stamps an author truly great,
Have we not Bristed's ponderous tomes? a treasure
For any man of patience and of leisure.

LVI.

Oxonian Bristed! many a foolscap page
    He, in his time, hath written, and moreover
(What few will do in this degenerate age)
    Hath read his own works, as you may discover
By counting his quotations from himself—
You'll find the books on any auction-shelf.

LVII.

I beg Great Britain's pardon; 'tis not meant
    To claim this Oxford scholar as our own;
That he was shipped off here to represent
    Her literature among us, is well known;
And none could better fill the lofty station
Of Learning's envoy from the British nation.

LVIII.

We fondly hope that he will be respected
  At home, and soon obtain a place or pension.
We should regret to see him live neglected,
  Like Fearon, Ashe, and others we could mention ;
Who paid us friendly visits to abuse
Our country, and find food for the reviews.

LIX.

But to return.—The Heliconian waters
  Are sparkling in their native fount no more,
And after years of wandering, the nine daughters
  Of poetry have found upon our shore
A happier home, and on their sacred shrines
Glow in immortal ink, the polished lines

LX.

Of Woodworth, Doctor Farmer, Moses Scott—
  Names hallowed by their reader's sweetest smile;
And who that reads at all has read them not?
  "That blind old man of Scio's rocky isle,"
Homer, was well enough ; but would he ever
Have written, think ye, the Backwoodsman? never.

LXI.

Alas! for Paulding—I regret to see
  In such a stanza one whose giant powers,

Seen in their native element, will be
  Known to a future age, the pride of ours.
There is none breathing that can better wield
The battle-axe of satire. On its field

LXII.

The wreath he fought for he has bravely won,
  Long be its laurel green around his brow !
It is too true, I'm somewhat fond of fun
  And jesting; but for once I'm serious now.
Why is he sipping weak Castalian dews ?
The muse has damned him—let him damn the muse.

LXIII.

But to return once more : the ancients fought
  Some tolerable battles. Marathon
Is still a theme for high and holy thought,
  And many a poet's lay. We linger on   ·
The page that tells us of the brave and free,
And reverence thy name, unmatched Thermopylæ.

LXIV.

And there were spirited troops in other days—
  The Roman legion and the Spartan band,
And Swartwout's gallant corps, the Iron Grays—·
  Soldiers who met their foemen hand to hand,
Or swore, at least, to meet them undismayed;
Yet what were these to General Laight's brigade

LXV.

Of veterans? nursed in that Free School of glory,
   The New York State Militia.   From Bellevue,
E'en to the Battery flag-staff, the proud story
   Of their manœuvres at the last review
Has rung; and Clinton's "order" told afar
He never led a better corps to war.

LXVI.

What, Egypt, was thy magic, to the tricks
   Of Mr. Charles, Judge Spencer, or Van Buren?
The first with cards, the last in politics,
   A conjuror's fame for years have been securing.
And who would now the Athenian dramas read,
When he can get "Wall Street," by Mr. Mead?

LXVII.

I might say much about our lettered men,
   Those "grave and reverend seigniors," who compose
Our learned societies—but here my pen
   Stops short; for they themselves, the rumor goes,
The exclusive privilege by patent claim,
Of trumpeting (as the phrase is) their own fame.

LXVIII.

And, therefore, I am silent.   It remains
   To bless the hour the Corporation took it

Into their heads to give the rich in brains
  The worn-out mansion of the poor in pocket,
Once "the old almshouse," now a school of wisdom,   -
Sacred to Scudder's shells and Dr. Griscom.

LXIX.

But whither am I wandering? The esteem
  I bear "this fairy city of the heart,"
To me a dear enthusiastic theme,
  Has forced me, all unconsciously, to part
Too long from him, the hero of my story.
Where was he?—waking from his dream of glory.

LXX.

And she, the lady of his dream, had fled,
  And left him somewhat puzzled and confused.
He understood, however, half she said;
  And that is quite as much as we are used
To comprehend, or fancy worth repeating,
In speeches heard at any public meeting.

LXXI.

And the next evening found him at the Hall;
  There he was welcomed by the cordial hand,
And met the warm and friendly grasp of all
  Who take, like watchmen, there, their nightly stand,
A ring, as in a boxing-match, procuring,
To bet on Clinton, Tompkins, or Van Buren.

LXXII.

'Twas a propitious moment ; for a while
    The waves of party were at rest. Upon
Each complacent brow was gay good-humor's smile:
    And there was much of wit, and jest, and pun.
And high amid the circle, in great glee,
Sat Croaker's old acquaintance, John Targee.

LXXIII.

His jokes excelled the rest, and oft he sang
    Songs, patriotic, as in duty bound.
He had a little of the " nasal twang
    Heard at conventicle ; " but yet you found
In him a dash of purity and brightness,
That spoke the man of taste and of politeness.

LXXIV.

For he had been, it seems, the bosom friend
    Of England's prettiest bard, Anacreon Moore.
They met, when he, the bard, came here to lend
    His mirth and music to this favorite shore;
For, as the proverb saith, "birds of a feather
Instinctively will flock and fly together."

LXXV.

The winds that wave thy cedar-boughs are breathing,
    "Lake of the Dismal Swamp !" that poet's name;

And the spray-showers their noonday halos wreathing
  Around "Cohoes," are brightened by his fame.
And bright its sunbeam o'er St. Lawrence smiles,
Her million lilies, and her thousand isles.

LXXVI.

We hear his music in her oarmen's lay,
  And where her church-bells "toll the evening
    chime;"
Yet when to him the grateful heart would pay
  Its homage, now, and in all coming time,
Up springs a doubtful question whether we
Owe it to Tara's minstrel or Targee.

LXXVII.

Together oft they wandered—many a spot
  Now consecrated, as the minstrel's theme,
By words of beauty ne'er to be forgot,
  Their mutual feet have trod; and when the stream
Of thought and feeling flowed in mutual speech,
'Twere vain to tell how much each taught to each.

LXXVIII.

But, from the following song, it would appear
  That he of Erin from the sachem took
The model of his " Bower of Bendemeer,"
  One of the sweetest airs in Lalla Rookh;

'Tis to be hoped that, in his next edition,
This, the original, will find admission :

SONG.

There's a barrel of porter at Tammany Hall,
　And the bucktails are swigging it all the night
　　long ;
In the time of my boyhood 'twas pleasant to call
　For a seat and cigar, 'mid the jovial throng.

That beer and those bucktails I never forget ;
　But oft, when alone, and unnoticed by all,
I think, is the porter-cask foaming there yet ?
　Are the bucktails still swigging at Tammany Hall ?

No ! the porter was out long before it was stale,
　But some blossoms on many a hose brightly
　　shone,
And the speeches inspired by the fumes of the ale,
　Had the fragrance of porter when porter was gone.

How much Cozzens will draw of such beer ere he
　dies,
　Is a question of moment to me and to all ;
For still dear to my soul, as 'twas then to my eyes,
　Is that barrel of porter at Tammany Hall.

SONG.

There's a bower of roses by Bendemeer's stream,
  And the nightingale sings round it all the night long ;
In the time of my childhood 'twas like a sweet dream
  To sit in the roses and hear the bird's song.

That bower and its music I never forget ;
  But oft, when alone, in the bloom of the year,
I think, is the nightingale singing there yet ?
  Are the roses still bright by the calm Bendemeer ?

No ! the roses soon withered that hung o'er the wave,
  But some blossoms were gathered when freshly they
    shone ;
And a dew was distilled from their flowers, that gave
  All the fragrance of summer when summer was gone.

Thus memory draws from delight ere it dies,
  An essence that breathes of it many a year ;
Thus bright to my soul, as 'twas then to my eyes,
  Is that bower on the banks of the calm Bendemeer.

LXXIX.

For many months my hero ne'er neglected
  To take his ramble there, and soon found out,
In much less time than one could have expected,
  What 'twas they all were quarrelling about.

He learned the party countersigns by rote,
And when to clap his hands, and how to vote.

LXXX.

He learned that Clinton became Governor
  Somehow by chance, when we were all asleep;
That he had neither sense, nor talent, nor
  Any good quality, and would not keep
His place an hour after the next election—
So powerful was the voice of disaffection:

LXXXI.

That he was a mere puppet made to play
  A thousand tricks, while Spencer touched the
    springs—
Spencer, the mighty Warwick of his day,
  " That setter up and puller down of kings,"
Aided by Miller, Pell, and Doctor Graham,
And other men of equal worth and fame:

LXXXII.

And that he'd set the people at defiance,
  By placing knaves and fools in public stations;
And that his works in literature and-science
  Were but a schoolboy's web of misquotations;
And that he quoted from the devil even—
" Better to reign in hell than serve in heaven."

LXXXIII.

To these authentic facts each bucktail swore ;
  But Clinton's friends averred, in contradiction,
They were but fables, told by Mr. Noah,
  Who had a privilege to deal in fiction,
Because he'd written travels, and a melo-
Drama ; and was, withal, a pleasant fellow.

LXXXIV.

And they declared that Tompkins was no better
  Than he should be ; that he had borrowed money,
And paid it—not in cash—but with a letter ;
  And, though some trifling service he had done, he
Still wanted spirit, energy, and fire ;
And was disliked by—Mr. McIntyre.

LXXXV.

In short, each one with whom in conversation
  He joined, contrived to give him different views
Of men and measures ; and the information
  Which he obtained, but aided to confuse
His brain.   At best, 'twas never very clear ;
And now 'twas turned with politics and beer.

LXXXVI.

And he was puffed, and flattered, and caressed
  By all, till he sincerely thought that Nature

Had formed him for an alderman at least —
  Perhaps, a member of the Legislature;
And that he had the talents, ten times over,
Of Henry Meigs, or Peter H. Wendover.

LXXXVII.

The man was mad, 'tis plain, and merits pity,
  Or he had never dared, in such a tone,
To speak of two great persons, whom the city
  With pride and pleasure points to as her own—
Men wise in council, brilliant in debate,
".The expectancy and rose of the fair state."

LXXXVIII.

The one—for a pure style and classic manner,
  Is—Mr. Sachem Mooney far before;
The other, in his speech about the banner,
  Spell-bound his audience until they swore
That such a speech was never heard till then,
And never would be—till he spoke again.

LXXXIX.

Though 'twas presumptuous in this friend of ours
  To think of rivalling these, I must allow
That still the man had talents; and the powers
  Of his capacious intellect were now
Improved by foreign travel, and by reading,
And at the Hall he'd learned, of course, good-breeding

XC.

He had read the newspapers with great attention,
    Advertisements and all; and Riley's book
Of travels—valued for its rich invention;
    And Day and Turner's Price Current; and took
The Edinburgh and Quarterly Reviews;
And also Colonel Pell's; and to amuse

XCI.

His leisure hours with classic tale and story,
    Longworth's Directory, and Mead's Wall Street,
And Mr. Delaplaine's Repository;
    And Mitchill's scientific works complete,
With other standard books of modern days,
Lay on his table, covered with green baize.

XCII.

His travels had extended to Bath races;
    And Bloomingdale and Bergen he had seen,
And Harlem Heights; and many other places,
    By sea and land, had visited; and been,
In a steamboat of the Vice-President's,
To Staten Island once—for fifty cents.

XCIII.

And he had dined, by special invitation,
    On turtle, with " the party" at Hoboken;

And thanked them for his card in an oration,
  Declared to be the shortest ever spoken.
And he had strolled one day o'er Weehawk hill:
A day worth all the rest—he recollects it still.

XCIV.

Weehawken !—In thy mountain scenery yet,
  All we adore of Nature, in her wild
And frolic hour of infancy, is met ;
  And never has a summer's morning smiled
Upon a lovelier scene, than the full eye
Of the enthusiast revels on—when high

XCV.

Amid thy forest solitudes, he climbs
  O'er crags, that proudly tower above the deep,
And knows that sense of danger which sublimes
  The breathless moment—when his daring step
Is on the verge of the cliff, and he can hear
The low dash of the wave with startled ear—

XCVI.

Like the death-music of his coming doom.
  And clings to the green turf with desperate force,
As the heart clings to life ; and when resume
  The currents in his veins their wonted course,
There lingers a deep feeling—like the moan
Of wearied ocean, when the storm is gone.

XCVII.

In such an hour he turns, and on his view,
 Ocean, and earth, and heaven, burst before him ;
Clouds slumbering at his feet, and the clear blue
 Of summer's sky in beauty bending o'er him—
The city bright below ; and far away,
Sparkling in golden light, his own romantic bay.

XCVIII.

Tall spire, and glittering roof, and battlement,
 And banners floating in the sunny air ;
And white sails o'er the calm blue waters bent,
 Green isle, and circling shore, are blended there
In wild reality.   When life is old,
And many a scene forgot, the heart will hold

XCIX.

Its memory of this ; nor lives there one
 Whose infant breath was drawn, or boyhood's days
Of happiness were passed beneath that sun,
 That in his manhood's prime can calmly gaze
Upon that bay, or on that mountain stand,
Nor feel the prouder of his native land.

C.

" This may be poetry, for aught I know,"
 Said an old, worthy friend of mine, while leaning

Over my shoulders as I wrote ; "although
  I can't exactly comprehend its meaning.
For my part, I have long been a petitioner
To Mr. John McComb, the Street Commissioner—

CI.

" That he would think of Weehawk, and would lay it
  Handsomely out in avenue and square ;
Then tax the land and make its owners pay it
  (As is the usual plan pursued elsewhere) ;
Blow up the rocks, and sell the wood for fuel—
'Twould save us many a dollar, and a duel."

. CII.

" The devil take you and John McComb," said I ;
  " Lang, in its praise, has penned one paragraph,
And promised me another.   I defy,
  With such assistance, yours and the world's laugh ;
And half believe that Paulding, on this theme,
Might be a poet—strange as it may seem."

CIII.

For even our traveller felt, when home returning
  From that day's tour, as on the deck he stood,
The fire of poetry within him burning ;
  " Albeit unused to the rhyming mood ; "
And with a pencil on his knee he wrote
The following flaming lines

TO THE HORSEBOAT.

1.

Away—o'er the wave to the home we are seeking,
   Bark of my hope! ere the evening be gone;
There's a wild, wild note in the curlew's shrieking;
   There's a whisper of death in the wind's low moan.

2.

Though blue and bright are the heavens above me,
   And the stars are asleep on the quiet sea;
And hearts I love, and hearts that love me,
   Are beating beside me merrily:

3.

Yet, far in the west, where the day's faded roses,
   Touched by the moonbeam, are withering fast;
Where the half-seen spirit of twilight reposes,
   Hymning the dirge of the hours that are past—

4.

There, where the ocean-wave sparkles at meeting
   (As sunset dreams tell us) the kiss of the sky,
On his dim, dark cloud is the infant storm sitting,
   And beneath the horizon his lightnings are nigh.

5.

Another hour—and the death-word is given,
  Another hour—and his lightnings are here;
Speed! speed thee, my bark; ere the breeze of even
  Is lost in the tempest, our home will be near.

6.

Then away o'er the wave, while thy pennant is stream-
      ing
  In the shadowy light, like a shooting-star;
Be swift as the thought of the wanderer, dreaming,
  In a stranger land, of his fireside afar.

7.

And while memory lingers I'll fondly believe thee
  A being with life and its best feelings warm;
And freely the wild song of gratitude weave thee,
  Blessed spirit! that bore me and mine from the storm.

CIV.

But where is Fanny? She has long been thrown
  Where cheeks and roses wither—in the shade.
The age of chivalry, you know, is gone;
  And although, as I once before have said,
I love a pretty face to adoration,
Yet, still, I must preserve my reputation,

CV.

As a true dandy of the modern schools.
   One hates to be old-fashioned; it would be
A violation of the latest rules,
   To treat the sex with too much courtesy.
'Tis not to worship beauty, as she glows
In all her diamond lustre, that the beaux

CVI.

Of these enlightened days at evening crowd,
   Where Fashion welcomes in her rooms of light
That "dignified obedience; that proud
   Submission," which, in times of yore, the knight
Gave to his "ladye-love," is now a scandal,
And practised only by your Goth and Vandal.

CVII.

·To lounge in graceful attitudes—be stared
   Upon, the while, by every fair one's eye,
And stare one's self, in turn : to be prepared
   To dart upon the trays, as swiftly by
The dexterous Simon bears them, and to take
One's share at least of coffee, cream, and cake,

CVIII.

Is now to be "the ton." The pouting lip,
   And sad, upbraiding eye of the poor girl,

Who hardly of joy's cup one drop can sip,
  Ere in the wild confusion, and the whirl,
And tumult of the hour, its bubbles vanish,
Must now be disregarded. One must banish

CIX.

Those antiquated feelings, that belong
  To feudal manners and a barbarous age.
Time was—when woman " poured her soul " in song,
  That all was hushed around. 'Tis now " the rage "
To deem a song, like bugle-tones in battle,
A signal-note, that bids each tongue's artillery rattle.

CX.

And, therefore, I have made Miss Fanny wait
  My leisure. She had changed, as you will see, as
Much as her worthy sire, and made as great
  Proficiency in taste and high ideas.
The careless smile of other days was gone,
And every gesture spoke "*qu'en dira-t-on ?*"

CXI.

She long had known that in her father's coffers,
  And also to his credit in the banks,
There was some cash ; and therefore all the offers
  Made her, by gentlemen of the middle ranks,
Of heart and hand, had spurned, as far beneath
One whose high destiny it was to breathe,

CXII.

Ere long, the air of Broadway or Park Place,
　And reign a fairy queen in fairy land ;
Display in the gay dance her form of grace,
　Or touch with rounded arm and gloveless hand,
Harp or piano.—Madame Catilani
Forgot awhile, and every eye on Fanny.

CXIII.

And in anticipation of that hour,
　Her star of hope, her paradise of thought,
She'd had as many masters as the power
　Of riches could bestow ; and had been taught
The thousand nameless graces that adorn
The daughters of the wealthy and high-born.

CXIV.

She had been noticed at some public places
　(The Battery, and the balls of Mr. Whale),
For hers was one of those attractive faces,
　That when you gaze upon them, never fail
To bid you look again ; there was a beam,
A lustre in her eye, that oft would seem

CXV.

A little like effrontery ; and yet
　The lady meant no harm ; her only aim

Was but to be admired by all she met,
　And the free homage of the heart to claim ;
And if she showed too plainly this intention,
Others have done the same—'twas not of her invention.

CXVI.

She shone at every concert ; where are bought
　Tickets by all who wish them, for a dollar ;
She patronized the Theatre, and thought
　That Wallack looked extremely well in Rolla ;
She fell in love, as all the ladies do,
With Mr. Simpson—talked as loudly, too,

CXVII.

As any beauty of the highest grade,
　To the gay circle in the box beside her ;
And when the pit—half vexed and half afraid,
　With looks of smothered indignation eyed her,
She calmly met their gaze, and stood before 'em,
Smiling at vulgar taste and mock decorum.

CXVIII.

And though by no means a *bas bleu*, she had
　For literature a most becoming passion ;
Had skimmed the latest novels, good and bad,
　And read the Croakers, when they were in fashion ;
And Dr. Chalmers' sermons of a Sunday ;
And Woodworth's Cabinet, and the new Salmagundi.

CXIX.

She was among the first and warmest patrons
  Of Griscom's *conversaziones,* where
In rainbow groups, our bright-eyed maids and matrons,
  On science bent, assemble ; to prepare
Themselves for acting well, in life, their part
As wives and mothers.   There she learned by heart

CXX.

Words, to the witches in Macbeth unknown.
  Hydraulics, hydrostatics, and *pneumatics,*
Dioptrics, optics, katoptrics, carbon,
  Chlorine, and *iodine,* and *aërostatics ;*
Also,—why frogs, for want of air, expire ;
And how to set the Tappan Sea on fire !

CXXI.

In all the modern languages she was
  Exceedingly well-versed ; and had devoted,
To their attainment, far more time than has,
  By the best teachers, lately been allotted ;
For she had taken lessons, twice a week,
For a full month in each ; and she could speak

CXXII.

French and Italian, equally as well
  As Chinese, Portuguese, or German ; and,

7

What is still more surprising, she could spell
  Most of our longest English words off-hand ;
Was quite familiar in Low Dutch and Spanish,
And thought of studying modern Greek and Danish.

CXXIII.

She sang divinely ; and in " Love's young dream "
  And " Fanny dearest," and " The soldier's bride ; "
And every song, whose dear delightful theme,
  Is " Love, still love," had oft till midnight tried
Her finest, loftiest " pigeon-wings " of sound,
Waking the very watchmen far around.

CXXIV.

For her pure taste in dress, I can appeal to
  Madame Bouquet, and Monsieur Pardessus ;
She was, in short, a woman you might kneel to,
  If kneeling were in fashion ; or if you
Were wearied of your duns and single life,
And wanted a few thousands and a wife.

CXXV.

     *   *   *   *   *   *

     *   *   *   *   *   *

CXXVI.

' There was a sound of revelry by night ; "
   Broadway was thronged with coaches, and within
A mansion of the best of brick, the bright
   And eloquent eyes of beauty bade begin
The dance ; and music's tones swelled wild and high,
And hearts and heels kept tune in tremulous ecstasy.

CXXVII.

For many a week, the note of preparation
   Had sounded through all circles far and near ;
And some five hundred cards of invitation
   Bade beau and belle in full costume appear ;
There was a most magnificent variety,
All quite select, and of the first society.

CXXVIII.

That is to say—the rich and the well-bred,
   The arbiters of fashion and gentility,
In different grades of splendor, from the head
   Down to the very toe of our nobility :
Ladies, remarkable for handsome eyes
Or handsome fortunes—learned men, and wise

CXXIX.

Statesmen, and officers of the militia—
   In short, the " first society "—a phrase,

Which you may understand as best may fit you ;
  Besides the blackest fiddlers of those days,
Placed like their sire, Timótheus, on high,
With horsehair fiddle-bows and teeth of ivory.

CXXX.

The carpets were rolled up the day before,
  And, with a breath, two rooms became but one,
Like man and wife—and, on the polished floor,
  Chalk in the artists' plastic hand had done
All that chalk could do—in young Eden's bowers
They seemed to tread, and their feet pressed on flowers.

CXXXI

And when the thousand lights of spermaceti
  Streamed like a shower of sunbeams—and free tresses
Wild as the heads that waved them—and a pretty
  Collection of the latest Paris dresses
Wandered about the room like things divine,
It was, as I was told, extremely fine.

CXXXII.

The love of fun, fine faces, and good eating,
  Brought many who were tired of self and home ;
And some were there in the high hope of meeting
  The lady of their bosom's love—and some
To study that deep science, how to please,
And manners in high life, and high-souled courtesies.

CXXXIII.

And he, the hero of the night was there,
  In breeches of light drab, and coat of blue.
Taste was conspicuous in his powdered hair,
  And in his frequent *jeux de mots*, that drew   .
Peals of applauses from the listeners round,
Who were delighted—as in duty bound.

CXXXIV.

'Twas Fanny's father—Fanny near him stood,
  Her power, resistless—and her wish, command ;
And Hope's young promises were all made good ;
  " She reigned a fairy queen in fairy land ; "
Her dream of infancy a dream no more,
And then how beautiful the dress she wore !

CXXXV.

Ambition with her sire had kept her word.
  He had the rose, no matter for its thorn,
And he seemed happy as a summer bird,
  Careering on wet wing to meet the morn.
Some said there was a cloud upon his brow ;
It might be—but we'll not discuss that now.

CXXXVI.

I left him making rhymes while crossing o'er
  The broad and perilous wave of the North River.

He bade adieu, when safely on the shore,
   To poetry—and, as he thought, forever.
That night his dream (if after-deeds make known
Our plans in sleep) was an enchanting one.

CXXXVII.

He woke, in strength, like Samson from his slumber,
   And walked Broadway, enraptured the next day;
Purchased a house there—I've forgot the number—
   And signed a mortgage and a bond, for pay.
Gave, in the slang phrase, Pearl Street the go-by,
And cut, for several months, St. Tammany.

CXXXVIII.

Bond, mortgage, title-deeds, and all completed,
   He bought a coach and half a dozen horses
(The bill's at Lawrence's—not yet receipted—
   You'll find the amount upon his list of losses),
Then filled his rooms with servants, and whatever
Is necessary for a " genteel liver."

CXXXIX.

This last removal fixed him : every stain
   Was blotted from his " household coat," and he
Now " showed the world he was a gentleman,"
   And, what is better, could afford to be;
His step was loftier than it was of old,
His laugh less frequent, and his manner told

CXL.

What lovers call "unutterable things "—
  That sort of dignity was in his mien
Which awes the gazer into ice, and brings
  To recollection some great man we've seen,
The Governor, perchance, whose eye and frown,
  'Twas shrewdly guessed, would knock Judge Skinner
    down.

CXLI.

And for "Resources," both of purse and head,
  He was a subject worthy Bristed's pen ‡
Believed devoutly all his flatterers said,
  And deemed himself a Crœsus among men ;
Spread to the liberal air his silken sails,
And lavished guineas like a Prince of Wales.

CXLII.

He mingled now with those within whose veins
  The blood ran pure—the magnates of the land—
Hailed them as his companions and his friends,
  And lent them money and his note of hand.
In every institution, whose proud aim
Is public good alone, he soon became

CXLIII.

A man of consequence and notoriety;
  His name, with the addition of esquire,

Stood high upon the list of each society,
 Whose zeal and watchfulness the sacred fire
Of science, agriculture, art, and learning,
Keep on our country's altars bright and burning.

CXLIV.

At Eastburn's Rooms he met, at two each day,
 With men of taste and judgment like his own,
And played " first fiddle " in that orchestra
 Of literary worthies—and the tone
Of his mind's music by the listeners caught,
Is traced among them still in language and in thought.

CXLV.

He once made the Lyceum a choice present
 Of muscle-shells picked up at Rockaway ;
And Mitchill gave a classical and pleasant
 Discourse about them in the streets that day,
Naming the shells, and hard to put in verse 'twas
 " Testaceous coverings of bivalve molluscas."

CXLVI.

He was a trustee of a Savings Bank,
 And lectured soundly every evil-doer,
Gave dinners daily to wealth, power, and rank,
 And sixpence every Sunday to the poor ;
He was a wit, in the pun-making line—
Past fifty years of age, and five feet nine.

CXLVII.

But as he trod to grandeur's pinnacle,
  With eagle eye and step that never faltered,
The busy tongue of scandal dared to tell
  That cash was scarce with him, and credit altered;
And while he stood the envy of beholders,
The Bank Directors grinned, and shrugged their shoul-
  ders.

CXLVIII.

And when these, the Lord Burleighs of the minute,
  Shake their sage heads, and look demure and holy,
Depend upon it there is something in it;
  For whether born of wisdom or of folly,
Suspicion is a being whose fell power
Blights every thing it touches, fruit and flower.

CXLIX.

Some friends (they were his creditors) once hinted
  About retrenchment and a day of doom;
He thanked them, as no doubt they kindly meant it,
  And made this speech when they had left the room:
"Of all the curses upon mortals sent,
One's creditors are the most impudent;

CL.

"Now I am one who knows what he is doing,
  And suits exactly to his means his ends;

How can a man be in the path to ruin,
  When all the brokers are his bosom friends?
Yet, on my hopes, and those of my dear daughter,
These rascals throw a bucket of cold water !

CLI.

" They'd wrinkle with deep cares the prettiest face,
  Pour gall and wormwood in the sweetest cup,
Poison the very wells of life—and place
  Whitechapel needles, with their sharp points up,
Even in the softest feather bed that e'er
Was manufactured by upholsterer."

CLII.

This said—he journeyed "at his own sweet will,"
  Like one of Wordsworth's rivers, calmly on ;
But yet, at times, Reflection, "in her still
  Small voice," would whisper, something must be done ;
He asked advice of Fanny, and the maid
Promptly and duteously lent her aid.

CLIII.

She told him, with that readiness of mind
  And quickness of perception which belong
Exclusively to gentle womankind,
  That to submit to slanderers was wrong,
And the best plan to silence and admonish them,
Would be to give " a party "—and astonish them.

CLIV.

The hint was taken—and the party given;
 And Fanny, as I said some pages since,
Was there in power and loveliness that even,
 And he, her sire, demeaned him like a prince,
And all was joy—it looked a festival,
Where pain might smooth his brow, and grief her
 smiles recall.

CLV.

But Fortune, like some others of her sex,
 Delights in tantalizing and tormenting;
One day we feed upon their smiles—the next
 Is spent in swearing, sorrowing, and repenting.
(If in the last four lines the author lies,
He's always ready to apologize.)

CLVI.

Eve never walked in Paradise more pure
 Than on that morn when Satan played the devil,
With her and all her race.   A love-sick wooer
 Ne'er asked a kinder maiden, or more civil,
Than Cleopatra was to Antony
The day she left him on the Ionian sea.

CLVII.

The serpent—loveliest in his coilèd ring,
 With eye that charms, and beauty that outvies

The tints of the rainbow—bears upon his sting
   The deadliest venom.   Ere the dolphin dies
Its hues are brightest.   Like an infant's breath
Are tropic winds before the voice of death

CLVIII.

Is heard upon the waters, summoning
   The midnight earthquake from its sleep of years
To do its task of woe.   The clouds that fling
   The lightning, brighten ere the bolt appears;
The pantings of the warrior's heart are proud
Upon that battle morn whose night-dews wet his shroud;

CLIX.

The sun is loveliest as he sinks to rest;
   The leaves of autumn smile when fading fast;
The swan's last song is sweetest—and the best
   Of Meigs's speeches, doubtless, was his last.
And thus the happiest scene, in these my rhymes,
Closed with a crash, and ushered in—hard times.

CLX.

St. Paul's tolled one—and fifteen minutes after
   Down came, by accident, a chandelier;
The mansion tottered from the floor to rafter!
   Up rose the cry of agony and fear!
And there was shrieking, screaming, bustling, fluttering,
Beyond the power of writing or of uttering.

CLXI.

The company departed, and neglected
  To say good-by—the father stormed and swore—
The fiddlers grinned—the daughter looked dejected—
  The flowers had vanished from the polished floor,
And both betook them to their sleepless beds,
With hearts and prospects broken, but no heads.

CLXII.

The desolate relief of free complaining
  Came with the morn, and with it came bad weather;
The wind was east-northeast, and it was raining
  Throughout that day, which, take it altogether,
Was one whose memory clings to us through life,
Just like a suit in Chancery, or a wife.

CLXIII.

That evening, with a most important face
  And dreadful knock, and tidings still more dreadful,
A notary came—sad things had taken place;
  My hero had forgot to " do the needful; "
A note (amount not stated), with his name on't,
Was left unpaid—in short, he had "stopped payment."

CLXIV.

I hate your tragedies, both long and short ones
  (Except Tom Thumb, and Juan's Pantomime);

And stories woven of sorrows and misfortunes
   Are bad enough in prose, and worse in rhyme:
Mine, therefore, must be brief.   Under protest
His notes remain—the wise can guess the rest.

CLXV.

*   *   *   *   *   *

*   *   *   *   *   *

CLXVI.

For two whole days they were the common talk;
   The party, and the failure, and all that,
The theme of loungers in their morning walk,
   Porter-house reasoning, and tea-table chat.
The third, some newer wonder came to blot them,
And on the fourth, the " meddling world " forgot them.

CLXVII.

Anxious, however, something to discover,
   I passed their house—the shutters were all closed;
The song of knocker and of bell was over;
   Upon the steps two chimney-sweeps reposed;
And on the door my dazzled eyebeam met
These cabalistic words—" This house to let."

*

CLXVIII.

They live now, like chameleons, upon air
　And hope, and such cold, unsubstantial dishes ;
That they removed, is clear, but when or where
　None knew.　The curious reader, if he wishes,
May ask them, but in vain.　Where grandeur dwells,
The marble dome—the popular rumor tells ;

CLXIX.

But of the dwelling of the proud and poor,
　From their own lips the world will never know
When better days are gone—it is secure
　Beyond all other mysteries here below,
Except, perhaps, a maiden lady's age,
When past the noonday of life's pilgrimage.

CLXX.

Fanny !　'twas with her name my song began ;
　'Tis proper and polite her name should end it ;
If, in my story of her woes, or plan
　Or moral can be traced, 'twas not intended ;
And if I've wronged het, I can only tell her
I'm sorry for it—so is my bookseller.

CLXXI.

I met her yesterday—her eyes were wet—
　She faintly smiled, and said she had been reading

The Treasurer's Report in the Gazette,
  McIntyre's speech, and Campbell's " Love lies bleed-
    ing; "
She had a shawl on, 'twas not a Cashmere one,
And, if it cost five dollars, 'twas a dear one.

CLXXII.

Her father sent to Albany a prayer
  For office, told how Fortune had abused him,
And modestly requested to be Mayor—
  The Council very civilly refused him ;
Because, however much they might desire it,
The " public good," it seems, did not require it.

CLXXIII.

Some evenings since, he took a lonely stroll
  Along Broadway, scene of past joys and evils ;
He felt that withering bitterness of soul,
  Quaintly denominated the " blue devils ; "
And thought of Bonaparte and Belisarius,
Pompey, and Colonel Burr, and Caius Marius,

CLXXIV.

And envying the loud playfulness and mirth
  Of those who passed him, gay in youth and hope,
He took at Jupiter a shilling's worth
  Of gazing, through the showman's telescope ;

Sounds as of far-off bells came on his ears—
He fancied 'twas the music of the spheres.

CLXXV.

He was mistaken, it was no such thing,
   'Twas Yankee Doodle played by Scudder's band ·
He muttered, as he lingered listening,
   Something of freedom and our happy land ;
Then sketched, as to his home he hurried fast,
This sentimental song—his saddest, and his last :

SONG.

1.

Young thoughts have music in them, love
   And happiness their theme ;
And music wanders in the wind
   That lulls a morning dream.
And there are angel-voices heard,
   In childhood's frolic hours,
When life is but an April day
   Of sunshine and of showers.

2.

There's music in the forest-leaves
   When summer winds are there,
And in the laugh of forest girls
   That braid their sunny hair.

The first wild-bird that drinks the dew,
From violets of the spring,
Has music in his song, and in
The fluttering of his wing.

3.

There's music in the dash of waves
When the swift bark cleaves their foam;
There's music heard upon her deck,
The mariner's song of home,
When moon and star beams smiling meet
At midnight on the sea—
And there is music—once a week—
In Scudder's balcony.

4.

But the music of young thoughts too soon
Is faint, and dies away,
And from our morning dreams we wake
To curse the coming day.
And childhood's frolic hours are brief,
And oft in after-years
Their memory comes to chill the heart,
And dim the eye with tears.

5.

To-day the forest-leaves are green,
They'll wither on the morrow,

And the maiden's laugh be changed ere long
  To the widow's wail of sorrow.
Come with the winter snows, and ask,
  Where are the forest birds?
The answer is a silent one,
  More eloquent than words.

6.

The moonlight music of the waves
  In storms is heard no more,
When the living lightning mocks the wreck
  At midnight on the shore;
And the mariner's song of home has ceased,
  His corse is on the sea—
And music ceases when it rains
  In Scudder's balcony.

THE RECORDER.

THE RECORDER.[1]

A PETITION.

BY THOMAS CASTALY.

December 20, 1828.

"On they move
In perfect phalanx to the Dorian mood
Of flutes and soft RECORDERS."
MILTON.

"Live in Settle's numbers one day more!"
POPE.

MY dear RECORDER, you and I
    Have floated down life's stream together,
And kept unharmed our friendship's tie
Through every change of Fortune's sky,
    Her pleasant and her rainy weather.
Full sixty times since first we met,
Our birthday suns have risen and set,
And time has worn the baldness now
Of Julius Cæsar on your brow ;
Your brow, like his, a field of thought,
With broad deep furrows spirit-wrought,

Whose laurel-harvests long have shown
As green and glorious as his own ;
And proudly would the CÆSAR claim
Companionship with RIKER'S name,
His peer in forehead and in fame.

Both eloquent and learned and brave,
  Born to command and skilled to rule,
One made the citizen a slave,
  The other makes him more—a fool.
The Cæsar an imperial crown,
  His slaves' mad gift, refused to wear ;
The Riker put his fool's-cap on,
  And found it fitted to a hair ;
The Cæsar, though by birth and breeding,
Travel, the ladies, and light reading,
A gentleman in mien and mind,
  And fond of Romans and their mothers,
Was heartless as the Arab's wind,
And slew some millions of mankind,
  Including enemies and others.
The Riker, like Bob Acres, stood
Edgewise upon a field of blood,
  The where and wherefore Swartwout knows,
Pulled trigger, as a brave man should,
  And shot—God bless them—his own toes !
The Cæsar passed the Rubicon
With helm, and shield, and breastplate on,
  Dashing his war-horse through the waters ;

The Riker would have built a barge
Or steamboat at the city's charge,
   And passed it with his wife and daughters.

But let that pass. As I have said,
There's naught, save laurels, on your head,
And time has changed my clustering hair,
And showered the snow-flakes thickly there;
And though our lives have ever been
As different as their different scene ;
Mine more renowned for rhymes than riches,
Yours less for scholarship than speeches ;
Mine passed in low-roofed leafy bower,
Yours in high halls of pomp and power,
Yet are we, be the moral told,
Alike in one thing—growing old,
Ripened like summer's cradled sheaf,
Faded like autumn's falling leaf—
And nearing, sail and signal spread,
The quiet anchorage of the dead.
For such is human life, wherever
   The voyage of its bark may be,
On home's green-banked and gentle river,
Or the world's shoreless, sleepless sea.

Yes, you have floated down the tide
Of time, a swan in grace and pride
And majesty and beauty, till
The law, the Ariel of your will,
   8

Power's best beloved, the law of libel
(A bright link in the legal chain)
Expounded, settled, and made plain,
By your own charge, the juror's Bible,
Has clipped the venomed tongue of slander,
That dared to call you " Party's gander,
The leader of the geese who make
   Our city's parks and ponds their home,
And keep her liberties awake
   By cackling, as their sires saved Rome.
Gander of Party's pond, wherein
Lizard, and toad, and terrapin,
Your ale-house patriots, are seen,
   In Faction's feverish sunshine basking : "
And now, to rend this veil of lies,
Word-woven by your enemies,
And keep your sainted memory free
From tarnish with posterity,
   I take the liberty of asking
Permission, sir, to write your life,
With all its scenes of calm and strife,
   And all its turnings and its windings,
A poem, in a quarto volume—
Verse, like the subject, blank and solemn,
   With elegant appropriate bindings,
Of rat and mole skin the one half,
The other a part fox, part calf.
Your portrait, graven line for line,
From that immortal bust in plaster,

The master-piece of Art's great master,
   Mr. Praxiteles Browere,[2]
Whose trowel is a thing divine,
Shall smile and bow, and promise there,
And twenty-nine fine forms and faces
   (The Corporation and the Mayor),
Linked hand in hand, like Loves and Graces,
   Shall hover o'er it, grouped in air,
With wild pictorial dance and song ;
The song of happy bees in bowers,
The dance of Guido's graceful Hours,
All scattering Flushing's garden flowers[3]
   Round the dear head they've loved so long.

I know that you are modest, know
   That when you hear your merit's praise,
Your cheeks' quick blushes come and go,
Lily and rose-leaf, sun and snow,
   Like maidens' on their bridal days.
I know that you would fain decline
To aid me and the sacred Nine,
In giving to the asking earth
The story of your wit and worth ;
For if there be a fault to cloud
   The brightness of your clear good sense,
It is, and be the fact allowed,
   Your only failing—DIFFIDENCE !

An amiable weakness—given
   To justify the sad reflection,

That in this vale of tears not even
   A Riker is complete perfection,
A most romantic detestation
Of power and place, of pay and ration ;
A strange unwillingness to carry
   The weight of honor on your shoulders,
For which you have been named, the very
   Sensitive-plant of office-holders,
A shrinking bashfulness, whose grace
   Gives beauty to your manly face.
Thus shades the green and glowing vine
The rough bark of the mountain-pine,
Thus round her freedom's waking steel
   Harmodius wreathed his country's myrtle :
And thus the golden lemon's peel
   Gives fragrance to a bowl of turtle.

True, " many a flower," the poet sings,
   " Is born to blush unseen ; "
But you, although you blush, are not
   The flower the poets mean.
In vain you wooed a lowlier lot ;
   In vain you clipped your eagle-wings—
Talents like yours are not forgot
   And buried with earth's common things.
No ! my dear Riker, I would give
My laurels, living and to live,
Or as much cash as you could raise on
Their value, by hypothecation,

To be, for one enchanted hour,
In beauty, majesty, and power,
What you for forty years have been,
The Oberon of life's fairy scene.

An anxious city sought and found you
   In a blessed day of joy and pride,
Sceptred your jewelled hand, and crowned
   Her chief, her guardian, and her guide.
Honors which weaker minds had wrought
   In vain for years, and knelt and prayed for,
Are all your own, unpriced, unbought,
   Or (which is the same thing) unpaid for.
Painfully great ! against your will
   Her hundred offices to hold,
Each chair with dignity to fill,
   And your own pockets with her gold :
A sort of double duty, making
Your task a serious undertaking.
With what delight the eyes of all
Gaze on you, seated in your Hall,
   Like Sancho in his island, reigning,
Loved leader of its motley hosts
Of lawyers and their bills of costs,
   And all things thereto appertaining,
Such as crimes, constables, and juries,
Male pilferers and female furies,
The police and the *polissons*,
Illegal right and legal wrong,

Bribes, perjuries, law-craft, and cunning,
Judicial drollery and punning ;
And all the *et ceteras* that grace
That genteel, gentlemanly place !
Or in the Council Chamber standing
    With eloquence of eye and brow,
Your voice the music of commanding,
    And fascination in your bow,
Arranging for the civic shows
    Your " men in buckram," as per list,
Your John Does and your Richard Roes,
    Those Dummies of your games of whist.
The Council Chamber—where authority
Consists in two words—a majority.
For whose contractors' jobs we pay
    Our last dear sixpences for taxes,
As freely as in Sylla's day
    Rome bled beneath his lictors' axes.
Where—on each magisterial nose
    In colors of the rainbow linger,
Like sunset hues on Alpine snows,
    The printmarks of your thumb and finger.
Where he, the wisest of wild-fowl,
Bird of Jove's blue-eyed maid—the owl,
    That feathered alderman, is heard
Nightly, by poet's ear alone,
To other eyes and ears unknown,
    Cheering your every look and word,
And making, room and gallery through,

The loud applauding echoes peal,
Of his *" où peut on être mieux*
Qu'au sien de sa famille ? " [4]

Oh, for a herald's skill to rank
    Your titles in their due degrees !
At Sing Sing—at the Tradesman's Bank,
    In Courts, Committees, Caucuses :
At Albany, where those who knew
    The last year's secrets of the great,
Call you the golden handle to
    The earthen Pitcher of the State. [5]
(Poor Pitcher ! that Van Buren ceases
    To want its service gives me pain,
'Twill break into as many pieces
    As Kitty's of Coleraine.)
At Bellevue, on her banquet-night,
    Where Burgundy and business [6] meet,
On others, at the heart's delight,
    The Pewter Mug [7] in Frankfort Street ;
From Harlem bridge to Whitehall dock,
    From Bloomingdale to Blackwell's Isles,
Forming, including road and rock,
    A city of some twelve square miles,
O'er street and alley, square and block,
    Towers, temples, telegraphs, and tiles,
O'er wharves whose stone and timbers mock
The ocean's and its navies' shock,
O'er all the fleets that float before her,

O'er all their banners waving o'er her,
Her sky and waters, earth and air—
You are lord, for who is her lord mayor?
Where is he?   Echo answers, where?
And voices, like the sound of seas,
Breathe in sad chorus, on the breeze,
The Highland mourner's melody—
Oh HONE [8] a rie !   Oh HONE a rie !
The hymn o'er happy days departed,
The Hope that such again may be,
When power was large and liberal-hearted,
And wealth was hospitality.

One more request, and I am lost,
If you its earnest prayer deny ;
It is, that you preserve the most
Inviolable secrecy
As to my plan.   Our fourteen wards
Contain some thirty-seven bards
Who, if my glorious theme were known,
Would make it, thought and word, their own,
My hopes and happiness destroy,
And trample with a rival's joy
Upon the grave of my renown.
My younger brothers in the art,
Whose study is the human heart—
Minstrels, before whose spells have bowed
The learned, the lovely, and the proud,
Ere their life's morning hours are gone—

Light hearts be theirs, the Muse's boon,
And may their suns blaze bright **at noon,**
　And set **without a cloud !**

HILLHOUSE,[9] whose music, like his **themes,**
Lifts earth to heaven—whose poet-dreams
Are pure and holy as the hymn
Echoed from harps of seraphim,
By bards that drank at Zion's fountains
　When glory, peace, and **hope, were hers,**
And beautiful **upon her mountains**
　The feet of angel messengers.
BRYANT, **whose songs** are thoughts that bless
　The heart, its teachers, and its joy,
As mothers blend with their caress
Lessons of truth and gentleness　　　.
　And virtue for the listening boy　　.
Spring's lovelier flowers for many a day
Have blossomed on his wandering **way.**
.Beings of beauty and decay,
　They slumber **in their autumn tomb ;**
But those that graced **his own Green River,**
　And wreathed the lattice **of** his home,
Charmed by his song from mortal doom,
　Bloom **on,** and will bloom on forever.
And HALLECK—who has made thy roof,
St. Tammany ! oblivion-proof—
Thy **beer illustrious, and thee**
A belted knight of chivalry !

And changed thy dome of painted bricks
And porter-casks and politics,
   Into a green Arcadian vale,
With Stephen Allen [10] for its lark,
Ben Bailey's voice its watch-dog's bark,
   And John Targee its nightingale.

These, and the other THIRTY-FOUR,
Will live a thousand years or more—
If the world lasts so long. For me,
I rhyme not for posterity,
Though pleasant to my heirs might be
   The incense of its praise,
When I, their ancestor, have gone,
And paid the debt, the only one
   A poet ever pays.
But many are my years, and few
Are left me ere night's holy dew,
And sorrow's holier tears, will keep
The grass green where in death I sleep.

And when that grass is green above me,
And those who bless me now and love me
   Are sleeping by my side,
Will it avail me aught that men
Tell to the world with lip and pen
   That once I lived and died?
No: if a garland for my brow
Is growing, let me have it now,

While I'm alive to wear it ;
And if, in whispering my name,
There's music in the voice of fame
   Like Garcia's,[11] let me hear it !

The Christmas holidays are nigh,
Therefore till New-Year's Eve, good-by,
   Then *" revenons à nos moutons,"*
Yourself and aldermen—meanwhile,
Look o'er this letter with a smile ;
And keep the secret of its song
As faithfully, but not as long,
As you have guarded from the eyes
Of editorial Paul Prys,
   And other meddling, murmuring claimants,
Those Eleusinian mysteries,
   The city's cash receipts and payments.
                              Yours ever,

                                    T. C.

YOUNG AMERICA.

YOUNG AMERICA.

I.

IT is a BOY whom fourteen years have seen,
   Smiling, with them, on spring's returning green,
A bonny boy, with eye-delighting eyes,
Sparkling as stars, and blue as summer's skies,
With face, like April's, bright in smiles or tears,
His laugh a song—his step the forest deer's,
With heart as pure and liberal as the air,
And voice of sweetest tone, and bright gold hair
In thick curls clustering round his even brow,
And dimpled cheek—how calm he slumbers now!

———

The sentry stars in heaven's blue above,
Sleep their sweet daybreak sleep, their watch withdrawn,
And lovely as a bride from dream of love,
Blushing and blooming, wakes the summer dawn;
Winds—woods—and waters of the brook and bay
Wake at the fanning of the wings of day,

And birds and bells, in garden, tree, and tower,
Bow to the bidding of the wakening hour,
And breathe, the Hamlet's happy homes among
Morn's fragrant music from their lips of Song.

———

Within the loveliest of wayside bowers,
The summer home of loveliest leaves and flowers,
Cradled on rose-leaves, curtained round with vines,
And canopied by branches of a tree
Whose buds and blossoms charm the wandering bee,
In deep and dreaming sleep the youth reclines.
Sunbeams, wind-cooled, their fond caressing glow,
Twine, with leaf-shadows, the green roof below,
In wedded love-clasp of sweet shade and light,
The unwoven harmony of the dark and bright,
And blend within, around it, and above,
Their balm, their bloom, their beauty, and their joy,
Their watching—sleepless as the brooding dove,
Their bounty—boundless as the fairy love
Of Queen Titania for her Henchman Boy.

———

II.

The doors are open in the house of prayer,
The morning worshippers are kneeling there
In supplicating harmony, beneath
The intoning organ's incense-bearing breath,

That aids their hymning voices, and around
Moves in the might and majesty of sound.
The pages of the Holy Book are read,
The solemn blessing of the Priest is said,
Departing footsteps gently press the floor,
And silence seals and guards the consecrated door.
Along his homeward pathway, lingering slow,
His dark weeds tokening a mourner's woe,
The Gospel-Teacher comes.   The path inclines
His steps beside the cradle-bower of vines
Where sleeps the boy.   A moment's mute surprise,
And the mazed mourner greets, with grateful eyes,
The enlivening presence of that cherub face,
Delighted in its loveliness to trace
The memorial beauty of his own lost boy,
A blossomed bud, death-doomed, in its spring-time of
      joy ;
And says, in whispers, " Would that I might wake,
And woo, and win him, for his soul's sweet sake,
To make my home his cloister, and entwine
All his life's hopes and happiness with mine.
And with him win, dear daughter of the sky !
Handmaid of Heaven ! immortal Piety !
Thy visitings, and joy to see thee bring
In sisterly embrace, wing folding wing,
Meek Faith, sweet Hope, and Charity divine,
With thee to consecrate that home a shrine
Among the holiest where the adorer kneels,
Listening the coming of thy chariot-wheels.

Then the gay sportive dreams, enwreathing now
Their frolic fancies round the slumberer's brow,
Should yield to dreams of angels entering in
His young heart's Eden, unprofaned by sin ;
Then should his pleasant couch of leaves and flowers
Yield willing homage to the bliss of bowers
More beautiful than hers, and only given
In visions of the scenery of heaven ;
Then should the music now around him heard,
The wind-harp's song, the song of bee and bird,
Yield to thy chorused carollings sublime,
And sky-endomed cathedral's chant and chime.

———

And then the longing of his life should be
To praise, to love, to worship thine and thee,
And when, my pastoral task of duty done,
I rest beneath the cold sepulchral stone,
Be his the delegated power to grace,
In surpliced sanctity, thy Altar-place ;
To feed thy chosen flock with heavenly food,
Be their kind Shepherd, gentle, generous, good,
And, in the language of the Minstrel's lay,
" Lure them to brighter worlds, and lead the way."

———

Hark ! a bugle's echo comes,
Hark ! a fife is singing,
Hark ! the roll of far-off drums
Through the air is ringing !

The mourner turns—looks—listens, and is gone,
In quiet heedlessness the Boy sleeps on.

·

III.

Nearer the bugle's echo comes,
　　Nearer the fife is singing,
Near and more near the roll of drums
　　Through the air is ringing.

War ! it is thy music proud,
　　Wakening the brave-hearted,
Memories—hopes—a glorious crowd,
　　At its call have started.

Memories of our sires of old,
　　Who, oppression-driven,
High their rainbow flag unrolled
　　To the sun and sky of heaven.

Memories of the true and brave,
　　Who, at Honor's bidding,
Stepped, their Country's life to save,
　　To war as to their wedding.

Memories of many a battle-plain,
　　Where, their life-blood flowing,
Made green the grass, and gold the grain,
　　Above their grave-mounds growing.

Hopes—that the children of their prayers,
    With them in valor vieing,
May do as noble deeds as theirs,
    In living and in dying.

And make, for children yet to come,
    The land of their bequeathing
The imperial and the peerless home
    Of happiest beings breathing.

For this the warrior-path we tread,
    The battle-path of duty,
And change, for field and forest-bed,
    Our bowers of love and beauty.

Music ! bid thy minstrels play
    No tunes of grief or sorrow,
Let them cheer the living brave to-day,
    They may wail the dead to-morrow.

———

Such were the words, unvoiced by lip or tongue,
The thought-enwoven themes, the mental song
Of One, high placed, beside the slumberer's bower,
In the stern, silent chieftainship of power.
A War-king, seated on his saddle throne,
A listener to no counsels but his own,
The soldier leader of a soldier band,
Whose prescient skill, quick eye, and brief command,

Have won for him, on many a field of fame,
The immortality of a victor's name.
His troops, in thousands, now are marching by,
Heart-homage seen in each saluting eye,
And sword, and lance, and banner, bowing down
In tributary grace, before his bright renown.
And on, and on, as rank on rank appears,
Come, fast and loud, the thrice-repeated cheers
From voices of brave men whose life-long cry
Has been with him to live, for him to die.
Their plumes and pennons dancing in the breeze,
With leaves and flowers of overarching trees,
Timing their steps to tunes of flute and fife,
And trump and drum, the joy of soldier life,
While o'er them wave, proud banner of the free !
Thy sky-born stars and glorious colors three,
All beauteous in each interwoven hue
Of summer's rainbow, spanning earth and sea,
The rose's red and white, the violet's heavenly blue,
Emblems of valor, purity, and truth,
Long may they charm the air in ever-smiling youth !
And now the rearmost files are hurrying by,
Closing the gorgeous scene of pomp and pageantry ;
And far, far off, on wings of distance borne,
Speed the faint echoes of the trump and horn,
Plaintively breathing partings and farewells,
Solemn and sad as tones of tocsin-bells,
But triumphed o'er by voices that prolong
The wild war-music of the manlier song,

That bids the soldier's heart beat quick and gay,
The song of " O'er the hills and far away."

And now, beside the slumberer's couch of leaves,
His parting web of thought the warrior chieftain weaves.

How sweetly the Boy in the beauty is sleeping
 Of Life's sunny morning of hope and of youth !
May his guardian angels, their watch o'er him keeping,
 Keep his evening and noon in the pathways of truth !
Ah me ! what delight it would give me to wake him,
 And lead him wherever my life-banners wave,
O'er the pathways of glory and honor to take him,
 And teach him the lore of the bold and the brave ;

And when the war-clouds and their fierce storm of water,
 O'er the land that we love their outpourings shall
  cease,
Bid him bear to her Ark, from her last field of slaughter,
 Upon Victory's wings, the green olive of Peace ;

And when the death-note of my bugle has sounded,
 And memorial tears are embalming my name,
By young hearts like his may the grave be surrounded
 Where I sleep my last sleep in the sunbeams of fame.

Summoned to duty by his charger's neighs,
The only summons that his pride obeys,
He bows his farewell blessing, and is gone—
In quiet heedlessness the Boy sleeps on.

IV.

Merrily bounds the morning bark
   Along the summer sea,
Merrily mounts the morning lark
   The topmost twig on tree,
Merrily smiles the morning rose
   The morning sun to see,
And merrily, merrily greets the rose
   The honey-seeking bee.
But merrier, merrier far are these,
Who bring, on the wings of the morning breeze,
   A music sweeter than her own,
  A happy group of loves and graces,
Graceful forms and lovely faces,
   All in gay delight outflown ;
Outflown from their school-room cages,
School-room rules, and school-room pages,
Lovely in their teens and tresses, ·
Summer smiles, and summer dresses,
   Joyous in their dance and song,

With sweet sisterly caresses,
  Arm in arm they speed along
("Now pursuing, now retreating,
  Now in circling troops they meet,
To brisk notes in cadence beating,
  Glance their many twinkling feet.
Slow melting strains their Queen's approach declare.
  Where'er she turns the Graces homage pay,
With arms sublime, that float upon the air) ; "
  She comes—the gentle Lady of my Lay,
Well pleased that, for her welcome to prepare,
  I borrow music from the Muse of Gray.

His heroine was the lovely Paphian Queen,
Mine seems the Huntress of the Sylvan scene,
The chaste Diana, with her Nymphs, in gay
And graceful beauty keeping holiday.
Sudden she pauses in the race of joy,
Around the Cradle Bower where sleeps the Boy,
And, with a sunny smile of gladness, sees
His golden ringlets, on the dancing breeze,
Shading his eyelids—and, with quick delight,
Bids her wild Nymphs to wing their merry flight
Home to their morning nests, and leave her care
To watch the slumberer in his rose-leafed chair.
He, in his beauty, to her fancy seems
To be the young Endymion of her dreams
Of yester-evening, when, alone and still,
Waiting the coming of the whip-poor-will,

Our climate's nightingale, her garden bird,
From lips unseen, unknown, this whispered song
   she heard:

———

" The summer winds are wandering here
   In mountain freshness, pure and free,
  And all that to the eye are dear
   In rock and torrent, flower and tree,
  Upon the gazing stranger come,
   Till, in his starlight dreams at even,
  It seems another Eden-home,
   Reared by the word—the breath of Heaven.

" To-morrow—and the stranger's gone,
   And other scenes, as bright as this,
  May win it from his bosom soon,
   And dim its wild-wood loveliness.
  But ever round this spot his thought
   Will be—while Memory's leaves are green;
  The fairy scene may be forgot,
   But not the Fairy of the scene.

" The song she sang, the lip that breathed it,
   The cheek of rose, the speaking eye,
  The brow of snow, the hair that wreathed it,
   In their young life and purity,
  Will dwell within his heart among
   His holiest, longest cherished things,
  9

Themes worthy of a worthier song,
  Dear Lady of the mountain springs."

———

And who is she—the Fairy of the scene?
A bright-eyed, beautiful maiden of eighteen,
Lovely and learnèd, and well " skilled to rule,"
The Lady-Mentor of a village school,
" Teaching young Girls' ideas how to shoot ;
A tree of knowledge, rich in flowers and fruit,
A model heroine in mien and mind,
An " Admirable Crichton " crinolined,
And author of a charming Book that sings
Delightfully concerning wedding-rings,
Tracing the progress of the lightning-dart
Between the bridal finger and the heart,
And proving the arithmetic untrue
Which teaches us that one and one make two,
Whereas the marriage-ring is worn to prove
That two are one—the Algebra of Love.

Such is the Lady of my song, and now
She gazes on her young Endymion's brow,
And, fancying—by a sudden thought beguiled,
Herself a mother bending o'er her child,
Unconsciously imprints upon his eyes
A kiss—brimful of all the charities,
Sacredly secret, eloquently mute,
Yet " Musical as is Apollo's lute,"

Of power to lure a swan from off the lake,
　Or wooing bluebird from an April tree,
Upsprings the Boy, exclaiming, " I'm awake ! "
　And shakes his golden locks in frolic glee.

One look—and, like an arrow from the string,
Away the maiden went, on laughing wing,
Graciously leaving, ere she homeward flew,
On the green turf impearled with drops of dew,
Farewell impressions of the prettiest foot
That ever graced and charmed a Gaiter Boot.

V.

The awakened Boy, not fond of early rising,
Resumed his pillow, thus soliloquizing :

" That Lady's pleasant smile and ruby lip
Might hope to win my heart's companionship,
But for the memory of that morn which proved
That he is happiest who has never loved.
That morn, when I, within a Lady's bower,
Offered my heart, hand, and a handsome dower
To ONE who, to my great and sad surprise,
Told me, with mischief in her laughing eyes,
That she was not at all inclined to marry,
　And added, in a most provoking tone,

That YOUNG AMERICA had better 'tarry
  At Jericho until his beard was grown,'
And like his eagle wear upon his wings
Feathers, before he proffered wedding-rings;
That purpling grapes looked lovely on their vines,
But she preferred them perfected in wines;
That on my cheek the down was fair to see,
But she admired the full-blown *favoris,*
And rather liked in men a modest pride
Of mustache—if artistically dyed."

She then, dismissing me in queenly state,
Locked of her Eden the unfeeling gate,
And I—a victim to Love's cruel dart,
Went—to the Opera—with a broken heart!

Along thy peopled solitude—Broadway!
I walked, a desolate man, day after day,
With downcast eyes and melancholy brow,
  Until a lady's letter asked me why
I passed her ladyship without a bow;
  To which I sent the following reply,
  My earliest-born attempt at poetry:

———

" The heart hath sorrows of its own,
    And griefs it veils from all,
  And tears, close-hidden from the world,
    In solitude will fall;

And when its thoughts of agony
   Upon the bosom lie,
Even Beauty in her loveliness
   May pass unheeded by.

"'Tis only on the happy
   That she never looks in vain,
To them her smiles are rainbow hopes,
   New-born of summer rain,
And their glad hearts will worship her,
   As one whose home is heaven;
A being of a brighter world,
   To earth a season given.

'That time with me has been and gone,
   And life's best music now
Is but the winter's wind that bends
   The leafless forest-bough.
And I would shun, if that could be,
   The light of young blue eyes—
They bring back hours I would forget,
   And painful memories.

"Yet, lady, though too few and brief,
   There are bright moments still;
When I can free my prisoned thoughts,
   And wing them where I will,
And then thy smiles come o'er my heart
   Like sunbeams o'er the sea,

And I can bow as once I bowed
When all was well with me."

And now farewell to Rhyme ! and welcome Reason !
'Tis past—my early manhood's pleasant season ;
If morning dreams, that visit our closed eyes,
Changed, when we wake to Life's realities,
I might become a SOLDIER of renown,
Or wear a PREACHER'S or a TEACHER'S gown ;
For all three in my dreams since rose the sun,
Have sought to make me their adopted one,
Destined to run the race that each has run ;
But my Ambition's leaves no more are green,
In one brief month my age will be FIFTEEN.
I've seen the world, and by the world been seen,
And now am speeding fast upon the way
To the calm, quiet evening of my day ;
There but remains one promise to fulfil,
I bow myself obedient to its will,
And am prepared to settle down in life
By wooing—winning—wedding A RICH WIFE.

ADDITIONAL POEMS.

A FRAGMENT.

* * * * * * * *

HIS shop is a grocer's—a snug, genteel place,
   Near the corner of Oak Street and Pearl;
He can dress, dance, and bow to the ladies with grace,
   And ties his cravat with a curl.

He's asked to all parties—north, south, east, and west,
   That take place between Chatham and Cherry;
And when he's been absent, full oft has the "best
   Society" ceased to be merry.

And nothing has darkened a sky so serene,
   Nor disordered his beauship's Elysium,
Till this season among our *élite* there has been
   What is called by the clergy "a schism."

'Tis all about eating and drinking—one set
   Gives sponge-cake, a few "kisses" or so,
And is cooled after dancing with classic sherbet,
   "Sublimed" (see Lord Byron) "with snow."

Another insists upon punch and *perdrix*,
  Lobster-salad, champagne, and, by way
Of a novelty only, those pearls of our sea,
  Stewed oysters from Lynn-Haven Bay.

Miss Flounce, the young milliner, blue-eyed and bright,
  In the front parlor over her shop,
" Entertains," as the phrase is, a party to-night,
  Upon peanuts and ginger-pop.

And Miss Fleece, who's a hosier, and not quite as young,
  But is wealthier far than Miss Flounce,
She " entertains " also to-night with cold tongue,
  Smoked herring, and cherry-bounce.

In praise of cold water the Theban bard spoke,
  He of Teos sang sweetly of wine ;
Miss Flounce is a Pindar in cashmere and cloak,
  Miss Fleece an Anacreon divine.

The Montagues carry the day in Swamp Place ;
  In Pike Street the Capulets reign ;
A *limonadière* is the badge of one race,
  Of the other a flask of champagne.

Now as each the same evening her *soirée* announces,
  What better, he asks, can be done
Than drink water from eight until ten with the Flounces,
  And then wine with the Fleeces till one !

        *   *   *   *   *   *

SONG.

BY MISS * * * *.

AIR: "To ladies' eyes a round, boy."

MOORE.

THE winds of March are humming
    Their parting song, their parting song,
And summer skies are coming,
    And days grow long, and days grow long.
I watch, but not in gladness,
    Our garden-tree, our garden-tree;
It buds, in sober sadness,
    Too soon for me, too soon for me.
      My second winter's over,
        Alas! and I, alas! and I
      Have no accepted lover:
        Don't ask me why, don't ask me why.

'Tis not asleep or idle
    That Love has been, that Love has been;
For many a happy bridal
    The year has seen, the year has seen;
I've done a bridemaid's duty,
    At three or four, at three or four;
My best bouquet had beauty,
    Its donor more, its donor more.

My second winter's over,
　　Alas! and I, alas! and I
　Have no accepted lover:
　　Don't ask me why, don't ask me why.

His flowers my bosom shaded
　One sunny day, one sunny day;
The next they fled and faded,
　Beau and bouquet, beau and bouquet.
In vain, at balls and parties,
　I've thrown my net, I've thrown my net;
This waltzing, watching heart is
　Unchosen yet, unchosen yet.
　　My second winter's over,
　　　Alas! and I, alas! and I
　　Have no accepted lover:
　　　Don't ask me why, don't ask me why.

They tell me there's no hurry
　For Hymen's ring, for Hymen's ring;
And I'm too young to marry:
　'Tis no such thing, 'tis no such thing.
The next spring-tides will dash on
　My eighteenth year, my eighteenth year;
It puts me in a passion,
　Oh, dear, oh dear! oh dear, oh dear!
　　My second winter's over,
　　　Alas! and I, alas! and I
　　Have no accepted lover:
　　　Don't ask me why, don't ask me why.

SONG.

FOR THE DRAMA OF "THE SPY."

THE harp of love, when first I heard
   Its song beneath the moonlight tree,
Was echoed by his plighted word,
   And ah, how dear its song to me!
But wailed the hour will ever be
   When to the air the bugle gave,
To hush love's gentle minstrelsy,
   The wild war-music of the brave.

For he hath heard its song, and now
   Its voice is sweeter than mine own ;
And he hath broke the plighted vow
   He breathed to me and love alone.
That harp hath lost its wonted tone,
   No more its strings his fingers move,
Oh would that he had only known
   The music of the harp of love !

ADDRESS.

AT THE OPENING OF A NEW THEATRE

November, 1831.

WHERE dwells the Drama's spirit? not alone
Beneath the palace roof, beside the throne,
In learning's cloisters, friendship's festal bowers,
Art's pictured halls, or triumph's laurelled towers,
Where'er man's pulses beat, or passions play,
She joys to smile or sigh his thoughts away:
Crowd times and scenes within her ring of power,
And teach a life's experience in an hour.

To-night she greets, for the first time, our dome,
Her latest, may it prove her lasting home;
And we her messengers delighted stand,
The summoned Ariels of her mystic wand,
To ask your welcome.   Be it yours to give
Bliss to her coming hours, and bid her live
Within these walls new hallowed in her cause,
Long in the nurturing warmth of your applause.

'Tis in the public smiles, the public loves,
His dearest home, the actor breathes and moves,

Your plaudits are to us and to our art
As is the life-blood to the human heart:
And every power that bids the leaf be green,
In Nature acts on this her mimic scene.
Our sunbeams are the sparklings of glad eyes,
Our winds the whisper of applause, that flies
From lip to lip, the heart-born laugh of glee,
And sounds of cordial hands that ring out merrily,
And heaven's own dew falls on us in the tear
That woman weeps o'er sorrows pictured here.
When crowded feelings have no words to tell
The might, the magic of the actor's spell.

These have been ours; and do we hope in vain •
Here, oft and deep, to feel them ours again?
No! while the weary heart can find repose
From its own pains in fiction's joys or woes;
While there are open lips and dimpled cheeks,
When music breathes, or wit or humor speaks;
While Shakespeare's master-spirit can call up
Noblest and worthiest thoughts, and brim the cup
Of life with bubbles bright as happiness,
Cheating the willing bosom into bliss;
So long will those who, in their spring of youth,
Have listened to the Drama's voice of truth,
Marked in her scenes the manners of their age,
And gathered knowledge for a wider stage,
Come here to speed with smiles life's summer years,
And melt its winter snow with pleasant tears;

And younger hearts, when ours are hushed and cold,
Be happy here as we have been of old.

Friends of the stage, who hail it as the shrine
Where music, painting, poetry entwine
Their kindred garlands, whence their blended power
Refines, exalts, ennobles hour by hour
The spirit of the land, and, like the wind,
Unseen but felt, bears on the bark of mind;
To you the hour that consecrates this dome,
Will call up dreams of prouder hours to come,
When some creating poet, born your own,
May waken here the drama's loftiest tone,
Through after-years to echo loud and long,
A Shakespeare of the West, a star of song,
Bright'ning your own blue skies with living fire,
All times to gladden and all tongues inspire,
Far as beneath the heaven by sea-winds fanned,
Floats the free banner of your native land.

THE RHYME OF THE ANCIENT COASTER.

WRITTEN WHILE SAILING IN AN OPEN BOAT ON THE HUDSON RIVER,
BETWEEN STONY POINT AND THE HIGHLANDS, ON SEEING
THE WRECK OF AN OLD SLOOP, JUNE, 1821.

"And this our life, exempt from public haunt,
  Finds tongues in trees, books in the running brooks,
  Sermons in stones, and good in every thing."
                                        SHAKESPEARE.

HER side is in the water,
    Her keel is in the sand,
And her bowsprit rests on the low gray rock
    That bounds the sea and land.

Her deck is without a mast,
    And sand and shells are there,
And the teeth of decay are gnawing her planks,
    In the sun and the sultry air.

No more on the river's bosom,
    When sky and wave are calm,
And the clouds are in summer quietness
    And the cool night-breath is balm,

Will she glide in the swan-like stillness
    Of the moon in the blue above,

A messenger from other lands,
    A beacon to hope and love.

No more, in the midnight tempest,
    Will she mock the mounting sea,
Strong in her oaken timbers,
    An d her white sail's bravery.

She hath borne, in days departed,
    Warm hearts upon her deck;
Those hearts, like her, are mouldering now,
    The victims, and the wreck

Of time, whose touch erases
    Each vestige of all we love;
The wanderers, home returning,
    Who gazed that deck above,

And they who stood to welcome
    Their loved ones on that shore,
Are gone, and the place that knew them
    Shall know them never more.

        *   *   *   *   *

        *   *   *   *   *

It was a night of terror,
    In the autumn equinox,
When that gallant vessel found a grave
    Upon the Peekskill rocks.

Captain, mate, cook, and seamen
    (They were in all but three),
Were saved by swimming fast and well,
    And their gallows-destiny.

But two, a youth and maiden,
    Were left to brave the storm,
With unpronounceable Dutch names,
    And hearts with true-love warm.

And they, for love has watchers
    In air, on earth, and sea,
Were saved by clinging to the wreck,
    And their marriage-destiny.

From sunset to night's noon
    She had leaned upon his arm,
Nor heard the far-off thunder toll
    The tocsin of alarm.

Not so the youth—he listened
    To the cloud-wing flapping by;
And low he whispered in Low Dutch,
    " It tells our doom is nigh.

" Death is the lot of mortals,
    But we are young and strong,
And hoped, not boldly, for a life
    Of happy years and long.

" Yet 'tis a thought consoling,
　　That, till our latest breath,
We loved in life, and shall not be
　　Divided in our death.

" Alas, for those that wait us
　　On their couch of dreams at home,
The morn will hear the funeral-cry
　　Around their daughter's tomb.

" They hoped " ('twas a strange moment
　　In Dutch to quote Shakespeare)
" Thy bride-bed to have decked, sweet maid,
　　And not have strewed thy bier."

But sweetly-voiced and smiling,
　　The trusting maiden said,
" Breathed not thy lips the vow to-day,
　　To-morrow we will wed?

" And I, who have known thy truth
　　Through years of joy and sorrow,
Can I believe the fickle winds?
　　No! we shall wed to-morrow!"

The tempest heard and paused—
　　The wild sea gentler moved—
They felt the power of woman's faith
　　In the word of him she loved.

All night to rope and spar
　　They clung with strength untired,
Till the dark clouds fled before the sun,
　　And the fierce storm expired.

At noon the song of bridal bells
　　O'er hill and valley ran;
At eve he called the maiden his,
　　" Before the holy man."

They dwelt beside the waters
　　That bathe yon fallen pine,
And round them grew their sons and daughters,
　　Like wild-grapes on the vine.

And years and years flew o'er them,
　　Like birds with beauty on their wings,
And theirs were happy sleigh-ride winters,
　　And long and lovely springs—

Such joys as thrilled the lips that kissed
　　The wave, rock-cooled, from Horeb's fountains,
And sorrows, fleeting as the mist
　　Of morning, spread upon the mountains,

Till, in a good old age,
　　Their life-breath passed away ;
Their name is on the churchyard page—
　　Their story in my lay.

＊　　　＊　　　＊　　　＊
＊　　　＊　　　＊　　　＊

And let them rest together,
   The maid, the boat, the boy,
Why sing of matrimony now,
   In this brief hour of joy?

Our time may come, and let it—
   'Tis enough for us now to know
That our bark will reach West Point ere long,
   If the breeze keep on to blow.

We have Hudibras and Milton,
   Wines, flutes, and a bugle-horn,
And a dozen cigars are lingering yet
   Of the thousand of yester-morn.

They have gone, like life's first pleasures,
   And faded in smoke away,
And the few that are left are like bosom friends
   In the evening of our day.

We are far from the mount of battle,*
   Where the wreck first met mine eye,
And now where twin forts † in the olden time rose,
Through the Race, like a swift steed, our little bark
     goes,
And our bugle's notes echo through Anthony's Nose,
   So wrecks and rhymes—good-by.

---

* Stony Point.   † Forts Clinton and Montgomery.

LINES

TO HER WHO CAN UNDERSTAND THEM.

AIR: "To ladies' eyes a round, boy!"

THE song that o'er me hovered,
   In summer's hour, in summer's hour,
To-day with joy has covered
   My winter bower, my winter bower.
Blest be the lips that breathe it,
   As mine have been, as mine have been,
When pressed in dreams beneath it,
   To hers unseen, to hers unseen.
And may her heart, wherever
   Its hope may be, its hope may be,
Beat happily, though never
   To beat for me, to beat for me!

Is she a spirit given
   One hour to earth, one hour to earth,
To bring me dreams from heaven,
   Her place of birth, her place of birth?
Or minstrel maiden hidden,
   Like cloistered nun, like cloistered nun,
A bud, a flower forbidden,
   To air and sun, to air and sun?

For had I power to summon,
  With harp divine, with harp divine,
The angel or the woman,
  The last were mine, the last were mine.

If earth-born beauty's fingers
  Awaked the lay, awaked the lay,
Whose echoed music lingers
  Around my way, around my way,
Where smiles the hearth she blesses
  With voice and eye, with voice and eye?
Where binds the night her tresses,
  When sleep is nigh, when sleep is nigh!
Is Fashion's bleak cold mountain
  Her bosom's throne, her bosom's throne?
Or love's green vale and fountain,
  With one alone, with one alone?

Why ask! why seek a treasure
  Like her I sing, like her I sing?
Her name nor pain nor pleasure
  To me should bring, to me should bring.
Love must not grieve or gladden
  My thoughts of snow, my thoughts of snow,
Nor woman soothe or sadden
  My path below, my path below.
Before a worldlier altar
  I've knelt too long, I've knelt too long;
And if my footsteps falter,
  'Tis but in song, 'tis but in song.

Nor would I break the vision
  Young fancies frame, young fancies frame,
That lights with stars Elysian
  A poet's name, a poet's name.
For she whose gentle spirit
  Such dreams sublime, such dreams sublime,
Gives hues they do not merit
  To sons of rhyme, to sons of rhyme,
But place the proudest near her,
  Whate'er their pen, whate'er their pen,
She'll say (be mute who hear her)
  Mere mortal men, mere mortal men!

Yet though unseen, unseeing,
  We meet and part, we meet and part,
Be still my worshipped being,
  In mind and heart, in mind and heart.
And bid thy song that found me,
  My minstrel-maid, my minstrel-maid!
Be winter's sunbeam round me,
  And summer's shade, and summer's shade.
I could not gaze upon thee,
  And dare thy spell, and dare thy spell,
And when a happier won thee,
  Thus bid farewell, thus bid farewell.

TRANSLATION FROM THE FRENCH OF VICTOR HUGO.

E Poëte, inspiré lorsque la terre ignore,
    Ressemble á les grands monts que la nou-
      velle aurore
Dore avant tous á son réveil,
Et qui, longtemps vainqueur de l'ombre,
Gardent jusque dans la nuit sombre
    Le dernier rayon du soleil.

Moorland and meadow slumber
    In deepest darkness now,
But the sunrise hues of the wakened day
    Smile on the mountain's brow.

And when eve's mists are shrouding
    Moorland and meadow fast,
That mountain greets day's sunset light,
    Her loveliest and her last.

And thus the God-taught minstrel,
    Above a land untaught,
Smiles lonely in the smiles of heaven
    From his hill-tops of thought.

ITHIN a rock, whose shadows linger,
    At moonlight hours, on Erie's sea,
Some unseen, Indian spirit's finger
    Woke in far times sweet minstrelsy.
'Twas in the summer twilight only,
    When evening winds the green leaves stirred,
And all beside was mute and lonely
    Its wild aërial tones were heard.

So I—that fabled rock resembling,
    With heart as cold, and head as hard—
Appear, although with fear and trembling,
    At Beauty's call, as Beauty's bard.
Yet why despair if winds can summon
    Minstrels and music when they please?
For who but deems the lips of woman
    More potent than an evening breeze?

Her lips the magic word have spoken,
    That bids me call from far and near
Each minstrel-pen, to leave its token
    Of fealty and of friendship here.
These consecrated leaves are given
    To you, ye rhyme-composing elves;

To poets who were taught by Heaven,
   And poets who have taught themselves.

To wits, whose thistle-shafts by flowers
   Are hid, their points in balsam dipped;
To humor, in his happiest hours,
   And punsters—if their wings are clipped.
But friendship, with her smiling features,
   Will come, 'tis hoped, without a call;
For though your wits are clever creatures,
   One line of hers is worth them all.

Let names of heroes and of sages,
   On history's leaf eternal be;
A few brief years on Beauty's pages
   Are worth their immortality.
At least this charmèd book permits us
   To brave oblivion's withering power,
Till she who summons us, forgets us;
   And who would live beyond that hour?

ODE TO GOOD-HUMOR.

MAID of the sweet, engaging smile!
   Companion of our hours of peace!
Whose soothing arts can care beguile,
   And bid discordant passions cease;
Virtue in thee her favorite hails,
And dwells where'er thy sway prevails,
Life's fairest charms to thee we owe,
The source of pure delight, the healing balm of woe!

Can rapture thrill congenial hearts,
   Entwined by Friendship's wreath divine?
If aught of bliss its bond imparts,
   The praise, enchanting maid! be thine.
Can we a soft attractive grace
In the bright beam of Beauty trace?
'Tis only when with thee combined,
Her powers can justly claim the homage of the mind!

When the first pair in Eden's bower
   Enjoyed the favoring smile of Heaven,
Thy influence brightened every flower,
   And blessed the balmy breeze of even.
And since in Love's connubial ties,
We best can learn thy sweets to prize,

'Tis in affection's fond domain,
Where still unruffled joys denote thy golden reign.

Deprived of thee, does earth possess
    One charm to bind us here below?
In vain may pomp and power caress,
    Or wealth its glittering gifts bestow.
Lost is their worth when thou art fled,
When Discord lifts her sceptre dread,
And pallid Envy, Care, and Strife
Unite their darkening clouds to veil the noon of life.

But when thy welcome steps appear,
    This dreaded train of evil flies,
Gay Cheerfulness is ever near,
    And calm Content with placid eyes;
And all that to the soul endears
This dreary wilderness of years,
All that our happiest hours employ,
When beats the willing heart to transport and to joy.

Where'er I tread this varied scene,
    Good-Humor! on my path attend;
Alike when pleasure smiles serene,
    Or pain and grief my bosom rend,
Do thou infuse thy sovereign power,
In youth's gay morn, in manhood's hour,
Or when, in age, life's parting ray
But faintly lingers low ere yet it fades away!

1811.

TRANSLATED FROM THE FRENCH OF
GENERAL LALLEMAND.

SWEET maid! whose life the frost of destiny
    Withered while yet its first spring-leaves were
        green;
Pure, sainted being! from thy home on high,
Look with thine eyes of love, upon the scene
Where, for one little hour, thy spirit moved,
A visitant—to love, and to be loved,
And where thy song of youth to virtue gave
The music of its praises—the green bowers
Of home and friendship wreathed with fadeless flowers,
And made the laurel dearer to the brave.

Still do the hearts that loved thee, beat for thee
Warmly, as when they beat beside thy bier.
And still to them, of earthly things most dear
And sacred, is thy pledge of memory—
A father's gift, whose every cherished word
Bids the sweet echo of thy song be heard;
And fain would bid their sorrows cease to be.
Would it could soothe a mother's griefs, but they
Are graven deep, and will not pass away!

Blest spirit! long as at the name alone
Of their Eliza, tears are seen to start,
And sighs are breathed, whose birthplace is the heart.
Look on thy friends from thine ethereal throne,
With smiles that greeted them in happier days;
And pardon one to thee, and thine unknown,
Whose Stranger hand strews flowers upon thy tomb,
For he hath heard the music of thy lays,
And who can listen to its tones, nor raise
His thoughts to thee, and thine Eternal home?

THE VISION OF ELIPHAZ.

PARAPHRASED FROM JOB

'TWAS in the solemn midnight hour,
   When sleep extends its balmy power,
     The slumbering world around;
When Darkness, o'er the extensive globe
Spreads, far and wide, its sable robe,
     And Silence reigns profound!

As wrapped in lonely solitude,
The starry canopy I viewed,
     In pensive thought reclined;
A sudden tremor chilled my blood,
My hair, with horror, upright stood,
     And terror filled my mind.

Before mine eyes a spirit passed—
I gazed, with trembling looks, aghast!
     As o'er the path it flew;
It stood, but naught could I descry,
The gloom, that veiled the midnight sky,
     Concealed it from my view.

Dread Silence reigned! I, shuddering, feared!
When suddenly a voice I heard,
   In slow and solemn tone:
"Shall man," it cried, "presume to vie
In justice, and in majesty,
   With Heaven's Eternal Throne?

"Can man more purity display
Than He, who formed him from the clay,
   The offspring of the dust?
Behold! to those that round Him stand,
Attentive to His dread command,
   He gives no charge, or trust.

"Even angels, next in might to God,
Submissive at His footstool nod,
   And own superior power;
And ah! how much! how far below
Are mortals, doomed to pain and woe,
   The pageants of an hour.

"Before the meanest worm they die,
And, mouldering into dust, they lie,
   Within the earth's cold bed.
Many, on whom the morn arose,
Before the evening shades, repose
   In mansions of the dead.

" And soon their memory is no more,
Long ages roll successive o'er,
 And other scenes arise;
And, leagued with their departing breath,
Before the fatal shaft of death,
 Their boasted knowledge flies."

1809.

A POETICAL EPISTLE.

TO MRS. RUSH.

LADY, I thank you for your letter;
   Would that these rhymes it asks were better
  Worthy of her who taught
My song, when life was in its June,
To mingle heart with word and tune,
  And melody with thought.

Gone are the days of sunny weather
  (I quote remembered words), when we
"Revelled in poetry" together;
  And frightened leaves from off their tree,
With declamation loud and long,
From epic sage and merry song,
  And odes, and madrigals, and sonnets,
Till all the birds within the wood,
And people of the neighborhood
  Said we'd "a bee in both our bonnets."
And he [1] sat listening, he the most
Honored and loved, and early lost—
He in whose mind's brief boyhood hour
Was blended by the marvellous power

[1] Joseph Rodman Drake.

That Heaven-sent genius gave,
The green blade with the golden grain;
Alas! to bloom and beard in vain,
Sheafed round a sick-room's bed of pain,
　And garnered in the grave.

They are far away, those sunny days,
And since we watched their setting rays,
The music of the voice of praise
From many a land, and many a clime,
Has greeted my astonished rhyme;
Till half in doubt, half pleased, it curled
Its queerest lip upon the world,
But never heard I flattery's tone
Sounding around me, "Bard, well done!"
Without a blessing on the One
Who flattered first—the bonnie nurse
Whose young hand rocked my cradled verse.

Long may her voice, as now, be near
To prompt, to pardon, and to cheer;
And long be smiles for goodness' sake,
　Upon her best of happy faces,
Like Spenser's Una's given to make
　A sunshine in the shadiest places!

THE BLUEBIRD.

HAIL! warbling harbinger of Spring!
    How soft thy wild notes fill the breeze!
Raptured, I hear thy fluttering wing,
    Low murmuring 'mong the leafless trees.
        Now when all lone and drear
Bleak Winter holds her gloomy reign,
And spreads afar her wide domain,
O'er brake and dell, and lawn and plain,
        With joy thy notes we hear;
Their simple strains a charm impart,
Dear to the languid, aching heart.

Say, hast thou left yon mountains mild,
    Where southern gales ambrosial blow?
To cheer our fields now lone and wild,
    And ice-chained valleys clad in snow,
        The opening spring to hail?
To bring the rosy charms of May,
The feathered choir of warblers gay,
And clothe in Nature's green array,
        The mountain and the vale?

Then welcome to our groves once more,
Thou token sure that winter's o'er.

Sweet Bird ! the grateful muse shall pay
  Her homage and her love to thee;
To thee attune her earliest lay,
  And wake the lyre's soft harmony;
    While each exulting mind
Shall join, accordant with her lays,
And every hand unite to raise
A wreath of honorary bays,
    Around thy plumes to bind;
To crown thee first of all the train
Whose sportive warblings glad the plain.

Ye wintry clouds ! that o'er the heart
  A shade of sable horror threw !
Ye shadowy sorrows ! hence ! depart—
  Ye heart-corroding thoughts—adieu !
    With all your gloomy train,
On wings of stormy tempests fly
To Zembla's coasts or Scythia's sky;
Then deep in trackless deserts lie,
    And ne'er return again.
Let life a cheerful prospect wear,
Uncurtained by thy clouds' despair !

The mournful grove, in weeds forlorn,
  Bewails her festive summer bower:

No warblers now to wake the morn,
  Or charm the lonely evening hour !
    The warblers all are gone.
Wild is the dreary prospect round,
Hushed is the murmuring torrents' sound,
And solemn silence reigns profound,
    Terrific and alone !
Wild the deserted groves appear,
Untuneful, desolate, and drear !

But ah ! yon songster's glad return
Proclaims thy reign will soon be o'er ;
And bids the heart no longer mourn,
The Spring will soon return once more,
    And Nature smile serene.
Her smiles shall dissipate the gloom,
Again the fairest flowers shall bloom,
And Summer soon her seat resume,
    Her robes of brightest green ;
Again the groves in state shall rise,
And purest azure gild the skies.

Hail ! grateful songster, tuneful bird !
  Thou earliest pledge of spring, all hail !
How sweet thy plaintive notes are heard
Floating adown the balmy gale !
    How sweet thy morning song !

As wildly trembling—soft and slow,
Its wood-notes fill yon vale below,
Or, on resounding echoes, flow
    The distant hills along.
Then welcome, lovely warbler, here
Thy lay announcing, *" Spring is near!"*

HONOR TO WOMAN.

FROM THE GERMAN OF GOETHE.

ALL honor to WOMAN, the Sweetheart, the Wife,
    The delight of our homesteads by night and
      by day,
The darling who never does harm in her life,
    Except when determined to have her own way.

TO ELLEN.

THE Scottish Border Minstrel's lay
　　Entranced me oft in boyhood's day;
　　　His forests, glens, and streams,
Mountains, and heather blooming fair,
And Highland lake, and lady, were
　　　The playmates of my dreams.

Years passed away—my dreams were gone;
My pilgrim footsteps passed at noon
　　　Loch Katrine's storied shores:
In silence slept the fairy lake,
Nor did the mountain-echoes wake
　　　At music of my oars.

No tramp of warrior-men I heard;
Welcome-song, or challenge-word,
　　　I listened, but in vain;
And, moored beside his favorite tree,
As vainly wooed the minstrelsy
　　　Of gray-haired Allan Bane.

I saw the Highland heath-flower smile
In beauty, upon Ellen's isle;

And, couched in Ellen's bower,
I watched, beneath its latticed leaves,
Her coming, through a summer eve's
    Youngest and loveliest hour.

She came not—lonely was her home;
Herself of airy shapes "that come
    Like shadows, so depart."
Are there two Ellens of the mind?
Or have I lived at last to find
    The Ellen of my heart?

For music, like Sir Walter's, now
Rings round me, and again I bow
    Before the shrine of song,
Devoutly as I bowed in youth;
For hearts that worship there, in truth
    And joy, are ever young.

And dear the harp that sings to-day,
And well its gladdened strings obey
    Its minstrel's loved command—
A minstrel-maid's, whose infant eyes
Looked on Ohio's woods and skies,
    My youth's unheard-of land.

And beautiful that wreath she twines
Round Albi cottage bowered in vines,
    Or blest in sleigh-bell mirth;

And loveliest is her song that seems
To bid me welcome in my dreams,
    Beside its winter hearth.

And must I deem her beckoning smile
But pleasant mockery, to beguile
    Some lonely hour of care?
And will this Ellen prove to be
But like her namesake o'er the sea,
    A BEING OF THE AIR?

Or shall I take the morning wing,
Armed with a parson and a ring,
    Speed hill and dale along;
And, at her cottage-fire ere night,
Change into flutterings of delight,
Or what's more likely, of affright,
    The merry mockbird's song?

MEMORY.

STRONG as that power whose strange control
    Impels the torrent's force;
Directs the needle to the pole,
And bids the waves of ocean roll
    In their appointed course;
So powerful are the ties that bind
The scenes of childhood to the mind;
So firmly to the heart adheres
The memory of departed years.

Whence is this passion in the breast?
    That when the past we view,
And think on pleasures, once possessed,
In Fancy's fairest colors dressed,
    Those pleasures we renew?
And why do memory's pains impart
A *pleasing sadness* to the heart?
What potent charm to all endears
The days of our departed years?

True—many a rose-bud, blooming gay,
    Life's opening path adorns;
But all who tread that path will say
That, 'mid the flowers which strew its way,
    Are care's corroding thorns.

Yet still the bosom will retain
Affection even for hours of pain;
And we can smile, though bathed in tears,
At memory of departed years.

'Tis distance, our bewildered gaze
    On former scenes, beguiles,
And memory's charm the eye betrays:
For while enjoyments it displays
    And robes the past in smiles,
Its flattering mirror proves untrue,
Conceals the sorrows from our view,
And hides the griefs, the doubts, and fears,
That darkened our departed years!

Time, when our own, we oft despise;
    When gone, its loss deplore;
Nor, till the fleeting moment flies,
Do mortals learn its worth to prize,
    When it returns no more.
For this, an anxious look we cast,
With fond regret, on hours long past—
For this, the feeling heart reveres
The memory of departed years!

1810.

RELIGION.

WRITTEN ON A BLANK LEAF OF MY PRAYER-BOOK.

WHEN Misery's tear and Sorrow's sigh
    Oppress the feeling mind,
Say—where for refuge shall we fly ?
    And where a refuge find ?

The morn of life may open fair,
    And charm the view awhile ;
The world around us then may wear
    A universal smile ;

But Life's a transitory scene,
    Its prospects all are vain ;
The bosom that now beats serene,
    Too soon may throb with pain.

Though Pleasure Youth's gay hours adorn,
    The wayward heart to please,
'Tis fleeting as the dew of morn,
    'Tis fickle as the breeze.

Uncertain is our mortal breath,
    On swiftest wings it flies ;

And soon the iron hand of death
Shall close our dying eyes.

Such is our state—then, tell me, where,
Oppressed with care and grief,
The anxious bosom can repair,
To seek and find relief?

To mild Religion—heavenly maid!
Belongs the power alone,
To dissipate the deepest shade,
That shrouds the dark unknown.

She gives the glad inquiring mind
This solemn truth to know:
" The soul of man is not confined
To this short space below."

Then cherish well the hopes she gives,
To banish all our fears:
" The disembodied spirit lives
Beyond the vale of tears.

" Though want, contempt, and scorn, attend
The virtuous here below,
Their future bliss shall far transcend
Their present pain and woe.

" In realms of everlasting rest,
 Where cares and sorrows cease,
The sainted spirits of the blest
 Shall find eternal peace."

Then be to Heaven's will resigned,
 And own Religion's power,
For there a sure resource we find,
 In sorrow's darkest hour.

1810.

MILD beamed the sun's departing ray,
   Low sinking in the rosy west;
Still was the closing hour of day
   Sacred to silence, peace, and rest!
When a poor Wanderer, bent with woe,
O'er the moor travelled, sad and slow.

By dire misfortune forced to roam,
   He rambled on—he knew not where;
In hopes to find a tranquil home,
   To find relief from want and care.
The noonday of his life was past,
And Age his mantle o'er him cast.

He stopped, and, lingering on his road,
   Admired the lovely prospect round;
Slowly the lonely heath he trod,
   And gazed, in pleasing thought profound!
Enraptured at the enchanting scene,
His bosom heaved with joy serene.

But sudden-lowering clouds arise,
   And blackening mists the scene deform;
Terrific darkness veils the skies,
   Foreboding an impending storm!

The traveller sees the danger near,
And shuddering stands, appalled with fear !

Now raged the bleak wind o'er the plain,
   The billows bounded on the shore ;
Swift fell the cold and pelting rain,
   And loud the storm began to roar.
The unhappy wanderer mourned his fate—
He mourned—but ah ! alas ! too late.

Wild was the prospect, far and wide,
   And all was dreadful, dark, and drear ;
No shepherd's sheep-pent fold he spied,
   No friendly roof or shelter near ;
While fiercer still the tempest grew,
As o'er the lonely heath it flew.

Yet Hope still cheered him on his way :
   " Night soon will fly with its dark shade ;
Aurora soon will ope the day,
   And sweep the dew-drops down the glade.
Soon will the fearful storm be o'er,
And soon you'll see the cottage door."

But ah ! delusive Hope ! how vain
Are all thy fond, enrapturing dreams ;
Loud howled the raging wind, the rain
   Still poured in swift-descending streams.
Before the blast the forest yields,
And shivered branches strew the fields.

At length, worn down with toil and cold,
   The Wanderer sunk upon the heath;
And ere the shepherd loosed his fold,
   His weary eyes were closed in death.
The last, the dreaded pang is o'er,
And low he lies, to rise no more !

Such is Life's journey—'tis a scene
   Where joy and grief alternate reign ;
Where mixed emotions intervene,
   Of hope and fear, of bliss and pain ;
Where sunbeams dart, and tempests rage,
In every season, every age.   .

As through this wilderness we roam,
   Fond Hope may wear her sweetest smile,
And tell of happier days to come,
   The wearied bosom to beguile ;
But vanished is her soothing power,
In disappointment's languid hour.

Then happiest he whose hopes sublime
   Are centred in the joys of heaven ;
Calmly adown the stream of time
   His peaceful bark shall then be driven.
Firm as the adamantine rock,
His heart shall brave " Misfortune's rudest shock."

   1804.

LINES

WRITTEN ON A BLANK LEAF IN OSSIAN'S POEMS.

IN all that Genius calls its own,
  The "*Bard of Cona*" soars sublime !
And where the Muses' powers are known,
  His fame shall brave the blast of Time !

His was the soft persuasive art !
  Whene'er his fingers touched the lyre ;
To melt in sympathy the heart,
  Or thrill the soul with Glory's fire.

Unblest with Learning's ray refined,
  He warbled—Nature's favorite child—
His notes bespoke his feeling mind,
  Sublimely simple—sweetly wild.

Sweet Poet ! while the Muses' flame
  Within my heart enrapturing glows,
That heart shall pay thy honored name
  The homage which it justly owes.

1810.

IN HER ISLAND HOME.

WRITTEN IN MISS BRONSON'S ALBUM.

[In the olden time, a sect of Persian philosophers formed a society dedicated to Silence. Their number was limited to ten. One of the brotherhood, a personage who was never known to speak in his lifetime, and of whom no one has ever been heard to speak since, died. Among the applicants for the vacant chair was "Sadi," a "*sage grave man*," remarkable for saying nothing, at least nothing to the purpose. Unfortunately, ere he reached the place of meeting, the choice had fallen on another. The president announced this by placing a wineglass on the table, and filling it up to the brim. As Sadi entered, he pointed toward it. Sadi bowed, as is usual on such occasions, then took a roseleaf from the floor, and placed it so lightly on the bubbles of the wine, that not a drop was spilt. They received him.—COTTON MATHER.]

IN her island home, her home of flowers,
 The Queen of Beauty sat at noon,
In the shade of one of her wild-rose bowers,
Watching the spray of the bright sea-showers,
 As it sparkled in the sun of June.

And the smile of delight round her lip that played
 Was as sweet as a smile can be,
For that day had her minstrel-worshippers laid
On her altar a book where each pen had paid
 Its vows to their island-deity.

Its words still breathed, though the ink was cold
  As the hopes of the hearts she had fettered,
A magical name on the book was enrolled,
And its hot-pressed pages were tipped with gold,
  And 'twas bound in green, and lettered.

As she counted the leaves, and counted o'er
  The victims her frowns had killed,
A stranger-bard, from a far-off shore,
Came blushing, and said, "Here is one song more;"
  She answered, "The pages are filled."

He sighed, of course, but he manfully strove
  To check the sigh as it rose;
And, plucking a roseleaf, he tremblingly wove
Into very bad verses the tale which, above,
  Is written in good plain prose.

And added, "In coming hours, Lady, when you
  On the tears of your victims are feeding,
As the sunbeam feeds upon drops of dew,
Keep this withered leaf in the book—'twill do
  To mark where you left off reading."

THERE'S one who long will think of thee,
  Though thou art cold in death's last sleep;
There's one will love thy memory
  Till his own grave the night-dews steep.
And if no outward tears he weep,
  And none his silent sorrows know,
Still doth his heart its vigils keep
  Beside the spot where thou art low.

Sad was thy mortal pilgrimage,
  And bitter tears thine eyes have shed;
But now the storm hath spent its rage;
  The turf is green above thy head,
And, loveliest of the buried dead,
  Sweet may thy dreamless slumbers be;
Thy grave the summer's bridal bed,
  Her evening winds thy minstrelsy.

As withered on thy cheek the rose,
  I cursed the hour when love betrayed thee;
'Twas mine, in death, thine eyes to close,
  And watch till on the bier they laid thee.

No gloomy cypress-boughs shall shade thee,
   No marble thy sad story tell ;
The cruel world shall ne'er upbraid thee
   With having loved—and loved too well.

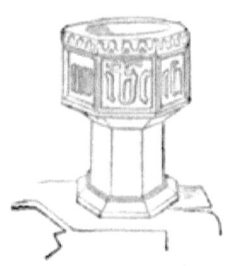

FORGET-ME-NOT.

WHERE flows the fountain silently,
   It blooms a lovely flower;
Blue as the beauty of the sky,
It speaks, like kind fidelity,
   Through fortune's sun and shower—
           " Forget-me-not ! "

'Tis like thy starry eyes, more bright
   Than evening's proudest star ;
Like purity's own halo-light,
It seems to smile upon thy sight,
   And says to thee from far—
           " Forget-me-not ! "

Each dew-drop on its morning leaves
   Is eloquent as tears,
That whisper, when young passion grieves,
For one beloved afar, and weaves
   His dream of hopes and fears—
           " Forget-me-not ! "

THE PILGRIMS.

THEY came—a life-devoting band—
  In winter o'er the sea ;
Tearless they left their fatherland,
  Home of their infancy.
And when they battled to be free,
  'Twas not for us and ours alone:
Millions may trace their destiny
  To the wild beach they trod upon.

The brave on Bunker's Hill who stood,
  And fearless fought and died,
Felt in their veins the pilgrims' blood,
  Their spirit, and their pride.
That day's last sunbeam was their last,
  That well-fought field their death-bed scene ;
But 'twas that battle's bugle-blast
  That bade the march of mind begin.

It sounded o'er the Atlantic waves:
  " One struggle more, and then
Hearts that are now to tyrants slaves,
  May beat like hearts of men.

The pilgrims' names may then be heard,
In other tongues a battle-word—
   The gathering war-cry of the free,
And other nations, from their sleep
Of bondage waking, long may keep,
   Like us, the pilgrims' jubilee."

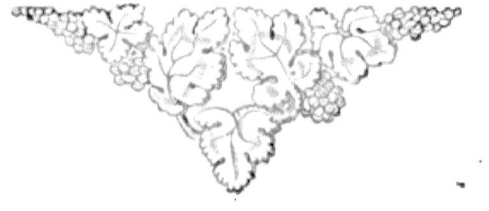

A FAREWELL TO CONNECTICUT.

TURNED a last look to my dear native moun-
    tain,
  As the dim blush of sunset grew pale in the sky ;
All was still, save the music that leaped from the fountain,
  And the wave of the woods to the summer-wind's
    sigh.

Far around, the gray mist of the twilight was stealing,
  And the tints of the landscape had faded in blue,
Ere my pale lip could murmur the accents of feeling,
  As it bade the fond scenes of my childhood adieu.

Oh! mock not that pang, for my heart was retracing
  Past visions of happiness, sparkling and clear :
My heart was still warm with a mother's embracing,
  My cheek was still wet with a fond sister's tear.

Like an infant's first sleep on the lap of its mother,
  Were the days of my childhood—those days are no
    more ;
And my sorrow's deep throb I had struggled to smother
  Was that infant's wild cry when it's first sleep was
    o'er.

Years have gone by, and remembrance now covers,
  With the tinge of the moonbeam, the thoughts of
        that hour;
Yet still in his day-dream the wanderer hovers
  Round the cottage he left and its green woven bower.

And Hope lingers near him, her wildest song breathing,
  And points to a future day, distant and dim,
When the finger of sunset, its eglantine weaving,
  Shall brighten the home of his childhood for him.

TO LOUIS GAYLORD CLARK, ESQ.

'VE greeted many a bonny bride
  On many a bridal day,
In homes serene and summer-skied,
Where Love's spring-buds, with joy and pride
  Had blossomed into May;
But ne'er on lovelier bride than thine
Looked these delighted eyes of mine,
And ne'er in happier bridal bower
Than hers, smiled rose and orange-flower
  Through green leaves glad and gay,
When bridesmaids, grouped around her room,
In youth's, in truth's, in beauty's bloom,
Entwined, with merry fingers fair,
Their garlands in her sunny hair;
Or bosomed them, with graceful art,
Above the beatings of her heart.

I well remember, as I stood,
Among that pleasant multitude,
A stranger, mateless and forlorn,
Pledged bachelor and hermit sworn,
That, when the holy voice had given,
  In consecrated words of power,

The sanction of approving Heaven
　To marriage-ring, and roof, and dower;
When she, a Wife, in matron pride,
Stood, life-devoted, at thy side ;
When happy lips had pressed her cheek,
　And happiest lips her " bonny mou',"
And she had smiled with blushes meek,
　On my congratulating bow,
A sunbeam, balmy with delight,
Entranced, subdued me, till I quite
　Forgot my anti-nuptial vow,
And almost asked, with serious brow
　And voice of true and earnest tone,
The bridesmaid with the prettiest face
To take me, heart and hand, and grace
　A wedding of my own.

Time's years, it suits me not to say
How many, since that joyous day,
Have watched and cheered thee on thy way
　O'er Duty's chosen path severe,
And seen thee, heart and thought full grown,
Tread manhood's thorns and tempters down,
　And win, like Pythian charioteer,
The wreaths and race-cups of renown —
Seen thee, thy name and deeds, enshrined
Within the peerage-book of mind —
And seen my morning prophecy
Truth-blazoned on a noonday sky,

That he, whose worth could win a wife
    Lovely as thine, **at life's beginning,**
Would always wield the power, through **life,**
    Of winning all things **worth the winning.**

Hark! there are songs on Summer's breeze,
And dance and song in Summer's trees,
And choruses of birds and bees
    In Air, their world of happy wings;
What far-off minstrelsy, **whose tone**
And words are sweeter than their own,
    Has waked these cordial welcomings?
'Tis nearer now, and now more near,
And now rings out like clarion clear.
They come—the merry bells of Fame!
They come—to glad me with thy name,
And borne upon their music's sea,
From wave to wave melodiously,
Glad **tidings bring of thine and thee.**
They tell me that, Life's tasks well done,
Ere shadows mark thy westering sun,
Thy Bark has reached a quiet **shore,**
And rests, with slumbering **sail and oar,**
Fast anchored near a cottage door,
    Thy home of pleasantness and peace,

Of Love, with eyes of Heaven's blue,
And Health, with cheek of rose's **hue,**
    And Riches, with "the Golden Fleece:"

Where she, the Bride, a Mother now,
   Encircled round with sons and daughters,
Waits my congratulary bow
   To greet her cottage woods and waters ;
And thou art proving, as in youth,
By daily kindnesses, the truth
And wisdom of the Scottish rhyme—
" To make a happy fireside clime
   For children and for wife,
Is the true pathos and sublime,"
   And green and gold of Life.

From long-neglected garden-bowers
Come these, my songs' memorial flowers,
With greetings from my heart, they come
To seek the shelter of thy home ;
Though faint their hues, and brief their bloom,
And all unmeet for gorgeous room
Of " honor, love, obedience,
   And troops of friends," like thine.
I hope thou wilt not banish thence
   These few and fading flowers of mine,
But let their theme be their defence,
The love, the joy, the frankincense,
   And fragrance o' LANG SYNE.

THE CROAKERS.[1]

BY

FITZ-GREENE HALLECK AND JOSEPH RODMAN DRAKE.

TO ENNUI.

AVAUNT! arch-enemy of fun,
  Grim nightmare of the wind;
Which way, great Momus! shall I run,
  A refuge safe to find?
My puppy's dead—Miss Rumor's breath
  Is stopped for lack of news,
And Fitz' is almost hypped to death,
  And Lang' has got the blues.

I've read friend Noah's book quite through,
  Appendix, notes, and all;
I've swallowed Lady Morgan's' too,
  And blundered through De Staël;'
The Edinburgh Review—I've seen't
  The last that has been shipped;
I've read, in short, all books in print,
  And some in manuscript.

I'm sick of General Jackson's toast,
  Canals are naught to me:
Nor do I care who rules the roast,
  Clinton—or John Targee:
No stock in any Bank I own,
  I fear no Lottery shark,
And if the Battery were gone,
  I'd ramble in the Park.

Let gilded Guardsmen[4] shake their toes,
  Let Altorf[5] please the pit,
Let Mister Hawkins blow his nose
  And Spooner[6] publish it:
Insolvent laws let Marshall[7] break,
  Let dying Baldwin cavil;
And let Tenth-Ward Electors shake
  Committees to the devil.

In vain—for like a cruel cat
  That sucks a child to death,
Or like the Madagascar bat
  Who poisons with his breath,
The fiend—the fiend is on me still,
  Come, doctor, here's your pay—
What potion, lotion, plaster, pill,
  Will drive the beast away?

                  D.

THE FREEDOM OF THE CITY

In a gold box to a great General.[8]

THE Board is met—the names are read·
   Elate of heart, the glad committee
Declare the mighty man has said
   He'll take " the freedom of the city."
He thanks the Council, and the Mayor,
   Presents 'em all his humble service;
And thinks he's time enough to spare
   To sit an hour or two with Jervis.[9]

Hurra! hurra! prepare the room—
   Skaats![10] are the ham and oysters come?
Go—make some savory whiskey-punch,
   The General takes it with his lunch;
For a sick stomach, 'tis a cure fit,
   And vastly useful in a surfeit.

But see! the Mayor is in the chair;
   The Council is convened again;
And ranged in many a circle fair,
   The ladies and the gentlemen

Sit mincing, smiling, bowing, talking
  Of Congress—balls—the Indian force—
Some think the General will be walking,
  And some suppose he'll ride, of course:
And some are whistling—some are humming,
  And some are peering in the Park
To try if they can see him coming;
  And some are half asleep—when, hark!

A triumph on the warlike drum,
  A heart-uplifting bugle-strain,
A fife's far flourish—and "They come!"
  Rung from the gathered train.
Sit down—the fun will soon commence—
  Quick, quick, your Honor, mount your place,
Present your loaded compliments,
  And fire a volley in his face!

They're at it now—great guns and small—
  Squib, cracker, cannon, musketry;
Dear General, though you swallow all,
  I must confess it sickens me.

                                        D.

THE SECRET MINE,

SPRUNG AT A LATE SUPPER

THE songs were good, for Mead and Hawkins
    sung 'em,
The wine went round, 'twas laughter all, and joke ;
When crack ! the General sprung *a mine* among 'em,
   And beat a safe retreat amid the smoke :
As fall the sticks of rockets when you fire 'em,
   So fell the Bucktails at that toast accurst ;
Looking like Korah, Dathan, and Abiram,
   When the firm earth beneath their footsteps burst.

Quelled is big Haff who oft has fire and flood stood,
   More pallid grows the snowy cheek of Rose,
Cold sweats bedew the leathern hide of Bloodgood,
   Deep sinks the concave of pug Edwards' nose.
But see the Generals Colden and Bogardus,
   Joy sits enthroned in each elated eye ;
While Doyle and Mumford clap their fists as hard as
   The iron mauls in Pearson's factory.

The midnight conclave met—good Johnny Targee
   Begins, as usual, to bestow advice :

"Declare the General a fool, I charge ye!
　And swear the toast was not his own free choice;
Tell 'em that Colden prompted, and maintain it:
　That is the fact, I'm sure, but we can see ·
By sending Aleck[11] down to ascertain it."
　The hint was taken, and accordingly

A certain member had a conversation,
　And asked a certain surgeon all about it:
Some folks assert he got the information;
　'Tis also said, he came away without it.
Good people all! I'm up to more than you know;
　But prudence frowns, my coward goose-quill lingers,
For fear that flint-and-trigger Doctor Brunaugh
　Should slip a challenge in your poet's fingers!

D

BONY'S FIGHT.

"There was Captain Cucumber, Lieutenant Tripe, Ensign Pattyman and myself."

FOOTE.

WHEN Bony fought his host of foes,
   Heroes and generals arose
  Like mushrooms when he bade them ;
Europe, while trembling at his nod,
Thought him a sort of demi-god,
  So wondrous quick he made them.

But "every dog must have his day,"
And Bony's power has passed away,
  His track let others follow ;
Yet in that talent of the Great,
With dash of goose-quill to create,
  Our Clinton beats him hollow !

Alas ! thou little god[12] of war,
The proud effulgence of thy star
  Is dimmed, I fear, forever,
Though bright thy buttons long have shined,
And still thy powdered hair behind
  Is clubbed so neat and clever.

Yet round thee are assembled now
New chieftains, all intent as thou
　　On hard militia duty:
Here's King,[13] conspicuous for his hat,
And Ferris Pell, for God knows what,
　　And Bayard, for his beauty.

These are but colonels—there are hosts
Of higher grades, like Banquo's ghosts,
　　Upon my sight advancing;
In truth they made e'en Jackson stare,
When in the Park, up-tossed in air,
　　He saw their plumage dancing.

Yet I should wrong them not to name
Two Major-Generals, high in fame,
　　By Heaven! a gallant pair!
(They haven't any soldiers yet,)
His Honor, General by brevet,
　　Bogardus, brevet Mayor.

Should England dare to send again
Her scoundrel red-coats o'er the main,
　　I fear some sad disaster;
Each soldier wears an epaulette,
The Guards have turned a capering set,
　　And want a dancing-master.

Sam Swartwout![14] where are now thy Grays?
Oh, bid again their banner blaze
 O'er hearts and ranks unbroken! .
Let drum and fife your slumbers break,
And bid the devil freely take
 Your meadows at Hoboken!

II.

TO MR. POTTER,[16]

THE VENTRILOQUIST.

DEAR Sir, you've heard that Mr. Robbin[16]
    Has brought in, without rhyme or reason,
A bill to send you jugglers hopping;
    That bill will pass this very season.
Now, as you lose your occupation,
    And may perhaps be low in coffer,
I send for your consideration
    The following very liberal offer:

Five hundred down, by way of bounty
    Expenses paid (as shall be stated),
Next April to Chenango County,
    And there we'll have you nominated.
Your duty'll be to watch the tongues
    When Root's[16] brigade begins to skirmish,
To stop their speeches in their lungs,
    And bring out such as I shall furnish.

Thy ventriloquial powers, my Potter!
    Shall turn to music every word,

And make the Martling[17] Deists utter
    Harmonious anthems to our Lord;
Then, all their former tricks upsetting,
    To honey thou shalt change their gall,
For Sharpe[16] shall vindicate brevetting,
    And Root admire the great canal.

It will be pleasant, too, to hear a
    Decent speech among our swains;
We almost had begun to fear a
    Famine for the dearth of brains.
No more their tongues shall play the devil,
    Thy potent art the fault prevents;
Now German[16] shall, for once, be civil,
    And Bacon[16] speak with common-sense.

Poor German's head is but a leaker;
    Should yours be found compact and close,
As you're to be the only speaker,
    We'll make you SPEAKER of the House.
If you're in haste to "touch the siller,"
    Dispatch me your acceptance merely,
And call on trusty Mr. Miller,[18]
    He'll pay the cash—Sir, yours sincerely,

                           D.

TO MR. SIMPSON,

MANAGER OF THE PARK THEATRE.

'M a friend to your theatre, oft have I told you,
   And a still warmer friend, Mr. Simpson, to you;
And it gives me great pain, be assured, to behold you
   Go fast to the devil, as lately you do.
We scarcely should know you were still in existence,
   Were it not for the play-bills one sees in Broadway;
The newspapers all seem to keep at a distance;
   Have your puffers deserted for want of their pay?

Poor Woodworth! [19] his Chronicle died broken-hearted;
   What a loss to the drama, the world, and the age!
And Coleman [20] is silent since Philipps departed,
   And Noah's too busy to think of the stage.
Now, the aim of this letter is merely to mention
   That, since all your critics are laid on the shelf,
Out of pure love for you, it is my kind intention
   To take box No. 3, and turn critic myself.

Your ladies are safe—if you please you may say it,
   Perhaps they have faults, but I'll let them alone;

Yet I owe two a debt—'tis my duty to pay it—
　Of them I must speak in a kind, friendly tone.
Mrs. Barnes[21]—Shakespeare's heart would have beat
　　　had he seen her—
Her magic has drawn from me many a tear,
And ne'er shall my pen or its satire chagrin her,
　While pathos, and genius, and feeling are dear.

And there's sweet Miss Leesugg,[22] by-the-bye, she's not
　　　pretty,
　She's a little too large, and has not too much grace,
Yet, there's something about her so witching and witty,
　'Tis pleasure to gaze on her good-humored face.
But as for your men—I don't mean to be surly,
　Of praise that they merit they'll each have his share;
For the present, there's Olliff,[23] a famous Lord Bur-
　　　leigh,
　And Hopper and Maywood, a promising pair.

　　　　　　　　　　　　　　H.

WAKE! ye forms of verse divine;
   Painting! descend on canvas wing,
And hover o'er my head, Design!
   Your son, your glorious son, I sing!
At Trumbull's name, I break my sloth,
   To load him with poetic riches;
The Titian of a table-cloth!
   The Guido of a pair of breeches!

Come, star-eyed maid, Equality!
   In thine adorer's praise I revel;
Who brings, so fierce his love to thee,
   All forms and faces to a level:
Old, young, great, small, the grave, the gay,
   Each man might swear the next his brother,
And there they stand in dread array,
   To fire their votes at one another.

How bright their buttons shine! how straight
   Their coat-flaps fall in plaited grace!
How smooth the hair on every pate!
   How vacant each immortal face!

And then the tints, the shade, the flush,
   (I wrong them with a strain too humble,)
Not mighty Sherred's [26] strength of brush
   Can match thy glowing hues, my Trumbull !

Go on, great painter ! dare be dull—
   No longer after Nature dangle ;
Call rectilinear beautiful ;
   Find grace and freedom in an angle :
Pour on the red, the green, the yellow,
   " Paint till a horse may mire upon it,"
And while I've strength to write or bellow,
   I'll sound your praises in a sonnet.

                                 D.

" Twice twenty shoe-boys, twice two dozen guards,
Chairmen and porters, hackney-coachmen, dandies ! "

TOM THUMB.

" HERE, Dickens !—go fetch my great-coat and
    umbrella,
Tell Johnny and Robert to put on their shoes;
And Dickens—take something to drink, my good fellow,
    You may go with Tom Ostler, along, if you choose :
You must put your new coat on, but mind and be quiet,
    Till my clerk, Mr. Scribble, shall tip you the wink;
Then, roar like the devil—hiss—kick up a riot !
    I imagine we'll settle the thing in a twink."

Arrived at the Hall, they were nothing too early;
    Little Hartman was placed, like King Log, in the chair,
Supported, for contrast, by modest King Charlie;
    The General was speaking, who is to be Mayor :
Undaunted he stood in the midst of the bobbery,
    Clerks, footmen, and dandies—ye gods ! what a noise !
No thief in Fly-Market, just caught in a robbery,
    Could raise such a clatter of blackguards and boys.

Mercein and Bogardus each told a long story,
 Very fine, without doubt, to such folks as could hear;
Then the two kings resigned, and in high gig and glory
 The light-footed chief of the Guards took the chair :
So he made them a speech, about little or nothing,
 Except he advised them to go home to bed;
And the simple fact is, that, in spite of their mouthing,
 'Twas the only good, sensible thing that was said.

By-the-way, though, we've heard that these sons of sedi-
  tion,
 These vile Bonapartes (to quote Jemmy Lent),
Are about to bring forward a second edition,
 And Squire McGareaghan fears the event.
Now to let our wise Council their honest game play on
  yet,
 Just call out, your Honor, the Gingerbread Guards,
Bid them drive at the traitors with cutlass and bayonet,
 And then pick their pockets as bare—as your bard's.

        D.

TO CROAKER, JUNIOR.

OUR hand, my dear Junior! we're all in a flame
    To see a few more of your flashes;
The Croakers forever! I'm proud of the name—
But, brother, I fear, though our cause is the same,
    We shall quarrel like Brutus and Cassius.

But why should we do so? 'tis false what they tell
    That poets can never be cronies;
Unbuckle your harness, in peace let us dwell;
Our goose-quills will canter together as well
    As a pair of Prime" mouse-colored ponies.

Once blended in spirit, we'll make our appeal,
    And by law be incorporate too;
Apply for a charter in crackers to deal;
A fly-flapper rampant shall shine on our seal,
    And the firm shall be "Croaker & Co."

Fun! prosper the union—smile, Fate, on its birth!
    Miss Atropos, shut up your scissors;
Together we'll range through the regions of mirth,
A pair of bright Gemini dropped on the earth,
    The Castor and Pollux of quizzers.

                          D.

[MR. EDITOR: I wish you to precede the lines I send you enclosed, by republishing Mr. Hamilton's late letter to the Governor *verbatim*, in order that the world may see that, on this occasion, at least, the poet does not deal in fiction.]

" *To De Witt Clinton, Governor of the State of New York.*

" SIR : To your shame and confusion let it be recorded, that you dare not assume the responsibility of preserving to our national councils a patriotic and distinguished statesman, while you could advocate the publication of an insidious and base attack upon private character through the public organ of your administration.

" You know the motive of my visit to Mr. Root—you were not ignorant that the senatorial reëlection of Rufus King [26] was to me a subject of deep personal concern ; and on this occasion you declared that you had marked my course, and that this support should recoil with vengeance upon the Republican party. To those intimate with your pusillanimity and intrigues, you disappoint no expectation. The traducer of America's brightest ornaments can only be consistent within the sphere of his degeneracy. It is the pride of the name I bear, to be distinguished by your envenomed malignity—one and all, we are opposed to your administration and your character. I am induced to make this explanation as a permanent obligation to the public ; to my own feelings it is perfectly humiliating. I have the honor to remain,

" Your obedient servant, ALEXANDER HAMILTON. [29]

" ASSEMBLY CHAMBER, *March 8th*, 1819."

A VERY MODEST LETTER FROM ONE GREAT MAN TO ANOTHER.

" To be a well-favored man is the gift of fortune, but to write and read comes by nature."   DOGBERRY.

OW dare you, Sir, presume to say,
    And write and print the paltry thing,
That I did wrong the other day
    To give my vote for Mr. King?

'Twas natural that I should take a
　　Particular interest in it, Sir,
For I've been agent at Jamaica,
　　And he a foreign minister.

You say you've *marked my course* of late,
　　And mean to make what I've been doing
A means of breaking up the State,
　　And bringing on our party's ruin.

With all who've known your scoundrel tricks,
　　Since first you came to curse the nation,
The Lucifer of politics,
　　" *You disappoint no expectation.*"

It suits your mean and grovelling spirit
　　Thus to attack great men like me ;
You slander only chiefs of merit,
　　Stars in our country's galaxy !

Elijah, when his task was done,
　　His mantle o'er Elisha threw ;
Now I'm my father's eldest son,
　　And heir to all his talents too.

We're proud to say, the world well knows
　　You never liked our family ;

We, "*one and all,*" have been your foes,
  My brother Jim, and John, and I.

For my own sake, you well may wonder
  That I these lines to you have sent;
It is to lay the public under
  An "*obligation permanent.*"

Assembly Chamber, *March 8th.*

Done into English and verse by H.

TO THE SURGEON-GENERAL[10] OF THE STATE OF NEW YORK.

" Why, Tom ! he knows all things.   An it be not the devil himself, we may thank God."   VILLAGE WIZARD.

H ! Mitchill, lord of granite flints,
   Doctus in law—and wholesome dishes;
Protector of the patent splints,
   The foe of whales—the friend of fishes,
" Tom Codus,"—" Septon " " Phlogobombas ! "
   What title shall we find to fit you ?
Inquisitor of sprats and compost,
   Or Surgeon-General of militia !

We hail thee—mammoth of the State !
   Steam frigate on the waves of physic !
Equal in practice or debate,
   To cure the nation or the phthisic;
The amateur of Tartar dogs,
   Wheat-flies, and maggots that create 'em !
Of mummies, and of mummy chogs !
   Of brickbats, lotteries, and pomatum !

It matters not how low or high it is,
    Thou knowest each hill and vale of knowledge;
Fellow of forty-nine societies,
    And lecturer in Hosack's College.
And when thou diest, for life is brief,
    Thy name, in all its gathered glory,
Shall shine, immortal, as the leaf
    Of Delaplaine's Repository!"

D.

TO JOHN MINSHULL, ESQ.,[92]

POET AND PLAYWRIGHT: FORMERLY OF MAIDEN LANE, BUT NOW
ABSENT IN EUROPE.

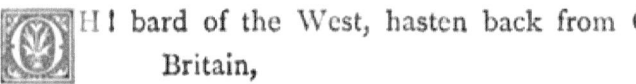H! bard of the West, hasten back from Great
    Britain,
  Our harp-strings are silent, they droop on the tree;
What poet among us is worthy to sit in
  The chair whose fair cushion was hallowed by thee?
In vain the wild clouds o'er our mountain-tops hover,
  Our rivers flow sadly, our groves are bereft;
They have lost, and forever, their poet, their lover!
  And Woodworth and Paulding are all we have left.

Great Woodworth, the champion of Buckets and Free-
    dom,
  Thou editor, author, and critic to boot,
I must leave thy rich volumes to those that can read 'em,
  For my part I never had patience to do't.
And as for poor Upham (who in a fine huff says
  He'll yield to no Briton the laurel of wit),
Alas! they have "stolen his ideas," as Puff says,
  I had read all his verses before they were writ.

But hail to thee, Paulding, the pride of the Backwood!
  The poet of cabbages," log huts, and gin,
God forbid thou shouldst get in the clutches of Black-
    wood!
  Oh, Lord! how the wits of old England would grin!
In pathos, oh! who could be flatter or funnier?
  Were ever descriptions more vulgar and tame?
I wronged thee, by Heaven! when I said there were
    none here
  Could cope with great Minshull, thou peer of his fame!

                      D.

THE MAN WHO FRETS AT WORLDLY STRIFE.

> " A merry heart goes all the way,
> A sad one tires in a mile-a."
>
> WINTER'S TALE.

THE man who frets at worldly strife,
 Grows sallow, sour, and thin ;
Give us the lad whose happy life
 Is one perpetual grin ;
He, Midas-like, turns all to gold,
 He smiles when others sigh,
Enjoys alike the hot and cold,
 And laughs through wet and dry.

There's fun in every thing we meet,
 The greatest, worst, and best,
Existence is a merry treat,
 And every speech a jest :
Be't ours to watch the crowds that pass
 Where Mirth's gay banner waves ;
To show fools through a quizzing-glass,
 And bastinade the knaves.

The serious world will scold and ban,
  In clamor loud and hard,
To hear Meigs called a Congressman,
  And Paulding styled a bard;
But, come what may, the man's in luck
  Who turns it all to glee,
And laughing, cries, with honest Puck,
  "Great Lord! what fools ye be."

                                 D.

TO E. SIMPSON, ESQ.,

ON WITNESSING THE REPRESENTATION OF THE NEW TRAGEDY
OF BRUTUS.

 HAVE been every night, whether empty or
  crowded,
And taken my seat in your Box No. 3 ;
In a sort of poetical Scotch mist I'm shrouded,
 As the far-famed Invisible Girl used to be.

As a critic professed, 'tis my province to flout you,
 And hiss as they did at poor Charley's³⁴ Macheath ;
But all is so right and so proper about you,
 That I'm forced to be civil in spite of my teeth.

In your dresses and scenery, classic and clever;
 Such invention ! such blending of old things and new !
Let Kemble's proud laurels be withered forever !
 Wear the wreath, my dear Simpson, 'tis fairly your
  due.

How *apropos* now was that street scene in Brutus,
 Where the sign "Coffee-House" in plain English
  was writ !

By-the-way, "Billy Niblo's"[35] would much better suit
    us,
  And box, pit, and gallery, roar at the wit.

How sparkled the eyes of the raptured beholders,
  To see Kilner,[36] a Roman, in robes "*à la Grec!*"
How graceful they flowed o'er his neatly-turned shoul-
    ders!
  How completely they set off his Johnny-Bull neck!

But to hint at the thousand fine things that amuse me,
  Would take me a month—so adieu till my next.
And your actors, they must for the present excuse me;
  One word though, *en passant*, for fear they'll be vexed.

Moreland, Howard, and Garner, the last importation!
  Three feathers as bright as the Prince Regent's plume!
Though puffing is, certainly, not my vocation,
  I always shall praise *them*, whenever I've room.

With manners so formed to persuade and to win you,
  With faces one need but to look on to love,
They're like Jefferson's "Natural Bridge" in Virginia—
  "*Worth a voyage across the Atlantic,*" by Jove!

                           H.

13

TO JOHN LANG, ESQ.[37]

E'VE twined the wreath of honor
 Round Doctor Mitchill's brow ;
Though bold and daring was the theme,
 A loftier waits us now.
In thee, immortal Lang ! have all
 The Sister Graces met,
Thou Statesman—Sage—and Editor
 Of the New-York Gazette !

A second Faustus in thine art !
 The Newton of our clime !
The Bonaparte of Bulletins !
 The Johnson of thy time !—
At thy dread name, the terriers bark,
 The *rats* fly to their holes !
Thou Prince of " *Petty Paragraphs,*"
 " *Red Notes,*" and " *Signal-Poles !* "

There's genius in thy speaking face,
 There's greatness in thine air ;
Take Franklin's Bust from off thy roof,
 And place thine own head there !

Eight corners within pistol-shot
  Long with thy fame have rang,
And bluebirds sung and mad cows lowed
  The name of Johnny Lang!

H.

TO DOMESTIC PEACE.

" Malbrook s'en va-t-en guerre."

H, Peace! ascend again thy throne,
   Resume the spotless olive-leaf,
Display thy snowy muslin gown,
And wave o'er this distracted town
   Thy cambric pocket-handkerchief!

Or, if thou dost not like the dress
   (We own we have our doubts upon it),
Come like some pretty Quakeress,
And let thine orbs of quietness
   Shine, dove-like, from a satin bonnet!

We need thee, row-abhorring maid!
   The dogs of party bark alarms,
And e'er the Battery tax is laid,
And e'er the next election's made,
   E'en Murray's Guards will rush to arms

Feds, Coodies, Bucktails,[38] all in flame,
   With peals of nonsense frighten thee;

Sweet Peace ! thou wert not much to blame,
If thou shouldst loathe the very name
   Of Clinton, or of John Targee.

For us, enthroned in elbow-chair,
   Thy foes alone with ink we sprinkle ;
We love to smooth the cheek of care,
Until we leave no furrow there,
   Save laughter's evanescent wrinkle.

With thee and mirth, we'll quit the throng—
   Each hour shall see our pleasures vary ;
Jarvis shall bring his Cats along,
And Lynch shall float in floods of song
   Pure as his highest-priced Madeira !

                                 D.

TO E. SIMPSON, ESQ.,

R. PHILIPPS has gone—and he carries away
with him
Much of my cash, and my hearty good-will;
To both he is welcome, and long may they stay with
him—
Poor as he's made me, I'll cherish him still.

For when the wild spell of his melody bound me,
I marked not the flight of the gay, happy hours;
His music created a fairy-land round me;
Above it, was sunshine—below it, were flowers.

But 'tis folly to weep—we must cease to regret him;
Look about—you have many as brilliant a star:
There's Barnes[20] (you may laugh if you will), but just
let him
Play Belino for once;—he'll beat Philipps by far!

When he sings "*Love's Young Dream*," every heart
will be beating,
The ladies shall wave their white kerchiefs in air;

The peals of applauses shall hail the repeating
  Of his " *Eveleen's Bower*," and his " *Robin Adair!* "

Fancy's sketch ! such fine *shakes* and such comic ex·
    pression
  He'll give it; 'twill put all the fiddles in tone !
And let Olliff (clean shaved, with a new hero dress on)
  Play Baron Toraldi *for that night alone.*

If you wish to give all your acquaintance delight,
  Fill your house to the brim, take this hint—it will
    go;
The humor will make e'en your candles burn bright,
  And crowd every seat, to the very fourth row.

Besides, *entre-nous*, there's another good reason—
  Perhaps 'twill the proud heart of Beekman beguile;
He *may* promise to lower your rent the next season,
  And, for once in his life,—take his hat off and smile.

                                        H.

TO CAPTAIN SEAMAN WEEKS,

CHAIRMAN OF THE TENTH WARD INDEPENDENT ELECTORS. [*]

APTAIN WEEKS, your right hand—though I
   never have seen it,
  I shake it on paper, full ten times a day:
I love your Tenth Ward, and I wish I lived in it;
  Do you know any house there to let against May?
I don't mind what the rent is, so long as I get off
  From these party-mad beings, these tongues without
    heads!
I'm ashamed to be seen, sir, among such a set of
  Clintonians, Tammanies, Coodies, and Feds!

Besides, I am nervous, and can't bear the racket
  These gentlemen make when they're begging for
    votes;
There's John Haff, and Ben Bailly, and Christian, and
    Bracket,
  Only think what fine music must come from *their*
    throats!
Colonel Warner calls Clinton a "star in the banner,"
  Mapes swears by his sword-knot he'll ruin us all;
While Meigs flashes out in his fine classic manner,
  " The meteor Gorgon of Clinton must fall!"

In vain I endeavor to give them a hint on
    Sense, reason, or temper—they laugh at it all ; ·
For sense is nonsense when it makes against Clinton,
    And reason is treason in Tammany Hall.
So I mean (though I fear I shall seem unto some a
    Strange, obstinate, odd-headed kind of an elf)
To strike my old tent in the Fourth, and become a
    " Tenth Ward independent elector " myself.

                                      D.

THE Surgeon-General by *brevet*,
   With zeal for public service burning,
Thinks this a happy time to get
   Another chance to show his learning;
He has in consequence collected
   His wits, and stewed them in retorts;
By distillation thus perfected,
   He hopes to shine, and so *reports*

That he has searched authorities
   From Johnson down to Ashe and Shelley,
And finds that a *militia* is
   What he is now about to tell ye:
Militia means—such citizens
   As e'en in peace are kept campaigning—
The gallant souls that shoulder guns,
   And, twice a year, go out a-training!

This point being fixed, we must, I think, sir,
   Proceed unto the second part,
Entitled Grog—a kind of drink, sir,
   Which, by its action on the heart,
Makes men so brave, they dare attack
   A bastion at its angle salient;

This is a well-established fact—
  The very **proverb says**—*pot-valiant.*

Grog—I'll define it in a minute—
  ·**Take** gin, rum, whiskey, **or peach-brandy,**
Put but a little water in it,
  And that is Grog—now understand me,
I mean to say, that should the spirit
  Be left out by some **careless dog,**
It is—I wish **the world may hear it!**
  It is plain water, and not Grog.

Having precisely fixed what Grog is
  (My reasoning, **sir,** that question settles!),
We next must ascertain what Prog is—
  Now Prog, in vulgar phrase, is **victuals:**
This will embrace all kinds of food,
  Which on the smoking board can **charm ye,**
And by digestion furnish blood,
  A thing essential in an army!

These things should all be swallowed·warm,
  For heat, digestion much facilitates;
Cold is a tonic, and does harm;
  A tonic always, sir, debilitates.
My *plan* then is to raise, as fast
  As possible, a *corps* of cooks,
And drill them daily from the **last**
  Editions of **your** cookery-books!

Done into English and likewise into verse by **H.** AND D.

TO AN ELDERLY COQUETTE

" Parcius junctas quatiunt fenestras."

HORACE, Book 1., Ode 25.

AH, Chloe! no more at each party and ball
　You shine the gay queen of the hour,
The lip, that alluringly smiled upon all,
　Finds none to acknowledge its power ;
No longer the hearts of the dandies you break,
　No poet adores you in numbers;
No billets-doux sweeten, nor serenades wake
　The peaceful repose of your slumbers.

Dissipation has clouded those eloquent eyes,
　That sparkled like gems of the ocean ;
Thy bosom is fair—but its billowy rise
　Awakens no kindred commotion :
And pale are those rubies of rapture, where Love
　Had showered his sweetest of blisses ;
And the wrinkles which Time has implanted above,
　Are covered in vain with false tresses.

The autumn is on thee—fell Scandal prepares
　To hasten the wane of thy glory ;

Too soon Disappointment will hand thee down-stairs,
    And old maidenhood end the sad story:
For me—long escaped from your trammels—I choose
    To enlist in the new corps of jokers;
Abandoning Chloe, I kneel to the Muse,
    And, instead of love-ditties, write Croakers.

D.

TO * * * *, ESQUIRE.

COME, shut up your Blackstone, and sparkle again
    The leader and light of our classical revels ;
While statues and cases bewilder your brain,
    No wonder you're vexed and beset with blue devils :
But a change in your diet will banish the blues ;
    Then come, my old chum, to our banquet sublime ;
Our wine shall be caught from the lips of the Muse,
    And each plate and tureen shall be hallowed in rhyme.

Scott, from old Albin, shall furnish the dishes
    With wild-fowl and ven'son that none can surpass ;
And Mitchill, who sung the amours of the fishes,
    Shall fetch his most exquisite tomcod and bass.
Leigh Hunt shall select, at his Hampstead Parnassus,
    Fine *greens*, from the hot-bed, the table to cheer ;
And Wordsworth shall bring us whole bowls of molasses
    Diluted with water from sweet Windermere.

To rouse the dull fancy and give us an appetite,
    Black wormwood bitters Lord Byron shall bear,
And Montgomery bring (to consumptives a happy sight)
    Tepid soup-meagre and " l'eau capillaire ; "

George Coleman shall sparkle in old bottled cider,
  Roast-beef and potatoes friend Crabbe will supply;
Rogers shall hash us an "olla podrida,"
    And the best of fresh "cabbage" from Paulding we'll
    buy.

Mr. Tennant—free, fanciful, laughing, and lofty,
  Shall pour out Tokay and Scotch whiskey like rain;
Southey shall sober our spirits with coffee,
    And Horace in London "flash up in champagne."
Tom Campbell shall cheer us with rosy Madeira,
  Refined by long keeping, rich, sparkling, and pure;
And Moore, "*pour chasse cafe*," to each one shall bear a
    Sip-witching bumper of *parfait amour.*

Then come to our banquet—oh! how can you pause
  A moment between merry rhyme and dull reason?
Preferring the wit-blighting "*Spirit of Laws*"
  To the spirit of verse, is poetical treason!
Judge Phœbus will certainly issue his writ,
  No quirk or evasion your cause can make good, man;
Only think what you'll suffer, when sentenced to sit
    And be kept broad awake till you've read the Back-
    woodsman!

                                              D.

ODE TO IMPUDENCE.

" Integer vitæ, scelerisque purus."

HORACE, Book 1., Ode 22.

THE man who wears a brazen face,
   Quite *à son aise* his glass may quaff;
And whether in or out of place,
  May twirl his stick, and laugh.
Useless to him the broad doubloon,
  Red note, or dollar of the mill;
Though all his gold be in the moon,
  His brass is current money still.

Thus, when my cash was at low water,
 . At Niblo's I sat down to dine;
And after a tremendous slaughter
  Among the wild-fowl and the wine,
The *bill* before mine eyes was placed—
  When, slightly turning round my head,
" *Charge it*," cried I—the man amazed,
  Stared, made his *congé*, and obeyed.

Oh! bear me to some forest thick,
  Where wampumed Choctaws prowl alone,

Where ne'er was heard the name of *tick*,
   And bankrupt laws are quite unknown ;
Or to some shop, by bucks abhorred,
   Where to the longing pauper's sorrow,
The cursed inscription decks the board
   Of "*Pay to-day and trust to-morrow.*"

Or plunge me in the dungeon-tower ;
   With bolts and turnkeys dim mine eyes ;
While, called from death by Marshall's power,
   The ghosts of murdered debts arise !
The easy dupes I'll wheedle still,
   With looks of brass and words of honey ;
And having scored a decent bill,
   Pay off my impudence for money.

                                   D.

TO MRS. BARNES,

DEAR Ma'am—we seldom take the pen
   To praise, for whim and jest our trade is '
We're used to deal with gentlemen,
To spatter folly's skirts, and then
   We're somewhat bashful with the ladies.

Nor is it meant to give advice;
   We dare not take so much upon us;
But merely wish, in phrase concise,
To beg you, Ma'am, and Mr. Price,
   For God's sake, to have mercy on us!

Oh! wave again thy wand of power,
   No more in melodramas whine,
Nor toil Aladdin's lamp to scour,
Nor dance fandangoes by the hour
   To Morgiana's tambourine!

Think, Lady, what we're doomed to feel—
   By Heaven! 'twould rouse the wrath of Stoics,
To see the queen of sorrows deal

In thundering "lofty-low" by Shiell,
  Or mad Maturin's mock-heroics.

Away with passion's withering kiss,
  A purer spell be thine to win us;
Unlock the fount of holiness
While gentle Pity weeps in bliss,
  And hearts throb sweetly sad within us.

Or call those smiles again to thee
  That shone upon the lip that won them,
Like sun-drops on a summer-sea,
When waters ripple pleasantly
  To wanton winds that flutter o'er them.

When Pity wears her willow-wreath,
  Let Desdemona's woes be seen;
Sweet Beverly's confiding faith,
Or Juliet, loving on in death,
  Or uncomplaining Imogen.

When wit and mirth their temples bind
  With thistle-shafts o'erhung with flowers,
Then quaint and merry Rosalind,
Beatrice with her April mind
  And Dinah's simple heart be ours.

For long thy modest orb has been
  Eclipsed by heartless, cold parade;

So sinks the light of evening's queen
When the dull earth intrudes between,
  Her beauties from the sun to shade.

Let Fashion's worthless plaudits rise
  At the deep toné and practised start;
Be thine true feeling's stifled sighs,
Tears wrung from stern and stubborn eyes,
  And smiles that sparkle from the heart.

H AND D.

TO SIMON,

THE OMNIPOTENT AND OMNIPRESENT CATERER FOR FASHIONABLE
SUPPER-PARTIES.

DEAR Simon! Prince of pastry-cooks,
   Oysters, and ham, and cold neat's tongue,
Pupil of Mitchill's cookery-books,
   And bosom friend of old and young!
Sure from some higher, brighter sphere
   In showers of gravy thou wert hurled,
To aid our routs and parties here,
   And grace the fashionable world!

Taught by thy art, we closely follow
   And ape the English lords and misses;
For music, we've the Black Apollo,
   And Mrs. Poppleton[42] for kisses.
We borrow all the rest, you know,
   Our glass from Christie[43] for the time,
Plate from our friends to make a show,
   And cash, to pay small bills from Prime.

What though old Squaretoes will not bless thee—
   He fears your power and dreads your bill;
Mother and her dear girls caress thee,
   And pat thy cheek, and praise thee still.

Oh, Simon ! how we envy thee,
    When belles that long have frowned on all,
Greet thee with smiles, and bend the knee,
    To beg you'll help them " give a ball ! "

Though it is ungenteel to think,
    For thought affects the nerves and brain !
Yet oft we think of thee, and drink
    Thy health in Lynch's best champagne.
'Tis pity that thy signal merit
    Should slumber in so low a station ;
Act, Simon, like a lad of spirit,
    And thou, in time, mayst rule the nation !

Break up your Saturdays "at home,"
    Cut Guinea and your sable clan,
Buy a new eye-glass and become
    A dandy and a gentleman.
You must speak French, and make a bow,
    Ten lessons are enough for that ;
And Leavenworth " will teach you how
    To wear your corsets and cravat.

Knock all your chambers into one,
    Hire fiddlers, glasses, Barons too,
And then invite the whole *haut-ton ;*
    Ask Hosack, he can tell you who.
The great that are, and—wish to be,
    Within your brilliant rooms will meet,

And belles of high and low degree,
   From Broadway up to Cherry Street.

This will insure you free admission
   To all our routs, for years to come;
And when you die, a long procession
   Of dandies shall surround your tomb.
We'll raise an *almond statue* where
   In dust your honored head reposes;
Mothers shall lead their daughters there,
   And bid them twine your bust with roses.

H. AND D.

A LOVING EPISTLE

TO MR. WILLIAM COBBETT,[45] OF NORTH HEMPSTEAD, LONG ISLAND.

> " Beloved of Heaven ! the smiling Muse shall shed
> Her moonlight halo on thy beauteous head ! "
>
> CAMPBELL.

RIDE, boast, and glory of each hemisphere !
    Well known and loved in both—great Cob-
bett, hail !
Hero of Botley there, and Hempstead here,
    Of Newgate, and a Pennsylvanian jail !
Long shall this grateful nation bless the hour,
    When, by the beadle and your debts pursued,
The victim, like famed Barrington,[46] of power,
    " *You left your country for your country's good !* "

Terror of Borough-mongers, Banks, and Crowns,
    Thorburn the seedsman, and Lord Castlereagh !
Potato-tops fall withering at your frowns,
    Grand *Ruta-Baga Turnip* of your day !
Banish the memory of Lockhart's cane,
    And Philadelphian *pole-cats* from your mind ;
Let the world scoff,—still you and Hunt remain,
    Yourselves a host—the envy of mankind !

Whether, as once in "Peter Porcupine,"
  You curse the country whose free air you breathe,
Or, as plain William Cobbett, toil to twine
  Around your brows Sedition's poisoned wreath,
Or, in your letter to Sir Francis, tear
  All moral ties asunder with your pen,
We trace your gentle spirit everywhere,
  And greet you prince of Slander's scribbling men.

Well may our hearts with pride and pleasure swell,
  To know that face to face we soon shall meet,
We'll gaze upon you as you stand and sell
  Grammars and *Garden Seeds* in Fulton Street!
And praise your book that tells about the weather,
  Our laws, religion, hogs, and things, to boot,
Where your unequalled talents teach together
  Turnips and "*young ideas how to shoot.*"

In recompense, that you've designed to make
  Choice of our soil above all other lands,
A purse we'll raise to pay your debts, and take
  Your unsold Registers all off your hands.
For this, we ask that you, for once will show
  Some gratitude—and, if you can, be civil;
Burn all your books, sell all your pigs, and go—
  No matter where—to England, or the devil!

14   H.

THE FORUM.

'TIS o'er—the fatal hour has come,
The voice of eloquence is dumb,
Mute are the members of the Forum !
We've shed what tears we had to spare,
There now remains the pious care
Of chanting a sad requiem o'er 'em.

The Roman drank the Tiber's wave,
Ilissus' stream its virtues gave
To bid the Grecian live forever ;
Our Forum orators a draught
Of greater potency have quaffed,
Sparkling and pure from the North River !

Proudly our bosoms beat to claim
Communion with our country's fame
From Bunker's Hill to Chippewa.
All who on battle-field or wave,
Have met the death that waits the brave,
Or pealed, above their foeman's grave,
The victor's wild hurrah !

The one that quelled a tyrant king,
And he who " grasped the lightning's wing,"
 Were nurtured in our country's bowers ;
But now a brighter gem is set
Upon her star-wrought coronet,
 The world's first orators are ours.

The name of every Forum chief [47]
Shall gleam upon our history's leaf,
 Circled with glory's quenchless fires ;
And poet's pen and painter's pallet
Shall tell of William Paxson Hallett,
 And Richard Varick Dey—Esquires !

Resort of fashion, beauty, taste,
The Forum-hall was nightly graced
With all who blushed their hours to waste
 At balls—and such ungodly places ;
And Quaker girls were there allowed
To show, among the worldly crowd,
 Their sweet blue eyes and pretty faces.

And thither all our wise ones went,
On charity and learning bent,
 With open ears—and purses willing,
Where they could dry the mourner's tear,
And see the world, and speeches hear,
 All, for "*a matter of two shilling !*"

Let Envy drop her raven quill,
Let Slander's venomed lip be still,
    And hushed Detraction's croaking song,
That dared, devoid of taste and sense,
To call these sons of Eloquence
    A spouting, stammering, schoolboy throng

In vain, for they in grave debate
Weighed mighty themes of church and state
    With words of power, and looks of sages;
While far diffused, their gracious smile
Soothed Bony in his prison-isle.
    And Turkish wives in harem-cages!

Heaven bless them! for their generous pity
Toiled hard to light our darkened city,
    With that firm zeal that never flinches;
And long, to prove the love they bore us,
With "more last words" they lingered o'er us,
    And died, like a tom-cat, by inches!

                        H.

FAIR lady with the bandaged eye !
    I'll pardon all thy scurvy tricks,
So thou wilt *cut* me, and deny
    Alike thy kisses and thy kicks :
I'm quite contented as I am,
    Have cash to keep my duns at bay,
Can choose between beefsteaks and ham,
    And drink Madeira every day.

My station is the middle rank,
    My fortune—just a competence—
Ten thousand in the Franklin Bank,
    And twenty in the six per cents. ;
No amorous chains my heart enthrall,
    I neither borrow, lend, nor sell;
Fearless I roam the City Hall,
    And "bite my thumb" at Sheriff Bell. [47]

The horse that twice a week I ride,
    At Mother Dawson's [49] eats his fill;
My books at Goodrich's [50] abide,
    My country-seat is Weehawk hill;

My morning lounge is Eastburn's shop,
   At Poppleton's I take my lunch,
Niblo prepares my mutton-chop,
   And Jennings[61] makes my whiskey-punch.

When merry, I the hours amuse
   By squibbing Bucktails, Guards, and Balls,
And when I'm troubled with the blues,
   Damn Clinton and abuse canals:
Then, Fortune! since I ask no prize,
   At least preserve me from thy frown!
The man who don't attempt to rise,
   'Twere cruelty to tumble down.

                           H. AND D.

THE LOVE OF NOTORIETY.

THERE are laurels our temples throb warmly to
    claim,
  Unwet by the blood-dripping fingers of War,
And as dear to the heart are the whispers of fame,
  As the blasts of her bugle rang fiercely and far ;
The death-dirge is sung o'er the warrior's tomb,
  Ere the world to his valor its homage will give,
But the feathers that form Notoriety's plume,
  Are plucked in the sunshine, and live while we live.

There's a wonderful charm in that sort of renown
Which consists in becoming *" the talk of the town ; "*
'Tis a pleasure which none but your " truly great " feels,
To be followed about by a mob at one's heels ;
And to hear from the gazing and mouth-open throng,
The dear words *" That's he,"* as one trudges along ;
While Beauty, all anxious, stands up on tip-toes,
Leans on her beau's shoulder, and lisps *" There he goes."*

For this the young Dandy, half whalebone, half starch,
Parades through Broadway with the stiff Steuben march ;
A new species of being, created, they say,
By nine London tailors, who ventured one day

To *cabbage* a spark of Promethean fire,
Which they placed in a German doll latticed with wire,
And formed of the scarecrow a Dandy divine,
But *mum* about tailors—I haven't paid mine.

And for this, little *Brummagem* mounts with a smile
His *own hackney* buggy, and dashes in style
From some livery stable to Cato's[62] Hotel,
And though 'tis a desperate task to be striving
With these sons of John Bull in the *science* of driving,
We have still a few Jockies who do it as well.

There are two, "*par example*," 'tis joy to behold,
    With their Haytian grooms trotting graceful behind
        them,
In their livery jackets of blue, green, and gold,
    Their bright varnished hats and the laces that bind
        them:
The one's an Adonis, who, since the sad day
    That he shot at himself[63] has been courted no more;
The other's a name it were treason to say,
    A very great man—with "*two lamps*[64] *at his door.*"

                                                H.

AN ODE TO SIMEON DE WITT, ESQ.,

SURVEYOR-GENERAL OF THE STATE OF NEW YORK.

When the Western District was surveyed, the power of naming its townships was intrusted to the Surveyor-General. Fancying the Indian appellations too sonorous and poetical, and conscious that his own ear was not altogether adapted for the musical combination of syllables, this gentleman hit upon a plan which for laughable absurdity has never been paralleled, except by the "Philosophy," "Philanthropy," and "Big Little Dry" system of Lewis and Clarke. It was no other than selecting from Lemprière and the "British Plutarch," the great names which these works commemorate. This plan he executed with the most ridiculous fidelity, and reared for himself an everlasting monument of pedantry and folly.

IF, on the deathless page of Fame,
    The warrior's deeds are writ,
If that bright record bear the name
Of each whose hallowed brow might claim
    The wreath of wisdom or of wit;
If even they, whose cash and care
Have nursed the infant arts, be there,
    What place remains for thee,
Who, neither warrior, bard, nor sage,
Has poured on this benighted age
    The blended light of all the three?

Godfather of the christened West!
    Thy wonder-working power

Has called from their eternal rest
The poets and the chiefs who blest
    Old Europe in her happier hour:
Thou givest to the buried great
A citizen's certificate;
    And, aliens now no more,
The children of each classic town
Shall emulate their sires' renown
    In science, wisdom, or in war.

The bard who treads on *Homer's* earth
    Shall mount the epic throne,
And pour, like breezes of the north,
Such spirit-stirring stanzas forth
    As Paulding would not blush to own.
And he, who casts around his eyes
Where *Hampden's* bright stone-fences rise,
    Shall swear with thrilling joint,
As German [56] did—" We yet are free,
And this accursed *tax* should be
    Resisted at the bayonet's point ! "

What man, where *Scipio's* praises skip
    From every rustling leaf,
But girds cóld iron on his hip,
With " Shoulder firelock ! " arms his lip
    And struts a bold militia chief!
And who that breathes where *Cato* lies,

But feels the Censor spirit rise
    At folly's idle pranks?
With voice that fills the Congress halls,
" Domestic manufactures " bawls,
    And damns the Dandies and the Banks !

Behold ! where *Junius town* is set,
    A Brutus is the judge ; [66]
'Tis true he serves the Tarquin yet,
Still winds his limbs in folly's net,
    And seems a very patient drudge.
But let the Despot fall, and bright
As morning from the shades of night,
    Forth in his pride he'll stand,
The guard and glory of our soil,
A head for thought, a hand for toil,
    A tongue to warn, persuade, command.

Lo ! *Galen* sends her Doctors round,
    Proficients in their trade ;
Historians are in *Livy* found,
Ulysses, from her teeming ground
    Pours politicians ready made ;
Fresh orators in *Tully* rise,
Nestor our counsellors supplies,
    Wise, vigilant, and close ;
Gracchus our tavern-statesmen rears,
And *Milton* finds us pamphleteers,
    As well as poets, by the gross.

Surveyor of the Western plains !
  The sapient work is thine ;
Full-fledged, it sprang from out thy brains,—
One added touch alone remains
  To consummate the grand design :
. Select a town—and christen it
With thy unrivalled name De Witt !
  Soon shall the glorious bantling bless us
With a fair progeny of *Fools*,
To fill our colleges and schools
  With tutors, regents, and professors.

H. AND D.

TO E. SIMPSON, ESQ.,

MANAGER OF THE PARK THEATRE.[57]

DEAR Simpson, since the day is near
    Destined to close your late campaign,
'Tis well to greet the coming year,
And learn how best you may appear
    Before the public eye again.
One thing, at least, whate'er you do,
For Heaven's sake give us something new !
For though your actors have not lost
    One lightning-flash of Thespian fire,
Yet beauties that delight us most,
    The wearied eye, in time, will tire.
'Tis thus the sated gaze of taste
    Holland's [58] drop-curtain heedless passes ;
And thus the schoolboy loathes at last
    His sugar-candy and molasses.

Now, if you will but take advice,
    Bank-notes shall fall like summer rain,
And next year you and Mr. Price
    May *cut* your cider for champagne.
Just hand your present *corps* down-stairs,
    Disband them all, and then create

Another army from the *Players*
    That figure on the *stage of State*.

A better set there cannot be
    For clap-trap and stage trickery,
And they'll be well content to quit
    Their present posts for higher pay;
For if they but good salaries get,
    It matters not what parts they play.
You'll have no quarelling about
The *characters* you deal them out;
Their public acts too well have shown
They care but little for *their own*.

How nicely would Judge Spencer fit
For "Overreach" and "Bajazet;"
Van Buren, nimble, sly, and thin,
Would make a noble "Harlequin;"
Clinton would play "King Dick the Surly,"
The learned "Pangloss" and grave "Lord Burleigh;"
Woodworth (whose name the Muse shall hallow)
Is quite at home in "Justice Shallow;"
And slippery, smooth-faced Tallmadge stands
A "Joseph Surface" at your hands.

Lo! where the *acting Council* sits,
A grand triumvirate of wits,
Cut out express by Nature's chisel
For "Noodle, Doodle, and Lord Grizzle;"

The *Members* who contrived to fill
The State purse from the steamboat-till,
Dressed out in turbans and white sleeves,
Would figure in the " Forty Thieves."

We'll linger with delighted grin
To see old Root in " Nipperkin,"
And gaze with reverential wonder
On Skinner's sapient face in " Ponder ! "
While Peter R——, the jovial soul,
Will toss off Jobson's " brimming bowl,"
 Fit for a Senator to swim in ;
And *bravos* rung from half the town,
Would tell the fame of Walter Bowne,
 In " Cacafogo" and old women.

Our *City Aldermen*, you know,
Are conjurors, *ex officio ;*
And, with the Mayor in his silk breeches,
Would do for " Hecate and the witches."
Christian and Warner, long the scourges
 Of Bucks and other " vagrom men,"
Would find in " Dogberry and Verges "
 Their very selves restored again.

Buckmaster, fat, and full of glee,
 Might rival Cooke in " Jack Falstaff ; "
" Pistol " and " Bobadil " would be
 Revived once more in Captain Half.

To classic Meigs, who soon, thank Heaven!
　In Congress, will illume the age,
The brightest wages should be given,
　To trim the lamps and *light* the stage.
Van Wyck will play the " Giant Wife,"
And " Death " in " Blue Beard " to the life ;
And surly German do, at least,
For " Bear " in " Beauty and the Beast."

Maxwell and Gardenier, you'll fix
　With strong indentures, by all means ;
They're used to *shifting* politics,
　And soon would learn to *shift* the scenes.
Bacon might bustle on in " Meddler,"
Gilbert play new tricks in " Diddler,"
　Good honest Peter H. Wendover
In " Vortex " read his *one* speech over,
While Pell would strike the critics dumb,
A perfect miniature " Tom Thumb ; "
And Mitchill, as in all the past,
Talk Science, and cut corns in " Last."

H. AND D.

THE COUNCIL OF APPOINTMENT AT ALBANY.

HERE'S magic in the robe of power,
  Ennobling every thing beneath it;
Its spell is like the Upas bower,
  Whose air will *puff up* all that breathe it.
Alike it charms the horse-hair tress
  That Turkey's three-tailed Bashaws wear,
And hallows Clinton's levee-dress
  Cut by the classic shears of Baehr.[59]

Before its witchery, of late,
  Our proudest politicians trembled,
When the five Heads that rule the State
  Around the Council-board assembled.
There, arbiter of fates and fortunes,
  Of brains it well supplied the loss,
Gave Bates[60] and Rosencrantz importance,
  And made a gentleman of Ross.

'Tis vain to win a great man's name
  Without some proof of having been one;

And *Killing's* a sure path to fame,
  Vide Jack Ketch and Mr. Clinton!
Our Council well this path have trod,
  Honor's immortal wreath securing;
They've dipped their hatchets in the blood,
  The patriot blood, of Mat Van Buren.

He bears, as every hero ought,
  The mandate of the powers that rule
(He's higher game in view, 'tis thought,
  All in good time; the man's no fool).
With him, some dozens prostrate fall,
  No friend to mourn, nor foe to flout them,
They die unsung, unwept by all,
  For no one cares a *sou* about them.

Wortman and Scott may grace the bar again,
  For them, a blest exchange we make;
We've dignity in Ned McGareaghan,
  And all, but that, in Jerry Drake.
And lo! the wreath of withered leaves
  That lately twined Van Buren's brow,
Oakley's pure, spotless hand receives;
  He's earned it—'tis no matter how.

Let office-holders cease to weep,
  And put once more their gala-dress on;

The Council's closed, and they may sleep
  In quiet, till the winter session.
Since all, or in or out of place,
  Wear Knavery's cloak or Folly's feather,
'Tis ours their *ups* and *downs* to trace,
  And laugh at *ins* and *outs* together.

H.

M̲R. CLINTON, whose worth we shall know when
    we've lost him,
Is delightfully free of his gifts, if they cost him
  But little or nothing, like smiles and brevets;
With what wonderful tact he appreciates merit
In bestowing on all our grown lads of high spirit
  His parchment commissions and gold epaulettes !

'Tis amusing to see these young nurslings of fame,
With their sashes of crimson and collars of flame;
Their cocked hats enchanting—their buttons divine,
And even the cloth of their coats superfine !
Displaying, around us, their new tinsel riches,
As proud as a boy in his first pair of breeches.

Ah ! who does not envy their steps of delight,
  Through the streets to their battle-drums prancing,
While scared at their "chimney-sweep" badges so
      bright,
Cartmen, pigs, and old women, seek safety in flight,
  As, in exquisite order, their lines are advancing !

Long live the Militia ! from sergeant to drummer
  They've the true soldier-aspect, chivalric and wild,

In their clothes of more hues than the rainbow of sum-
　　mer,
Or the dress which the Patriarch wore when a child.
Unawed by court-martials, by fines or by fears,
They glow with the feelings of free Volunteers.

Yes! long live the Militia! that free school of glory
　　Where Mapes, Colden, and Steddiford took their
　　　　degree;
Lives there a man who ne'er heard their proud story,
　　What an ignorant, unlettered cub he must be!
From the Battery flag-staff their fame has ascended
　　To the sand-hills of Greenwich and plains of Bellevue ·
And the belles of Park Place for the palm have con-
　　tended
　　Of rewarding the feats they have *promised to do!*
Let the poets of Europe still scribble as hard as
　　They please, of their Cæsars and Bonys to tell—
Be ours the bright names of Laight, Ward, and Bogar-
　　dus, ·
　　And that promising genius, the bold Colonel Pell.

　　　　　　　　　　　　　　　　　　H.

AN ADDRESS[61]

For the opening of the new Theatre, Sept. 1, 1821,
to be spoken by Mr. Olliff.

LADIES AND GENTLEMEN :
  Enlightened as you were, you all must know
Our playhouse was burnt down some time ago,
Without insurance.   'Twas a famous blaze,
Fine fun for firemen, but dull sport for plays ;
The proudest of our whole dramatic corps
Such *warm reception* never met before.
It was a woeful night for us and ours,
Worse than dry weather to the fields and flowers.
The evening found us gay as summer's lark,
  Happy as sturgeons in the Tappan Sea ;
The morning, like the dove from Noah's ark,
  As homeless, houseless, desolate as she.

But thanks to those who always have been known
To love the public interest, when their own—
Thanks to the men of talent and of trade,
Who joy in doing well when they're well paid—
Again our fireworn mansion is rebuilt,
Inside and outside, neatly carved and gilt,

With best of paint and canvas, lath and plaster,
The Lord bless Beekman [61] and John Jacob Astor !
As an old coat, from Jenning's [61] patent screw,
Comes out clean scoured and brighter than the new ;
As an old head in Saunders' [63] patent wig,
Looks wiser than when young, and twice as big ;
As Mat Van Buren in the Senate-hall,
Repairs the loss we met in Spencer's fall ;
As the new Constitution will (we're told)
Be worth, at least, a dozen of the old,
So is our new house better than its brother,
Its roof is painted yellower than the other,
It is insured at three per cent. 'gainst fire,
And cost three times as much, and is six inches higher.

'Tis not alone the house—the prompter's clothes
Are all quite new, so are the fiddlers' bows ;
The supernumeraries are newly shaved,
New drilled, and all extremely well behaved
(They'll each one be allowed, I pause to mention,
The right of suffrage by the new Convention).
We've some new thunder, several new plays,
And a new splendid carpet of green baize.
So that there's naught remains to bid us reach
The topmost bough of favor, but a speech—
A speech, the prelude to each public meeting,
Whether for morals, charity, or eating—
A speech, the modern mode of winning hearts,
And power, and fame, in politics and arts.

What made the good Monroe [64] our President?
'Twas that through all this blessed land he went
With his immortal cocked hat and short breeches,
Dining—wherever asked—and making speeches.
What, when Missouri stood on her last legs,
Revived her hopes? The speech of Henry Meigs. [65]
What proves our country wise, learned, and happy?
Mitchill's address to the Phi Beta Kappa.
What has convinced the world that we have men,
First with the sword, the chisel, brush, and pen,
Shaming all English rivals, men or madams?
The "Fourth of July" speech of Mr. Adams.
Yes, if our managers grow great and rich,
And players prosper, let them thank my speech,
And let the name of Olliff proudly go
With Meigs and Adams, Mitchill and Monroe!

H.

EPISTLE TO ROBERT HOGBIN, ESQ.,

*Chairman of the Committee of Working-Men, **etc.,** at the Westchester Hotel, Bowery, Nov.,* 1830.

MR. HOGBIN,—I work as a weaver—of rhyme—
    And therefore presume with a working-man's
grace,
To address you as one I have liked for some time,
    Though I know not (no doubt it's a fine one) your face.

There is much in a name, and I'll lay you a wager
    (Two ale-jugs from Reynolds' [66]), that Nature de-
signed,
When she formed you, that you should become the
    drum-major
    In that choice piece of music, the Grand March of
Mind.

A Hogbin! a Hogbin! how cheering the shout
    Of all that keep step to that beautiful air,
Which leads, like the treadmill, about and about,
    And leaves us exactly, at last, where we were!

Yes, there's much in a name, and a Hogbin's so fit is
    For that great moral purpose whose impulse divine
15

Bids men leave their own workshops to work in committees,
   And their own wedded wives to protect yours and
   mine !

That we working-men prophets are sadly mistaken,
   If yours is not, Hogbin, a durable fame,
As lasting as England's philosopher Bacon,
   Whom your ancestors housed, if we judge by his
   name.

When the moment arrives that we've won the good fight,
   And broken the chains of laws, churches, and mar-
   riages,
When no infants are born under six feet in height,
   And our chimney-sweeps mount up a flue in their
   carriages—

That glorious time when our daughters and sons
   Enjoy a *blue Monday* each day of the week,
And a clean shirt is classed with the mastodon's bones.
   Or a mummy from Thebes, an undoubted antique—

Then, then, my dear Hogbin, your statue in straw,
   By some modern *Pig*malion delightfully wrought,
Shall embellish the Park, and our youths' only law
   Shall be to be Hogbins in feeling and thought.

                                             H.

LAMENTINGS.

H ! where are now the lights that shed
   A lustre o'er my darkened hours,
The priests of pleasure's fane, who spread,
Each night beneath my weary head,
   Endymion's moonlight couch of flowers ?

No more in chains of music bound,
   I listen to those airy reels,
When quavering Philipps cuts around
Fantastic pigeon-wings of sound,
Like Byrne,[67] who, without touching ground,
   Eleven times can cross his heels.

No longer Cooper's tongue of tongues,
Pumps thunder from his stormy lungs;
   Turner [68] has shut his classic pages,
Southward his face Magenis [69] turns,
And for the halls of Congress spurns
   The mansion of our civic sages.

And Wallack,[69] too, no longer dips
   In bathos, for the tragic prize ;
And Bartley,[69] a melalogue that slips
Melodious from her honeyed lips,
   No more in murmured music dies.

Yet, though fell Fortune has bereft
My heart of all, one mode is left
   In slumber's vision to restore 'em ;
Weekly I'll buy with pious pence,
A dose of opiate eloquence,
   And sleep in quiet at the Forum.

                            D.

TO QUACKERY.

GODDESS ! for such thou art, who rules
    This honest and enlightened city;
True patroness of knaves and fools,
   To thee we dedicate our ditty.
Whether in Barclay Street thou sittest,
   Or, on papyrean pinions borne,
Dropping mercurial dews, thou flittest
   Around thine own anointed Horne :[70]

Whether, arrayed in gown and band,
   Thy pious zeal distributes Bibles,
Or, perched on Spooner's classic hand,
   Writes merry eulogistic libels ;
Where'er we turn our raptured eyes,
   We see this puffing generation,
Cheered by thy smile, propitious, rise
   To profit, power, and reputation.

Then come, ye Quacks ! the anthem swell ;
   Come, Allen, with thy lottery bills ;
Come, four-herbed Angelis,[70] who fell
   From heaven in a shower of pills ;
Come, Geib, whose potent word creates
   Prime analytical musicians ;

And come, ye hosts that hold brevets
  From Hosack's college of physicians.

And thou, botanic Hosack, bring
  Thy poppy-breathing lips along;
Thy name in steeple-bells shall ring,
  Thou monarch of the motley throng.
Yet Mitchill may the votes estrange,
  Or Doctor Clinton, to confound ye,
Again produce some queer melange
  Of scientific Salmagundi.

Clinton ! the name my fancy fires,
  I see him, with a sage's look,
Exhausting Nature, and whole quires
  Of foolscap, in his wondrous book.
Columbia's genius hovers o'er him,
  Fair Science, smiling, lingers near,
Encyclopædias lie before him,
  And Mitchill whispers in his ear.

Enough ! the swelling wave has borne
  Upon its bosom chiefs and kings—
From Mitchill, Clinton, Hosack, Horne,
  One cannot stoop to meaner things.
Yet once again we'll raise the song,
  And passing forums, banks, and brokers,
Join with the bubble-blowing throng,
  Seize Quackery's pipe, and puff the Croakers.

                                         D.

TO THE DIRECTORS OF THE ACADEMY
OF ARTS.

ILLUSTRIOUS autocrats of taste !
    Inspectors of the wonders traced
  By pencil, brush, or chisel !
Accept a nameless poet's lay,
Who longs to twine a sprig of bay
  Around his penny whistle.

Ye learned and enlightened few
Who keep the portal of *virtu*,
  I pray you now unlock it,
And grant a peep, for all my pains,
Within your oil-bedaubed domains,
The Dome where now the poor in brains
  Succeed the poor in pocket.

All honored be the rich repast
At which the sage decree was past
  Of pauper health so tender,
Which sent the beggars to Bellevue,
And left the classic fame to you
  And Scudder's Witch of Endor.

Obliging all, you fear no harm
From Disappointment's angry arm,
　No cudgels, sneers, or libels ;
Alike you smile on worst and best,
From great Rubens and Quaker West,
　To wooden cuts for Bibles.

Lo ! next the Gallic thunderbolt,
Some nameless, shapeless, ugly dolt,
　His plastic phiz advances ;
And vestal footsteps lightly tread,
And Cupids sport around the head
　Of gentle Doctor Francis.

While placed on high exalted pegs,
Apollo blushes for his legs,
　And mourns his severed fingers ;
Some amorous wight, with passion drunk,
O'er Cytherea's headless trunk
　Luxuriously lingers.

Here Danaë rolls her humid eyes
To meet the ruler of the skies
　In tricks that please old Satan ;
And there our eyes delighted trace
The scarlet coat and lily face
　Of gallant Captain Creighton. "

Here West's creative pencil shines,
And paints, in tear-compelling lines,
   Polony's frenzied daughter ;
A hang-dog king, and sheepish queen,
And her, who looks as if she'd been
   Just fished up from the water !

Thy glories, too, are blazoned there,
King Ben's first-born immortal heir—
   Apparent to the pallet ;
Orlando weighs his *cons* and *pros*,
Forgetting quite his heedless toes
   Are in the Phoca's gullet.

                                   D.

CUTTING.

THE world is not a perfect one,
All women are not wise or pretty,
All that are willing are not won—
More's the pity—more's the pity !
" Playing wall-flower's rather flat,"
L'Allegro or Penseroso—
Not that women care for that—
But oh ! they hate the slighting beau so !

Delia says my dancing's bad—
She's found it out since I have cut her ;
She says wit I never had—
I said she " smelt of bread and butter."
Mrs. Milton coldly bows—
I did not think her baby "cunning ; "
Gertrude says I've little " NOUS "—
I tired of her atrocious punning.

Tom's wife says my taste is vile—
I condemned her macarony ;
Miss McLush, my flirt awhile,
Hates me—I preferred her crony ;

Isabella, Sarah Anne,
  Fat Estella, and one other,
Call me an immoral man—
  I have cut their drinking brother.

Thus it is—be only civil—
  Dance with stupid, short and tall—
Know no line 'twixt saint and devil—
  Spend your wit on fools and all—
Simper with the milk-and-waters—
  Suffer bores, and talk of caps—
Trot out people's awkward daughters—
  You may scandal 'scape—perhaps!

But prefer the wise and pretty—
  Pass Reserve to dance with Wit—
Let the slight be e'er so petty,
  Pride will never pardon it.
Woman never yet refused
  Virtues to a seeming wooer—
Woman never yet abused
  Him who had been civil to her.

.   II.

OHNNY R * * * [72] gave a dinner last night,
    The best I have tasted this season;
The wine and the wit sparkled bright,
    'Twas a frolic of soul and of reason.
For the guests there was Cooper[73] and Kean;[74]
    Bishop Hobart[75] and Alderman Brasher,[76]
Buchanan,[77] that foe to the Queen,
    And Sherred the painter and glazier.

The beef had been warm, it is true,
    But when we sat down it was colder;
The wine when we entered was new;
    When we drank it, 'twas six hours older.
Mr. Kean, by-the-way, he's no dunce;
    His plate was so often repeating,
I thought he'd a genius at once
    Not only for acting but eating.

Mr. Cooper, a sensible man,
    Talked much of his scheme of rebuilding
The theatre on a new plan,
    With fantastical carving and gilding.

Said he, " I've a thought of my own :
　Of the people, so stupid the taste is,
I could fill the new playhouse in June
　If I only could furnish new faces."

In addition to those I have named,
　Harry Cruger [78] was there in his glory,
That *ci-devant jeune homme* so famed
　In Paris—but that's an old story.
And General Lewis, [79] by Jove !
　With two vests, and a new fashioned eye-glass,
He looked like the young god of love
　At distance beheld through a spy-glass.

I have read my first stanza again,
　And find that for once I have erred :
For Robert and Mat were the men,
　. Instead of Buchanan and Sherred.
Two Frenchmen, the best I have met,
　At home in bad English and flummery,
Were there—just to make up the set,
　Together with Master Montgomery. [80]

. Jack Nicholson [81] wanted to come
　With his pea-jacket on, but the ladies
Compelled him to leave it at home ;
　So he wore, as becoming his trade is,

Two epaulets—one on each arm,   *
  And a sword, once of laurels the winner,
Ever ready, in case of alarm,
  At carving a foe or a dinner.

Bishop Hobart said grace with an air
  'Twould have done your heart good to have seen him,
And Lewis so sweetly did swear,
  You'd have thought that the devil was in him.
And Alderman Brasher began
  A song, but he could not go through it.
When Johnny R * * * asks me again
  To a fête—by the Lord, I'll go to it!

H.

THE NIGHTMARE.

" Sure he was sent from heaven express to be the pillar of the State;
  So terrible his name, 'Clintonian' nurses frightened children with it."

TOM THUMB.

DREAMING, last night, of Pierre Van Wyck,
  I felt the *nightmare* creeping o'er me ;
In vain I strove to speak or strike,
  The horrid form was still before me ;
Till panting—struggling to be free,
  I raised my weak but desperate head,
And faintly muttered " John Targee ! "
  When—with a howl—the goblin fled.

I waked and cried in glad surprise:
  " The man is found ordained by Fate
To break our bonds, and exorcise
  The nightmare of the sleeping State.
He'll chase the demons great and small;
  They'll sink his withering gaze before.
Then rouse ! ye Sachems at the Hall,
  And nominate him Governor.

" Up with the name on Freedom's cause,
  Inscribe it, Bucktails, on your banner;

Fame's pewter trump shall sound applause,
  And blasts from party's furnace fan her.
Pledge high his health in mugs of beer,
  And, roaring like the boisterous sea,
Thunder in Clinton's frightened ear,
  The conquering name of John Targee!"

D.

THE MODERN HYDRA.

HERE is a beast sublime and savage,
   The Hydra by denomination;
Well doth he know his foes to ravage,
   And barks and bites to admiration.
Fox—wolf—cat—dog—of each, at least, he
   Has a full share, and never scants 'em;
But what is strangest in this beast, he
   Can make new heads whene'er he wants 'em.

But when our Tammany Alcides
   Had tomahawked his head political,
Straight from the bleeding trunk, out slid his
   Well-filled noddle scientifical.
Another comes—another! see—
   They rise in infinite variety;
One cries aloud, " Free-school trustee ! "
   The next exclaims, " Humane Society ! "

Behold the fourth—bewhiskered—big—
   A warlike cocked hat frowns upon it;
The fifth uprears a doctor's wig,
   The sixth displays the judgment-bonnet.

Herculean Noah! your strength you waste,
   Reserve your furious cuts and slashes,
Till Satan stands beside the beast
   With red-hot steel to sear the gashes.

D.

THE TEA-PARTY.

THE tea-urn is singing, the tea-cups are gay,
  And the fire sparkles bright in the room of D. K.
For the first time these six months, a broom has been
    there,
And the housemaid has brushed every table and chair ;
Drugs, minerals, books, are all hidden from view,
And the five shabby pictures are varnished anew ;
There's a feast going on, there's the devil to pay
In the furnished apartments of Doctor D. K.[2]

What magic has raised all this bustle and noise,
Disturbing the bachelor's still quiet joys ;
A pair of young witches have doomed them to death,
They are distant relations to those in Macbeth.
Not as ugly, 'tis true, but as mischievous quite,
And like them in teasing and talking delight ;
This morning they sent him a billet to say,
"To-night we take tea with you, Doctor D. K."

There is Mrs. J. D.,[3] in her high glee and glory,
And E. McC.,[4] with her song and her story ;

There's a smile on each lip, and a leer on each brow,
And they both are determined to kick up a row. .
They're mistaken for once, as they'll presently see,
For D. K.'s drinking whiskey with Langstaff and me:
They'll find the cage there, but the bird is away—
Catch a weasel asleep, and catch Doctor D. K.

H.

THE MEETING OF THE GROCERS.

THE knights of the firkin are gathered around,
 The rag-idols' rights to assert;
Each gatherer pricks up his ears at the sound,
Town rags are advancing a penny a pound,
 While country rags sink in the dirt.

Aghast stand the brokers—the carrying-trade
 Is lost if the butter-boys win—
The farmers are quaking, the worst is dismayed,
Omnipotent Fundable trembles afraid,
 And Wall Street is all in a din.

'Twasn't so when the banks in a body prepared
 To cut their own corporate throats;
And, biting their thumbs at the farmers, declared
To the thunderstruck dealers in butter and lard,
 They would handle no more of their notes.

Oh, Fundable! Fundable! look to thine own,
 Now, now, let thy management shine;
I fear the young Franklin will worry thee down,
And if all the bad paper be kicked out of town,
 Dear Fundable! where will be thine?

D.

OW stately yon palace uplifts its proud head,[6]
    Where Broadway and Barclay Street meet ;
Abhorring its old-fashioned tunic of red,
It shines in the lustre of chromate of lead,
    And its doors open—into the street !

No longer it rings to the merry sleigh-bells,
    The steeds' gallant neighings are o'er;
Instead of the pitchfork, we meet with scalpels,
And the throne of his medical majesty dwells
    Where the horse-trough resided before.

Oh, David ! how dreadful and dire was the note,
    When Rebellion beleaguered the place,
When the bull-dog of discord unbolted his throat,
And the hot Digitalis [87] unbuttoned his coat,
    And doubled his fist in your face !

Then Syncope seized thee; all wild with affright
    The Lord Chamberlain cried " God defend ye ! "
Mac [68] swung his shillelah in hopes of a fight,
While the brave Surgeon-General [89] exclaimed in de-
    light,
    " *Pugnatum est arte medendi.*"

But your wars are all ended, you're now at your ease,
    The Regents are bound for your debts;
You may fleece your poor students as much as you
       please,
Tax boldly, matriculate, double your fees,
    You can pay off all scores in brevets.

So a health to your highness, and long may you reign,
    O'er subjects obedient and true;
If the snaffle won't hold them, apply the curb-rein;
And if ever they prance, or go backward again,
    May you horsewhip them all black and blue !

                           D.

TO THE BARON VON HOFFMAN, [90]

Morrison's Hotel, Dublin, June 20, 1823.

AREWELL, farewell to thee, Baron von Hoffman,
    Thus warbled a creditor over his wine,
Of unmeaning faces I've gazed on enough, man,
    But never on one half as stupid as thine.

Oh, gay as the negro who trotted behind thee,
    How light was thy heart till thy money was gone !
But when all was gone, 'twas the devil to find thee ;
    The nest still remained, but the eagle was flown.

Yet long upon Harlem's gray rocks and green highlands
    Shall Burnham [91] and Cato remember the name
Of him who away in the far British Islands
    Now lights his cigar at the blaze of his fame.

And still when the bell at the Coffee-House ringing
    Assembles, of brokers, the young and the old,
The happiest there to his memory bringing
    Thy frolics, shall swear when thy story is told.

And Jacob, the tailor, as fondly he lingers
  O'er the leaves of his ledger by night and by day,
Will count the sums due him from thee on his fingers,
  And mournfully turn from their figures away.

Nor shall Carlo,[92] beloved of thy bosom, forget thee,
  In his merriest hour at thy name he will start ;
By the side of his chaise and his horses he'll set thee,
  Embalmed in the innermost shrine of his heart.

Farewell, farewell, while the spirit of evil
  Has power in a creditor's bosom, we swear
To be with thee on earth—if thou goest to the devil,
  He is an old friend of ours, and will visit thee there.

Farewell, be it ours to embitter thy pillow
  With thistles whose wounds are eternal and deep,
There are packets of letters afloat on the billow
  That shall poison thy whiskey and torture thy sleep.

Around thee shall hover the constable gentry,
  Those bloodhounds of law, ever thirsty and true—
Worse foes than the Frenchmen who saw you a sentry
  In a platoon of Dutchmen at red Waterloo.

We'll dine where the bailiffs in Bow Street are drinking,
  And bribe all their clubs to be aimed at thy head ;
And when of thy snug German home thou art thinking,
  Take out a *ca. sa.* and take thee out of bed.

       H.

A LAMENT FOR GREAT MEN DEPARTED.

" Hung be the heavens with black."
SHAKESPEARE.

THERE is a gloom on every brow,
  A sadness in each face we see;
The City Hall is lonely now,
  The Franklin Bank looks wearily.

The Surgeons' Hall in Barclay Street,
  Wears to the eye a ghastlier hue!
And Staten Island's *Summer-seat*
  Has lost its best attractions too!

Well may we mourn a stage-and-four
  (Our curse upon the rogue that drove it!)
From out our city lately bore
  All that adorn, and grace, and love it.

Ah, little knew each scoundrel horse
  How much they vexed, and grieved, and marred us;
They cared not sixpence for the loss
  We feel in Colden and Bogardus.

And Doctor Mitchill, LL. D.,
  And Tompkins, Lord of Staten Island !
Hushed be the strain of mirth and glee,
  'Twere reason now to laugh or smile.

Long has proud Albany, elate,
  Reared her two steeples[93] high in air,
And boasted that she ruled the State,
  Because the *Governor lives there.*

But loftier now will be her tone
  To know, within her walls are met
The brightest gems that ever shone
  Upon a city's coronet.

Though heavy is our load of pain
  To feel that Fate has so bereft us,
Some consolations yet remain,
  For Dicky Riker still is left us !

And Hope, with smile and gesture proud,
  Points to a day of triumph nigh,
When, like a sunbeam from the cloud,
  That dims awhile an April sky,

Our champions shall again return,
  Their pockets with new honors crowded,

That every heart may cease to mourn,
　And hats no more in crape be shrouded.

The Park shall throng with merry feet,
　And boys and beauties hasten there,
To place the new Judge on his seat !
　And hail the great Bogardus, Mayor !

H.

["Resolved that this Board will visit the Academy of Arts, for the purpose of viewing a painting, now on exhibition there, from the pencil of Mr. Rembrandt Peale, and that it be recommended to our fellow-citizens generally to go also."]

Extract from the Minutes of the Common Council, Dec. 26, 1820.

WHEN the wild waters from the deluged earth
    Retired, and Nature woke to second birth,
And the first rainbow met the patriarch's gaze,
In the blue west—a pledge of better days ;
What crowded feelings of delight were his
In that bright hour of hope and happiness !
What tears of rapture glistened in his eye,
His early tears forgot—his life's long agony !

So did the heart of Mr. Rembrandt Peale,
The "moral picture-painter," beat and feel,
When by the Mayor and Aldermen was passed
That vote which made his talent known at last,
And those wise arbiters of taste and fame
Pronounced him worthy of his *Christian name.*

Long did he linger anxiously, in vain,
Beside his painting in the classic fane
Of science (where, arranged by Scudder's hand,
The curiosities of every land,

From Babel brickbats, and the Cashmere goat,
Down to the famous Knickerbocker boat,
Applause and wonder from the gazer seek,
Aided by martial music once a week)—
Long did he linger there, and but a few
Odd shillings his *"Great Moral Picture"* drew.

In vain the newspapers its beauties told,
In vain they swore 'twas worth its weight in gold,
In vain invoked each patriotic spirit,
And talked of native genius, power, and merit;
In vain the artist threatened to lay by
His innate hope of immortality,
Grow rich by painting merely human faces,
Nor longer stay and starve in public places—
All would not do—his work remained unseen,
Taste, Beauty, Fashion, talked of Mr. Kean;
But of the Moral Picture not a word
From lips of woman or of man was heard.

The scene has changed, thanks to the Corporation,
And Peale has now a city's approbation.
"Resolved," the Council Records say, "that we
Untie the purse-strings of the Treasury,
Take out just five-and-twenty cents a head,
And by the Mayor in grave procession led,
Visit the Academy of Arts, and then,
Preceded by the Mayor—walk back again."

Hide your diminished heads, ye sage Reviewers !
Thank Heaven, the day is o'er with you and yours
No longer at your shrines will Genius bow,
For mayors and aldermen are critics now.
Alike to them the Crichtons of their age,
The painter's canvas, and the poet's page,
From high to low, from law to verse they stoop,
Judges of Sessions, Science, Arts, and Soup.

Time was, when Dr. Mitchill's word was law,
When monkeys, monsters, whales, and Esquimaux,
Asked but a letter from his ready hand,
To be the theme and wonder of the land.
That time is past,—henceforth each showman's doom
Must be decided in the Council Room ;
And there the city's guardians will decree
An artist's or an author's destiny,
Pronounce the fate of poem, song, or sonnet,
And shape the fashion of a lady's bonnet ;
Gravely determine when, and how, and where,
Bristed shall write, and Saunders shall cut hair,
'Till even the very buttons of a coat
Be settled, like assessment laws, by vote.

H.

At the opening of the New-York Legislature in January, 1825

TO Tallmadge[95] of the Upper House,
   And Crolius[96] of the lower,
After "*non nobis, Domine,*"
   Thus saith the Governor :

It seems by general admission,
   That, as a nation, we are thriving;
Settled in excellent condition,
   Bargaining, building, and beehiving ;
That each one fearlessly reclines
   Beneath his " fig-tree and his vines "
(The dream of philosophic man),
   And all is quiet as a Sunday,
From Orleans to the Bay of Fundy,
   From Beersheba to Dan.

I've climbed my country's loftiest tree,
   And reached its highest bough, save one.
Why not the highest?—blame not me ;
   " What man dare " do, I've done.

And though thy city—Washington!
  Still mocks my eagle wing and eye,
Yet is there joy upon a throne
  Even here at Albany.
For though but second in command,
  Far floats my banner in the breeze,
A Captain-General's on the land,
  An Admiral on the seas.
And if Ambition can ask more,
My very title—Governor—
  A princely pride creates,
Because it gives me kindred claims
To greatness with those glorious names
  A Sancho and a Yates!

As party spirit has departed,
  This life to breathe and blast no more,
The patriot and the honest-hearted
  Shall form my diplomatic *corps.*
The wise, the wittiest, the good,
  Selected from my band of yore,
My own devoted band, who've stood
Beside me, stemming faction's flood
  Like rocks on Ocean's shore—
Men, who, if now the field were lost,
  Again would buckle sword and mail on.
Followed by them, themselves a host,
Haines,[97] Hurtell, Herring, Pell, and Post,
Judge Miller, Mumford, and Van Wyck,

'Tis said I look extremely like
  A Highland chieftain with his tail on.

A clear and comprehensive view
  Of every thing in art or nature,
In this, my opening speech, is due
  To an enlightened Legislature.
I therefore have arranged with care,
  In orderly classification,
The following subjects, which should share
• Your most mature deliberation :

Physicians, senators, and makers
  Of patent medicines and machines,
The train-bands and the Shaking Quakers.
  Forts, colleges, and quarantines ;
Debts, cadets, coal-mines, and canals,
  Salt—the Comptroller's next report,
Reform within our prison walls,
  The customs and the Supreme Court ;
Delinquents, juvenile and gray,
  Schools, steamboats, justices of peace
Republics of the present day,
  And those of Italy and Greece ;
Militia-officers, and they
  Who serve in the police—
Madmen and laws, a great variety,
The horticultural society,

The rate of interests and of tolls,
The numbering of tax-worthy souls,
   Roads—and a mail three times a week,
From where the gentle Erie rolls
   To Conewango Creek.

These are a few affairs of state
   On which I ask your reasoning powers,
High themes for study and debate,
   For closet and for caucus hours.

This is my longest speech, but those
   Who feel, that, like a cable's strength
   Its power increases with its length,
Will weep to hear its close.
Weep not, my next shall be as long,
And that, like this, enbalmed in song,
Will be, when two brief years are told,
   Mine own no longer, but the Nation's,
With all my speeches, new and old,
And what is more, the place I hold,
   Together with its pay and rations.

                      H.

NOTES.

NOTES.

MISCELLANEOUS POEMS.

(1) Page 13.—MARCO BOZZARIS, one of the best and bravest of the modern Greek chieftains. He fell in a night attack upon the Turkish camp at Laspi, the site of the ancient Platæa, August 20, 1823, and expired in the moment of victory.

(2) Page 18.—ALNWICK CASTLE, Northumberlandshire, a seat of the Duke of Northumberland. Written in October, 1822, after visiting the " Home of the Percy's high-born race."

(3) Page 20.—*From him who once his standard set.*—One of the ancestors of the Percy family was an Emperor at Constantinople.

(4) Page 20.—*Fought for King George at Lexington.*—The late duke. He commanded a detachment of the British army, in the affair at Lexington and Concord, in 1775.

(5) Page 21.—*From royal Berwick's beach of sand.*—Berwick was formerly a principality. Richard II. was styled " King of England, France, and Ireland, and Berwick-upon-Tweed."

(6) Page 30.—WYOMING.—The allusion in the following stanzas can be understood by those only who have read Campbell's beautiful poem, " GERTRUDE OF WYOMING : " but who has not read it ?

(7) Page 46.—" RED JACKET " appeared originally in 1828, soon after the publication of Mr. Cooper's " NOTIONS OF THE AMERICANS."

(8) Page 57.—MAGDALEN.—Written in 1823, for a love-stricken young officer on his way to Greece. The reader will have the kindness to presume that he died there.

(9) Page 87.—Lieut. ALLEN.—He commanded the U. S. sloop-of-war Alligator, and was mortally wounded on the 9th of November, 1822, in an

action with pirates, near Matanzas, in the Island of Cuba. **His mother, a**
few hours after hearing of his death, died—literally of a broken heart.

(10) **Page** 89.—WALTER BOWNE, then, **and** for two years previous, a
Senator at Albany, and member of the Council of Appointment. **He was
afterward Mayor of** New York, where **he died in August, 1846.**

(11) Page 93.—During **the second war with Great Britain, Mr.** Halleck
joined **a** New-**York** infantry company, **"**Swartwout's **gallant** corps, the
Iron Grays," as he afterward wrote in " Fanny," **and** excited their martial
ardor by this spirited ode. Among the few survivors of **this much-admired**
corps, are Gouverneur S. **Bibby,** Stephen Cambreleng, **Dr. Edward Dela-**
field, Hickson W. Field, James W. Gerard, and Charles **W. Sandford.**

(12) Page 96.—CONTOIT'S GARDEN, open to the public under the au-
spices of a Frenchman of that name, on the west side of Broadway, between
Leonard and Franklin Streets.

(13) **Page 96.—**MADAME SAINT MARTIN, the proprietress of a milliner's
and perfumery shop on Broadway, next door to the Garden.

(14) **Page** 97.—The " OPERA FRANCAIS," **a name given during the
summer** season, while occupied by a troupe **of French actors from New
Orleans, to** the Chatham Garden Theatre of **Mr.** Palmo, situated **on the
west side of** Chatham Street, between Duane **and** Pearl. **The " Opera "
was a** place of fashionable resort, **and patronized particularly** by **the distin-**
guished personages named Mrs. **President J. Q.** Adams and Joseph Bonaparte, ex-King **of** Spain. The three **" danseuses " mentioned** were among
the principal performers attached **to the Opera.**

(15) Page 97.—"SWAMP PLACE," a name given, either in jest or earnest, to a plot of ground in the neighborhood of Jacob and Ferry Streets,
near which some medical Columbus of the time had found or fancied a
mineral spring of imperishable merit. Unfortunately, it proved itself to be
less than a " nine days' wonder," **by** vanishing one morning, **like a dream.**

(16) **Page 98.—The names of John** Quincy Adams, Henry Clay,
De Witt Clinton, Andrew Jackson, and Daniel Webster, which occur on
this page, belong to history.

(17) Page 98.—The " ANNUAL REGISTER," edited by Joseph Blunt, a
young lawyer of ability. The publication then in progress, was soon after
discontinued.

FANNY.

Stanza 1.—" FANNY."—Of this young lady and her worthy father, to whose exemplary and typical career the author was indebted for the theme of his story, we are not permitted to reveal more than that they wish to be known and remembered only in the words from Milton, on the title-page, among—

> " Gay creatures of the element,
> That in the colors of the rainbow live,
> And play in the plighted clouds."

Stanza 6, etc.—Doctors MITCHILL, HOSACK, and FRANCIS, then (1819) eminent physicians in New York, highly distinguished, not only in their profession, and as authors of popular works connected with medicine and general knowledge, but as active and useful leaders in the social, literary, and scientific institutions of the city. Doctor Mitchill, moreover, had won the name of a philosopher by his frequent discoveries, more or less important, in geology and other conjectural sciences.

Stanza 8, etc.—JAMES K. PAULDING, one of the best and most popular of early American authors. The quotation is from his poem, " The Back-woodsman," then recently published. He afterward rose, or fell, from literature to politics, and became navy agent at New York, and Secretary of the Navy during President Van Buren's administration.

Stanza 13.—The " MODERN SOLOMON," a *nom de plume* given to Mr. Lang by the pleasantry of his brethren of the press. The front door of his office was surmounted by the figure-head of his assumed prototype, Doctor Franklin, mentioned in stanza 49. The bust and statue therein named as specimens of the fine arts in America at the period were to be seen, the one in plaster at the Academy of Arts (stanza 51), the one in wax at Scudder's Museum (stanza 68). Poor McDonald Clarke, the mad poet of New York, having been called in Lang's paper a person with " zig-zag brains," immediately responded in the following neat epigram :

> " I can tell Johnny Lang, in the way of a laugh,
> In reply to his rude and unmannerly scrawl,
> That in my humble sense it is better by half
> To have brains that are zig-zag than to have none at all."

Stanza 16, etc.—CADWALLADER D. COLDEN, then Mayor of the city, before whose door, in accordance with immemorial usage, two prominent lamps were placed, in token of his magisterial position, to remain during and after his mayoralty. His residence, and the office of Mr. Lang, the editor of the *New-York Gazette* (see stanzas 11 and 49), were in the neighborhood of Pearl Street and Hanover Square.

Stanza 23.—DOMINICK LYNCH, a popular importer of French wines, who ranked among the prominent merchants of the city. He was well known

in social circles by his elegant entertainments at his residence, No. 1 Greenwich Street. One of his sons sang Moore's melodies with taste and deep
feeling.

Stanza 25.—JOHN BRISTED, an English gentleman, then recently arrived
in America. He was a graduate of Oxford University, a highly accomplished scholar, and the author of several ably-written works on various
topics, published in New York, among them the one entitled "The
Resources of Great Britain in Time of Peace," alluded to in stanza 141.
He married a daughter of John Jacob Astor.

Stanza 29.—Monsieur GUILLÉ, an aeronaut, recently from France, whose
balloon ascensions, then a rare and exciting exhibition, had proved a failure.

Stanza 32.—DAVID GELSTON, the collector of the customs.

Stanza 38, etc.—DE WITT CLINTON, then Governor of the State of New
York; MARTIN VAN BUREN, then its Attorney-General, afterward President of the United States; and DANIEL D. TOMPKINS, Vice-President of the
United States. These prominent and popular statesmen require no intro-
duction to the reader.

Stanza 39, etc.—The "NATIONAL ADVOCATE," a daily newspaper, conducted by Mordecai M. Noah, a veteran editor, highly distinguished in the
political strife of words, for wielding, alike powerfully and playfully, the pen
of a "ready writer." As the champion of a party (his party, for the time
being), he was a faithful friend and a formidable antagonist. He was
favorably known as the author of an interesting book of travels in Europe,
etc., and of several dramas successful on the stage.

"PELL'S POLITE REVIEW."—A political pamphlet, by Ferris Pell, an
enterprising young lawyer and politician.

Stanza 47.—CHRISTIAN BAEHR, one of the fashionable tailors of the
period, and a colonel in the militia.

Stanza 51.—S. & M. ALLEN and WAITE & CO. (see stanza 55), dealers
in lottery tickets.

"THE ACADEMY OF ARTS."—A society of artists and amateurs, among
whose presiding officers and patrons, Doctor Hosack, John G. Bogart (see
stanza 49), and Colonel Trumbull, the celebrated painter, were honorably
conspicuous. On the formation, soon after, of the present "National Academy of the Arts of Design," it ceased to exist.

Stanza 52.—"CULLEN'S MAGNESIAN SHOP."—A soda-water, etc.,
establishment, on the corner of Broadway and Park Place, rivalled in its
embellishments by the cottage of Mr. Gautier, at Hoboken, near the ferry.

"The EUTERPIAN SOCIETY."—An association of amateur musicians
occasionally giving public concerts.

Stanza 53.—Doctor **Wm. James** McNeven.—One of the ablest and purest of the banished Irish patriots of '98. His excellent personal character, without reference to political antecedents, insured him a warm reception in New York, and soon placed him among the most cherished of her adopted citizens. His monument stands in St Paul's Churchyard, New York, near that of his friend Thomas Addis Emmet.

Doctor Quackenbos, in spite of his name, a young physician in **good** repute.

"The Forum."—A society of young and promising lawyers and others emulating the "Speculative Society" of Edinburgh. Their meetings for debate were public, **and** drew flattering and fashionable audiences.

Stanza 54.—Doctor John **L. Graham.**—The Nestor of the New-York bar. His **legal merits had gained him the diploma of Doctor of Laws.** He was among the last of the gentlemen of the "old school," and remarkable for the courtesy and dignity of his manners.

Stanza 55.—Doctor **George** T. Horne.—An **advertising physician of New-York City.** The motto at the head of his advertisements was "*Salus Populi Suprema Lex.*"

Stanza 60.—Samuel Woodworth, etc.—Popular authors of the period, then and previously beginning an honorable literary career.

Stanzas 64 and 65.—"General Laight's Brigade of State Militia." —A "corps d'armée" quite distinct from the uniformed volunteer companies of the time, and one that Falstaff "would not march through Coventry with." Its officers were the young aristocracy of the city, but its soldiers were men or boys, who, either from choice or necessity, declined paying a fine of twenty-five dollars for non-attendance on parade days— three times a year—the penalty **imposed** by the then existing militia law.

Stanza 66.—Monsieur Charles.—The travelling **magician and conjurer** of the time.

Ambrose Spencer.—Then Chief Justice **of** the State, a judge universally respected for integrity and ability in the discharge of his official duties, but accused by his political opponents of exercising in party politics a controlling power injurious to their interests.

Mead's "Wall Street," a drama whose characters were designed to **be played** by stock actors only.

Stanza 68.—Doctor John Griscom.—A highly-esteemed Quaker physician then delivering **lectures upon chemistry, etc.** His office was in the building called the "Old Alms-House," situated in the rear of the City Hall, facing Chambers Street. Its rooms facing Broadway were occupied by the museum of John Scudder, the "illustrious predecessor" **of** the late world-renowned showman P. T. Barnum. Among its attractions was the band of music commemorated in stanza 175.

Stanza 71.—TAMMANY HALL, corner of Nassau and Frankfort Streets. —Then the home of the "Saint Tammany Society," whose members still claim to represent, *par excellence*, the Democratic party of the country in its pristine purity. Their once famous appellation of "Bucktails" (see stanza 83), was derived from their custom of wearing, when on duty, a deer's tail in their hats as a badge of membership. Among their leading Sachems were William Mooney (stanza 78) and John Targee (see stanzas 72, etc). The latter gentleman, from his steadfast refusal to accept a money-making office in the gift of the society, an example of self-denial previously unrecorded in their annals, became a sort of mythical personage, like Shakespeare's "Cuckoo in June," "ne'er seen but wondered at." The fact, however, enlarged upon in stanzas 73, etc., of his political and musical intimacy with Tom Moore, is one that, in the newspaper phrase, wants confirmation. The Tammany Hall of 1819 is now known as the Sun Building, the Society having erected a more spacious edifice in Fourteenth Street, formally opened on the Fourth of July, 1868. Here the Democratic Convention was held which nominated Horatio Seymour, of New York, for President, and Francis P. Plair, Jr., of Missouri, as their candidate for the Vice-Presidency of the United States.

Song, Page 124.—WILLIAM B. COZZENS.—Then the proprietor of the "Tammany Hall Hotel"—more recently of the princely establishment at West Point known by his name, and now conducted by his son.

Stanza 81.—SYLVANUS MILLER.—An active and influential party leader, for many years surrogate of the city, and a gentleman who was never seen without his inseparable companion—a cigar. As a smoker, he even excelled General Grant.

Stanza 84.—Judge SKINNER and Mr. McINTYRE.—Members of the State Senate. The one a political opponent of Governor Clinton, the other of ex-Governor Daniel D. Tompkins.

Stanza 86.—HENRY MEIGS and PETER H. WENDOVER.—Members of Congress from the city. The former one of the original founders of the "American Institute," and for a long time its secretary. To the latter is owing the invention of the present legal arrangement of the stars and stripes in the United States flag.

Stanza 90.—Captain RILEY's book.—A somewhat Munchausen-like narrative of his shipwreck on the coast of Africa.

Stanza 91.—"DELAPLAINE'S REPOSITORY."—A biographical work published in Philadelphia, valuable for its engraved portraits of the most distinguished men of the day.

Stanza 92.—DANIEL D. TOMPKINS.—Then a resident of Staten Island.

Stanza 93.—"THE TURTLE CLUB."—From New York, whose frequent open-air festivities, at Hoboken, were devoted to punch and politics.

Stanza 107.—SIMON THOMAS.—A man of color, the orthodox and omni-present caterer for fashionable dinner and supper parties.

Stanza 114.—THOMAS WHALE.—An eminent dancing-master, and a fine specimen of the old-school gentleman. He always appeared in knee-breeches and silk stockings, and was a constant reader at the Society Library, of which venerable institution he was a member.

Stanza 116.—EDMUND SIMPSON and JAMES W. WALLACK, managers of the city theatres, and actors highly esteemed, then and now.

Stanza 118.—The "CROAKERS"—see note, page 377.
"WOODWORTH'S CABINET."—A periodical conducted by the poet of the name.
The "NEW SALMAGUNDI."—A continuation, by James K. Paulding, of a work under a similar title, published in 1808, the joint production of himself and his friend Washington Irving.

Stanza 124.—Madame BOUQUET and Monsieur PARDESSUS.—The fashionable milliner and ladies' slipper-maker of the day.

Stanza 138.—Mr. R. P. LAWRENCE.—A coach-maker in John Street.

Stanza 140.—DE WITT CLINTON.—Governor of the State of New York.

Stanza 141.—"EASTBURN'S ROOMS," in the building occupied by James Eastburn & Co., booksellers and publishers, on the corner of Broadway and Pine Street—a favorite resort of men of letters and leisure. Bishop Eastburn, of the Episcopal Church, and James W. Eastburn, the young poet, who died at twenty-two, are sons of the worthy bookseller, for whom Mr. Halleck entertained a great friendship, and to whose reading-room he was a constant visitor.

Stanza 144.—The "LYCEUM OF NATURAL HISTORY."—An association of men of science, and patronized by the most highly cultivated of the city scholars, still existing.

Stanza 172.—The "COUNCIL OF APPOINTMENT" at Albany.—Then an important department of the State government, abolished upon the revision of the Constitution in 1821, having become a notorious political machine.

Stanza 173.—Colonel AARON BURR, then Vice-President of the United States, the theme of one of the most interesting episodes in American history.

THE RECORDER.

(1) Page 161.—Richard Riker.—The Recorder of the city at the date of the poem. A gentleman of great merit, who had previously filled, and continued to fill through life, offices of the highest trust. In the poem he is sportively made to appear, not in his excellent and estimable personal character, but as the "burden of a merry song"—the embodied representative of a party leader, and of party men in general, in their proverbial obnoxiousness. Like the scape-goat of antiquity, he is forced to bear the sins of others, not his own, and is "sent out into the wilderness of criticism," with a heavy load of them upon his innocent shoulders. In the duel alluded to on page 162, which took place early in his political career, the result of a political difference of opinion between him and his antagonist, General Robert Swartwout, Mr. Riker was slightly wounded.

(2) Page 165.—A sculptor, rather mechanical than artistic, famous, for a time, for moulding the busts of notorious men into the immortality of plaster in lieu of marble.

(3) Page 165.—"Garden Flowers."—An allusion to those of Mr. William Prince, near Flushing, Long Island.

(4) Page 169.—A favorite French air. In English, "Where can one be more happy than in the bosom of one's family?"

(5) Page 169.—Nathaniel Pitcher, then Governor of the State, accused, in like manner, of being under the political control of Martin Van Buren, then on his way to the presidency of the United States.

(6) Page 169.—"Burgundy and Business."—Mr. Riker was a director in the Tradesmen's Bank, and "ex officio" a visitor to the Sing-Sing Prison, the Bellevue Hospital, etc., and was accused, by his party opponents, of making the civic and social meetings there, of himself and his colleagues, subservient to party purposes.

(7) Page 169.—The "Pewter Mug."—The sign conspicuous over the door of a tavern in Frankfort Street, in the rear of Tammany Hall, the frequent resort of politicians in general, and of the Tammany-Hall party in particular.

(8) Page 170.—An allusion to Philip Hone, then the LATE Mayor of the city, recently, by the party rule of rotation, displaced from an office in which for several preceding years he had won, by his conduct as an upright magistrate, and a noble and generous man, "honor, love, obedience, troops of friends," from the highest as well as from the humblest of his constituents.

(9) Page 171.—Hillhouse, Bryant, and Halleck.—Three names

honestly drawn out **from a lottery comprising those of** the thirty-seven city **poets,** and impartially representing the whole lot. Where the writings of **all were** of equal value, choice was impossible, and chance the only arbiter except the account-sales of their several publishers—a class of accountants whose hieroglyphics are proverbially difficult to decipher.

(10) Page 172.—Stephen Allen, Benjamin Bailey, and John Targee, prominent members of the Tammany Society. Mr. Allen became in after-years Mayor of the city.

(11) Page 173.—Signorina Garcia, then attached to her father's **opera** company, soon after to become the world-renowned and lamented cantatrice

---

THE CROAKERS.

(1) Page 253.—A signature adopted by Halleck and Drake, from an amusing character in Goldsmith's comedy of "The Good-natured Man," and attached to a series of verses appearing from time to time in the *New-York Evening Post*, and in other periodicals, in and after the month of **March, 1819.** The letters H. and D. represent the names of Fitz-Greene **Halleck and** Joseph Rodman Drake, and indicate the respective authorship **of the poems.**

(2) Page 255.—Fitz and Lang, the names abbreviated of Fitz-Greene Halleck and Dr. William Langstaff, intimate friends of the writer, and in daily intercourse with him. The latter studied medicine with Drs. Bruce and Romayne, Drake and DeKay being fellow-pupils. Langstaff not being successful as a physician, his friend Henry Eckford aided him in establishing an apothecary and drug store at No. 360 Broadway, which business he carried on for many years. **By the** liberality **of the same gentleman Lang-** staff **accompanied Dr. and Mrs. Drake** in **their tour through Europe in 1818.**

(3) Page 255.—" **Lady** Morgan and Madame De Stael."**—The** "France" of the one, **and the** "French Revolution" of the other, had been recently published.

(4) Page 256.—"Guardsmen," **the Governor's Guard.—A** company of young gentlemen, in scarlet and gold, **commanded by James B.** Murray, then an active and able young merchant; in after-life an alderman of the **city,** and among her most public-spirited magistrates.

(5) **Page** 256.—"Altorf."--A drama founded on the tradition of William Tell, and unsuccessfully played at the Park Theatre. Its author, Miss Fanny Wright, a Scottish lady, was for a time a public lecturer on morals and religion, from a somewhat infidel point of view. Her chief theme was "just knowledge," **which** she pronounced "joost nolidge."

(6) Page 256.--" SPOONER and BALDWIN," editors of newspapers, the one in Brooklyn, the other in New York. The former had quoted in his columns the three words alluded to from the chorus to a song, to the tune of " Yankee Doodle," gracing a comic and comical opera, entitled the " Saw-mill "--the work of Mr. Micah Hawkins, a merry and musical genius from Long Island—performed once, and, I believe, but once, at the Chatham Garden Theatre.

(7) Page 256.--Chief-Justice MARSHALL, of the United States Supreme Court, whose recent decision had denied the validity of the New-York State Insolvent Laws.

(8) Page 257.--General JACKSON, since President of the United States, on his first visit to New York. At the dinner with which he was welcomed (see the "Secret Mine ") by the Tammany Society, its Grand Sachem, Mr. Mooney, eloquently assured him that, at the announcement of his intended visit, the hearts of its members had "expanded to explosion." In reply to which the General gave as a toast, "De Witt Clinton, the Governor of the great and patriotic State of New York." As a large proportion of the guests were bitterly opposed to Mr. Clinton in politics, a compliment so flattering to him alike surprised and annoyed them. The gentlemen named in the verses were all prominent leaders in the two adverse parties, and designated, by their approval or non-approval of the toast, their party attachments.

(9) Page 257.--JOHN WESLEY JARVIS, the popular portrait-painter of the day, a favorite of his patrons and of many social circles for his genial drollery of song and story. Most of the portraits of our officers, civil and military, then winning honorable distinction, and now gracing our public halls and chambers, we owe to his admired and admirable pencil. Halleck's portrait, painted by Jarvis for Dr. DeKay (now in the possession of Drake's daughter, Mrs. Commodore DeKay), is by many esteemed the best likeness we have of the poet.

(10) Page 257.--BARTHOLOMEW SKAATS, or " BARTY SKAATS," as he was familiarly known—superintendent and curator of the City Hall, and for many years crier of the courts which were held in the old City Hall in Wall Street.

(11) Page 260.--" ALECK," the name of Alexander Hamilton abbreviated, a member of the Legislature at the time, and especially opposed to Mr. Clinton; the eldest son of the illustrious soldier and statesman of the same name, whose death, a few years previous, in the duel with Colonel Burr, had put the hearts of his countrymen in mourning.

(12) Page 261.—Major-General MORTON, commanding the militia of the city.--In dignity and courtesy, a worthy representative of the old

school, and retaining in many respects its costume, particularly in the arrangement of his hair.

(13) Page 262.—CHARLES KING.—The lately lost and lamented president of Columbia College ; her model of an accomplished scholar and gentleman. In early life an aide to a military commander.

ROBERT BAYARD.—A young officer in a similar military position. He was one of the firm of Le Roy, Bayard, and McEvers, prominent merchants of New York, and a brother-in-law of the late General Stephen Van Rensselaer. Mr. Bayard is still a resident of this city.

(14) Page 263.—" SAMUEL SWARTWOUT " (see previous note).—He was for a time the proprietor of the meadows between Weehawken and Jersey City.

(15) Page 264.—"Mr. POTTER."—Then exhibiting his powers as a ventriloquist in Washington Hall, corner of Broadway and Chambers Street, where A. T. Stewart's store now stands.

(16) Page 264.—LEVI ROBBINS, ERASTUS ROOT, PETER SHARPE, OBADIAH GERMAN, and EZEKIEL BACON, members of the New-York Legislature, and leading politicians.

(17) Page 265.—"ABRAHAM B. MARTLING."—The proprietor of the Tammany-Hall Hotel, and successor of *Barty Skaats* as the keeper of the City Hall.

(18) Page 265.—SYLVANUS MILLER, Surrogate.—See previous note to " Fanny," on page 374.

(19) Page 266.—" WOODWORTH'S CHRONICLE."—A periodical conducted by that popular poet for a brief period.

(20) Page 266.—WILLIAM COLEMAN.—The editor of the *New-York Evening Post.* He died during the summer of 1829.

(21) Page 267.—Mrs. JOHN BARNES appeared for the last time in Philadelphia, July 25, 1851, as Lady Randolph, which character she sustained with almost undiminished excellence.

(22) Page 267.—Miss CATHERINE LEESUGG, afterward Mrs. James H. Hackett and Mrs. Barnes. As ladies and actresses, well meriting the poet's eulogiums, and highly estimated in public and private life.

(23) Page 267.—OLLIFF, etc.—Actors of merit in various departments of their profession.

(24) Page 268.—The national painting, "The Declaration of Independence," by Colonel Trumbull.

(25) Page 269.—JACOB SHERRED.—A wealthy painter and glazier.

17

(26) Page 270.—A public meeting concerning the enlargement of the Battery, over which Lewis Hartman, a politician of some note, and Charles King, presided. Thomas R. Mercein and Robert Bogardus were lawyers of distinction, James Lent was city Register, and Edward McGaraghan a magistrate.

(27) Page 272.—NATHANIEL PRIME.—A wealthy and worthy banker of the house of Prime, Ward & Sands, in Wall Street.

(28) Page 273.—RUFUS KING, then recently chosen United-States Senator from the State of New York, an eminent statesman and diplomatist.

(29) Page 273.—"Mr. HAMILTON'S LETTER."—See previous note for that gentleman's position.

(30) Page 276.—"THE SURGEON-GENERAL."—An office held by Doctor Mitchill.—See previous references to him.

(31) Page 277.—See previous note to "Fanny," page 374.

(32) Page 278.—JOHN MINSHULL.—An Englishman by birth, who was a butt of the critics of the day. His plays were performed at the Park Theatre, and afterward published.

(33) Page 279.—"So have I seen in gardens rich and rare
    A stately cabbage waxing fat each day;
    Unlike the lively foliage of the trees,
    Its stubborn leaves ne'er wave in summer breeze,
    Nor flower, like those that prank the walks around,
    Upon its clumsy stem is ever found:
    It heeds not noontide heats, or evening's balm,
    And stands unmov'd in one eternal calm.
    At last, when all the garden's pride is lost,
    It ripens in drear autumn's killing frost;
    And in a savory sourkrout finds its end,
    From which detested dish, me Heaven defend!"
      PAULDING's "Backwoodsman," Book II.

(34) Page 282.—"CHARLEY MACHEATH."—In which character in the Beggars' Opera the celebrated English singer, Mr. Charles Incledon, during his engagement some time previous at the Park Theatre, had been favorably received.

(35) Page 283.—WILLIAM NIBLO.—The proprietor of the then most popular hotel and restaurant in New York, on the corner of William and Pine Streets, and still a highly-respected resident of this city.

(36) Page 283.—THOMAS KILNER, etc., etc.—Comedians at the theatre

The three latter had been recently engaged in England by Mr. Simpson during a professional visit there.

(37) **Page** 284.—Mr. LANG.—See previous notes. The **words in** italics are quotations from his paper, *The New-York Gazette.*

(38) Page 286.—" FEDS," etc.—The assumed or imputed titles of various party factions at war with each other.

(39) Page 288.—JOHN BARNES, a comedian of much excellence, the great favorite of laughter-loving audiences, and the husband of the lady mentioned in notes **21** and **22.**

(40) Page 290.—TENTH-WARD ELECTORS.—Those composing a party in opposition for a short time to the regular nominees at Tammany Hall.

(41) **Page 292.—The Surgeon-General, Doctor** SAMUEL L. MITCHILL.

(42) **Page 303.—Mrs.** POPPLETON, the fashionable confectioner at No. 206 Broadway.

(43) **Page 303.—Messrs.** CHRISTIAN, china and glass **dealers in Maiden Lane.**

(44) Page 304.—NATHANIEL LEAVENWORTH.—A young gentleman of fortune and fashion, recently returned from his travels abroad, then residing at 30 Greenwich Street, which, strange as it **may** now appear, was fifty years ago a fashionable place of residence.

(45) Page 306.—WILLIAM COBBETT.—The career of this very powerful writer and political agitator, here and in England, is too prominent in the records of both countries to be other **than** slightly mentioned. At the time of the appearance of the verses, he was a resident **of** Hempstead, Long Island.

(46) Page 306.—GEORGE BARRINGTON, the celebrated burglar and light-fingered gentleman. The line is said to have been written by him when a convict at Botany Bay.

(47) Page 309.—The FORUM.—See previous note. Mr. Hallett and Mr. Dey were young lawyers. Mr. Dey afterward became a clergyman. The career of Napoleon, and Turkish social life, were among their subjects of debate.

(48) Page 311.—JAMES L. BELL, the High Sheriff of the County.

(49) **Page 311.—**ROBERT DAWSON, the keeper of a livery stable at No. 9 Dey Street.

(50) Page 311.—A. T. GOODRICH & **Co.**, booksellers at the corner of Broadway and Cedar Street, who kept a popular circulating library.

(51) Page 312.—CHESTER JENNINGS, the lessee of the City Hotel, on Broadway, between Cedar and Thames Streets.

(52) Page 314.—For nearly half a century, Cato Alexander kept a house of entertainment on the old post-road, about four miles from the City Hall. It was the fashionable out-of-town resort for the young men of the day.

(53) Page 314.—The Baron VON HOFFMAN.—An adventurer styling himself a Dutch nobleman of high distinction, and by the fashionable circles courted and caressed accordingly, until detected as an impostor. "A fish can as vell live out of water as I can live out of de ladies," was a favorite remark of the bogus baron, who came very near winning the hand of a noted New-York belle and heiress. Among his attempts at notoriety was that of shooting at himself with the wad of a pistol. He soon after disappeared from New York, and when last heard from was at Morrison's Hotel, Dublin, quietly luxuriating in the blaze of his fame.

(54) Page 314.—Two lamps, or gaslights, are always placed before the door of the house occupied by a Mayor of New-York City.

(55) Page 316.—" Mr. GERMAN."—From a speech of his when a member of the Legislature.

(56) Page 317.—JOHN MCLEAN.—A judge of the county court in the town of " Junius," recently appointed by Governor Clinton.

(57) Page 319.—" LINES TO Mr. SIMPSON."—A twofold knowledge, that of the then acted plays, and of the personal peculiarities of the political gentlemen named, is requisite for the understanding and enjoying of these verses. For many of the names, and for the existing Council of Appointment, see previous notes. Among them, Peter R. Livingston was distinguished for persuasive and genial oratory, Charles Christian and James Warner were police justices, Pierre C. Van Wyck was City Recorder, and Hugh Maxwell City Attorney. Barent Gardenier was a member of Congress. He was renowned for a time as an eloquent speaker, and is noticed for all time in that matchless specimen of the pleasantry of genius, the " Knickerbocker " of Washington Irving.

The " STEAMBOAT BILL."—The members who had voted a tax on passengers on board the North-River boats.

(58) Page 319.—JOHN JOSEPH HOLLAND, the scene-painter of the theatre.

(59) Page 323.—CHRISTIAN BAEHR, a fashionable Wall-Street tailor.

(60) Page 323.—STEPHEN BATES, etc., were members of the Legislature ; TUNIS WORTMAN, etc., city judges and lawyers of party eminence.

(61) Page 328.—This amusing burlesque address, first published in the New-York *Evening Post*, was included in a small volume containing the Rejected Addresses, together with the prize address, written by Charles Sprague, and spoken by Edmund Simpson, on the reopening of the Park Theatre, September 1st, 1821.

(62) Page 329.—Messrs. JOHN K. BEEKMAN and JOHN JACOB ASTOR were joint proprietors of the Park Theatre. The former, from his love of theatricals, was familiarly known as "Theatre Jack."

(63) Page 329.—ISAAC JENNINGS, was a well-known dealer in old clothes, and GEORGE SAUNDERS was a fashionable wig-maker. ⸍

(64) Page 330.—The PRESIDENT, James Monroe, had a short time previously made a tour through the Middle and Eastern States.

(65) Page 330.—HENRY MEIGS, when a member of Congress, had advocated the admission of Missouri into the Union, on Southern terms.

(66) Page 331.—WILLIAM REYNOLDS, the proprietor of a celebrated English ale-house in Thames Street, in the rear of the City Hotel. He pronounced Mr. Halleck the only gentleman that ever came into his house, "because he never interferes with my fire."

(67) Page 333.—Mr. BYRNE, a dancer from Paris, was performing at the Park Theatre.

(68) Page 333.—Mr. TURNER and Mr. MAGENIS were public lecturers in the rooms of the City Hotel.

(69) Page 334.—JAMES W. WALLACK and Mrs. BARTLEY were great favorites with the theatre-goers of that day. The melologue referred to in the poem was written for Mrs. B. by Thomes Moore.

(70) Page 335.—Doctor HORNE and Doctor GIDEON DE ANGELIS, well-known advertising physicians. The latter's *Four-herb Pills* were announced as a panacea for all the diseases that flesh is heir to.

(71) Page 338.—Captain OGDEN CREIGHTON, an officer in the British service, and a brother of the late Rev. Dr. Creighton, of Tarrytown.

(72) Page 342.—JOHN R. LIVINGSTON.—A wealthy gentleman, who dispensed liberal hospitalities both at his city residence and at his country-seat on the Hudson. Among the notabilities whom he entertained at the latter place was the Prince of Saxe-Weimar, who visited the United States in 1825-'26. Mr. Livingston was a brother of the Chancellor, and at one time a member of the New-York Assembly.

(73) Page 342.—THOMAS A. COOPER.—The celebrated actor, and for a time manager of the Park Theatre. His daughter married a son of President Tyler, who gave him an appointment in the New-York Custom-House, which he held for several years.

(74) Page 342.—EDMUND KEAN, who ranks among the greatest of modern actors, second only to Garrick and John Philip Kemble. He visited

the United States in 1820 and again in 1825. His last appearance in public was at Covent Garden Theatre, London, in 1833, when he played Othello to the Iago of his son Charles, but, on repeating the words "Othello's occupation's gone," he sank exhausted, and died soon after, in his forty-sixth year.

(75) Page 342.—The Right Rev. JOHN HENRY HOBART, D. D., who, in 1811, was elected Bishop of the Diocese of New-York, and was consecrated in Trinity Church—where a full-length effigy of him is to be seen—by Bishops White, Provost, and Jarvis. His episcopate lasted twenty-nine years.

(76) Page 342.—PHILIP BRASHER.—A New-York alderman, a member of the Legislature for eight years, and a noted *bon-vivant.*

(77) Page 342.—JAMES BUCHANAN.—For many years British Consul at New York, and bitterly opposed to Queen Caroline, wife of George the Fourth, by whom he was appointed to his office through the influence of his friend Lord Castlereagh. He died in 1851, at Montreal.

(78) Page 343.—HENRY CRUGER, a native of New York, was educated in England, where he became a successful merchant, and was, in 1774, elected to the British Parliament as the colleague of Edmund Burke. He returned to his native land on a visit in 1783, and seven years later became a permanent resident of this city. Upon the first senatorial election after his return, he was chosen to the State Senate. He died at his residence in Greenwich Street—then a fashionable locality—in 1827, in his eighty-eighth year.

(79) Page 343.—MORGAN LEWIS held many honorable positions, among which were those of Chief-Justice of the State, Governor, and the command of the forces destined for the defence of New York, with the rank of Major-General. In 1835 he was elected President of the New-York Historical Society. He lived to the same age as Lord Brougham, of whom he was a great admirer.

(80) Page 343.—MONTGOMERY LIVINGSTONE, a son of the gentleman whose entertainment is described by the poet.

(81) Page 343.—Captain J. R. NICHOLSON, a gallant officer, who served under Decatur; like Halleck, a bachelor, and, like his poet-friend, always an admirer of, and admired by, the ladies.

(82) Page 349.—JAMES E. DEKAY was educated a physician, but devoted himself from his early years to natural history, and, in the State Survey of New York, the Department of Zoology was assigned to him. It was through Dr. DeKay that Halleck and Drake became acquainted in the summer of 1813. He died August 8th, 1851, at his residence, Oyster Bay, Long Island.

(83) Page 349.—Mrs. Joseph Rodman Drake, wife of the poet, and daughter of Henry Eckford, the celebrated ship-builder, of New York.

(84) Page 349.—Miss Eliza McCall, a young lady of many accomplishments, and a charming singer, who was much admired by Halleck and Drake. Both the poets wrote songs for her. The, beautiful lines by the former, "The world is bright before thee," were written for Miss McCall, and Drake's "Yes, Heaven protect thee," and "Though fate upon this faded flower," were also inscribed to the same young lady.

(85) Page 352.—Doctor David Hosack.—See previous notes.

(86) Page 352.—The college was originally a stable, on the walls of which a wag of a student inscribed these lines:

"Once a stable for horses,
Now a college for asses."

(87) Page 352.—William Hamersley, Professor of Clinical Medicine, whose almost universal remedy for the cure of pulmonary consumption and heart disease was *digitalis.* Hence his *sobriquet.*

(88) Page 352.—Dr. Macnevan.—See note to "Fanny," page 371.

(89) Page 352.—Dr. Samuel L. Mitchill.—See previous notes.

(90) Page 354.—Baron Von Hoffman. The New-York *Evening Post*, of June 12, 1823, says: "Baron Von Hoffman of Sirony, who used to serenade our ladies with the Tyrolese air so merrily, under their windows in Broadway, a year or two ago, and one day took French leave of them all, now shows away as one of the 'nobility and persons of distinction in Dublin.'"—Vide also note to the Croakers, No. 53.

(91) Page 354.—James Burnham kept a famous hostelry on the Bloomingdale road, still extant. Few New Yorkers of the past fifty years are unacquainted with "Burnham's," which was for many years as well known and popular as Cato's, already referred to in another note.

(92) Page 355.—Carlo, the Baron's colored groom.

(93) Page 357.—The North Dutch Church.—The only fane at the State capital that could then boast of two spires.

(94) Page 359.—The "Court of Death," which the Common Council of New York pronounced an effort of uncommon genius, deserving the patronage of an enlightened public.

(95) Page 362.—James Tallmadge, of Dutchess County, Lieutenant-Governor of the State, and president of the Senate, afterward appointed American Minister to Russia. "Veracity of history," says Hammond

in his Political History of New-York, "compels me to state that in no part of New York were political bargains more common than among some of the politicians of Dutchess County, and that Mr. Livingston (Peter R.), and Mr. Tallmadge (James), were prominent party leaders in that county."

(96) **Page** 362.—CLARKSON CROLIUS, Speaker of the State Assembly at Albany, and for many years Grand Sachem of the Tammany Society.

(97) **Page** 363.—Colonel CHARLES G. HAINES and the others mentioned were zealous and devoted partisans of De Witt Clinton.

INDEX TO FIRST LINES.

THE END.

Fitz-Greene Halleck's Poetical Works.

Edited by JAMES GRANT WILSON.

COMPLETE POETICAL WORKS. 1 vol., 12mo. Cloth, $2.50; half
calf, extra, $4.50; morocco, antique, $6.00.

LARGE-PAPER COPY OF THE SAME. 8vo. Cloth, $10.00;
morocco, antique, $15.00.

COMPLETE POETICAL WORKS. 1 vol., 18mo. In blue-and-gold,
$1.00; morocco, antique, $3.00.

THE

Life and Letters of Fitz-Greene Halleck.

By JAMES GRANT WILSON.

*With a fine Steel Portrait from Inman's Picture, and Views of
the Poet's Residence and Monument at Guilford.*

One volume, 12mo, gilt. Uniform with the new edition of "Halleck's
Poems." Cloth, $2.50; half calf, extra, $4.50; morocco, $6.00.

The Halleck Memorial:

*A Description of the Dedication of the Monument erected to his Mem-
ory at Guilford, Connecticut; and of the Proceedings connected with the unveiling of the Poet's Statue in
the Central Park, New York.*

Edited by EVERT A. DUYCKINCK.

With 22 Steel Portraits and Illustrations. Only 100 Copies printed.
1 vol, quarto, cream-colored paper. Cloth, price, $5.00.
Privately printed, and to Subscribers only.

Copies mailed, post-paid, to any part of the United States, on receipt of
the price, by

D. APPLETON & CO., Publishers, 1, 3, & 5 Bond Street, N. Y.

WORKS
OF
WILLIAM CULLEN BRYANT.

Illustrated 8vo Edition of Bryant's Poetical Works. 100 Engravings by Birket Foster, Harry Fenn, Alfred Fredericks, and other Artists. 1 vol., 8vo. Cloth, gilt side and edge, $4.00; half calf, marble edge, $6.00; full morocco, antique, $8.00; tree calf, $10.00.

Household Edition. 1 vol., 12mo. Cloth, $2.00; half calf, $4.00; morocco, $5.00; tree calf, $5.00.

Red-Line Edition. With 24 Illustrations, and Portrait of Bryant, on Steel. Printed on tinted paper, with red line. Square 12mo. Cloth, extra, $3.00; half calf, $5.00; morocco, $7.00; tree calf, $8.00.

Blue-and-Gold Edition. 18mo. Cloth, gilt edge, $1.50; half calf, marble edge, $3.00; morocco, gilt edge, $4.00.

Letters from Spain and other Countries. 1 vol., 12mo. Price, $1.25.

The Song of the Sower. Illustrated with 42 Engravings on Wood, from Original Designs by Hennessy, Fenn, Winslow Homer, Hows, Griswold, Nehlig, and Perkins; engraved in the most perfect manner by our best Artists. Elegantly printed and bound. Cloth, extra gilt, $5.00; morocco, antique, $9.00.

The Story of the Fountain. With 42 Illustrations by Harry Fenn, Alfred Fredericks, John A. Hows, Winslow Homer, and others. In one handsome quarto volume. Printed in the most perfect manner, on heavy calendered paper. Uniform with "The Song of the Sower." Square 8vo. Cloth, extra gilt, $5.00; morocco, antique, $9.00.

The Little People of the Snow. Illustrated with exquisite Engravings, printed in Tints, from Designs by Alfred Fredericks. Cloth, $5.00; morocco, $9.00.

D. APPLETON & CO., PUBLISHERS, 1, 3, & 5 BOND STREET, N. Y

THE

HOUSEHOLD BOOK OF POETRY.

Edited by CHARLES A. DANA.

New edition, enlarged, **with additions from recent authors.** Illustrated **with steel engravings.**

1 vol., royal 8vo., cloth, **gilt extra $5.00;** Half Calf, $8.00; Morocco, antique, or extra, $10.00; Crushed Levant, $15.00.

New cheap edition. **Cloth, extra, red edges, $3.50.**

"The purpose of this book is to comprise within the bounds of a single volume whatever is truly beautiful and admirable among the minor poems of the English language. . . . Especial care has also been **taken to give every** poem entire and unmutilated, as well as in the **most authentic form** which could be procured."—*Extract from Preface.*

"**This work is an** immense improvement **on all its** predecessors. The entire number **of** poems given is about **two** thousand, taken from **the writings** of English and American poets, and including some of **the finest** versions of poems from ancient and modern languages. **The** selections appear to be admirably made, nor do we think that it would be possible for any one to **improve upon this** collection."—*Boston Traveller.*

"It is almost needless to say that it is a mine of poetic wealth."—*Boston Post.*

"By the exercise **of a sound** and skillful judgment, and **a thorough** familiarity with the poetical productions of all nations, the compiler of this work has succeeded in combining, within the space of a single volume, nearly every poem of established worth and compatible length in the English language."—*Philadelphia Journal.*

"Among the similar works which have appeared we do not hesitate **to give** this the highest place."—*Providence Journal.*

"**This is a choice** collection of the finest poems in the English language, and supplies in some measure the place of an extensive library. —*Chicago Press.*

D. APPLETON & CO., PUBLISHERS, 1, 3, & 5 BOND STREET, N. Y.

THE GLOBE EDITION OF THE POETS.

Illustrated. 16mo.

Price per volume, Cloth, $1.25; Half Calf, $3.25; Antique
Morocco, $4.00

ANY VOLUME SOLD SEPARATELY.

Volumes already published:

CAMPBELL,	DANTE,	KIRKE WHITE,
SCOTT,	TASSO,	SPENSER,
POPE,	BURNS,	BUTLER,
DRYDEN,	COWPER,	HERBERT,
MILTON,	CHAUCER,	Mrs. HEMANS.

(2 vols.)

THE POPULAR EDITION OF THE

STANDARD POETS.

SIXTY CENTS A VOLUME.

Volumes already published:

I. SCOTT'S POETICAL WORKS.
II. MILTON'S POETICAL WORKS.
III. BURNS'S POETICAL WORKS.
IV. DANTE'S POEMS.
V. TASSO'S JERUSALEM DELIVERED.
VI. CAMPBELL'S POETICAL WORKS.
VII. POPE'S POETICAL WORKS.
VIII. DRYDEN'S POETICAL WORKS.
IX. KIRKE WHITE'S POETICAL WORKS.

D. APPLETON & CO., PUBLISHERS, 1, 3, & 5 BOND ST., N. Y.

THE VERBALIST:

A MANUAL

Devoted to Brief Discussions of the Right and the Wrong Use of Words,

AND TO

SOME OTHER MATTERS OF INTEREST TO THOSE WHO WOULD SPEAK AND WRITE WITH PROPRIETY.

By ALFRED AYRES.

"We remain shackled by timidity till we have learned to speak with propriety."—JOHNSON.

"As a man is known by his company, so a man's company may be known by his manner of expressing himself."—SWIFT.

Uniform with "The Orthoepist."

---

1 vol., 18mo, cloth. Price, $1.00.

For sale by all booksellers; or sent by mail, post-paid, on receipt of price.

New York: D. APPLETON & CO., 1, 3, & 5 Bond Street.

THE ORTHOËPIST.

A PRONOUNCING MANUAL,

CONTAINING

About Three Thousand Five Hundred Words,

INCLUDING

A Considerable Number of the Names of Foreign Authors, Artists, etc., that are often mispronounced.

By ALFRED AYRES.

"As a remedial agency, for popular application to an evil which we all know to be widespread and constantly operative, this is one of the most timely issues from the press which we have had the good fortune to welcome for many a day. Within the compass of this little volume is placed at the command of every speaker of the English tongue an aid to correct pronunciation which, if used, will be really invaluable. Scarcely one person in five thousand, or ten thousand, can claim to be without occasion for resort to the corrections offered in the pages before us. Indeed, whoever will take the pains to examine those pages will enjoy a continued succession of surprises at the multiplicity of the blunders of which he or she is constantly guilty in the use of the mother-tongue. This conviction is carried home to the comprehension, not only by the arrangement of contrasted correct and incorrect pronunciations, but also in explanatory notes which make clear the relations of the vowel-sounds, the uses of the diphthong, methods of using the unaccented syllables, proper accentuation, correct employment of the aspirates, etc. The arrangement of the words is alphabetical, thus rendering reference particularly easy. The entire presentation is at once simple and direct, so that while the ripest scholar will find constant reward for study, the youngest student, or the man of affairs and the mother in her home, can not fail to comprehend the nature of their own faulty pronunciations, and how they may, if they will, promptly apply a remedy. Such a manual ought to be in the hands of every intelligent person in the country, and at ready command in every household."—*Davenport Daily Gazette.*

"The book is an excellent one, which is likely to do more for the cause of good speech by directing attention to common errors than any work with which we are acquainted."—*New York Evening Post.*

"It furnishes what will serve at once as a guide and as a standard for those who desire to have their practice in speaking English conform to the most approved orthoëpical usage."—*Eclectic Magazine.*

One volume, 18mo. Cloth, price, $1.00.

For sale by all booksellers; or sent by mail, post-paid, on receipt of price.

D. APPLETON & CO., Publishers, 1, 3, & 5 Bond Street, N. Y.

MISCELLANEOUS PUBLICATIONS.

The Land of Gilead.

With Excursions in the Lebanon. By LAURENCE OLIPHANT. With Illustrations and Maps. Crown 8vo. Cloth, $2.00.

"His journeys took him quite off the beaten tracks of tourists and archæological explorers; he got an 'inside view,' so to call it, of native life and manners; he saw something of the wandering Bedouins; and we know of no recent book on Palestine which is really so instructive, from which the reader can derive so large a fund of entertainment."—*Eclectic Magazine.*

Anecdotal History of the British Parliament.

From the Earliest Periods to the Present Time, with Notices of Eminent Parliamentary Men and Examples of their Oratory. Compiled by G. H. JENNINGS. Crown 8vo. Cloth, $2.50.

"As pleasant a companion for the leisure hours of a studious and thoughtful man as anything in book shape since Selden."—*London Telegraph.*

Young Ireland.

A Fragment of Irish History, 1840–1850. By the Hon. Sir CHARLES GAVAN DUFFY, K. C. M. G. New cheap edition. 12mo. Cloth, $1.50.

"'Young Ireland' is a memoir of the few stormy years in Ireland during which O'Connell was tried and convicted of conspiracy, and Smith O'Brien tried and convicted of high treason, written by one who was in succession the fellow-prisoner of each of them, and has seen since a remarkable career in Australia. The book is founded on the private correspondence of the leading men of the period, and throws a searching light on the Irish politics of the present day.

"Never did any book appear so opportunely. But, whenever it had appeared, with so lucid and graphic a style, so large a knowledge of the Irish question, and so statesmanlike a grasp of its conditions, it would have been a book of great mark."—*London Spectator.*

Great Singers.

Second Series. MALIBRAN—SCHRÖDER-DEVRIENT—GRISI—VIARDOT—PERSIANI—ALBONI—JENNY LIND—CRUVELLI—TITIENS. By GEORGE T. FERRIS, author of "Great Singers," First Series, "The Great German Composers," etc. Appletons' "New Handy-Volume Series." 18mo. Paper, 30 cents; cloth, 60 cents.

D. APPLETON & CO., Publishers,

1, 3, & 5 Bond Street, New York.

MISCELLANEOUS PUBLICATIONS.

NEW VOLUMES OF "THE INTERNATIONAL SCIENTIFIC SERIES."

Sight:

An Exposition of the Principles of Monocular and Binocular Vision. By JOSEPH LE CONTE, LL. D., author of "Elements of Geology," "Religion and Science," and Professor of Geology and Natural History in the University of California. With numerous Illustrations. 12mo. Cloth, $1.50.

"It is pleasant to find an American book which can rank with the very best of foreign works on this subject. Professor Le Conte has long been known as an original investigator in this department ; all that he gives us is treated with a master-hand."—*The Nation.*

Animal Life,

As affected by the Natural Conditions of Existence. By KARL SEMPER, Professor of the University of Würzburg. With 2 Maps and 106 Woodcuts, and Index. 12mo. Cloth, $2.00.

"It appears to me that, of all the properties of the animal organism, Variability is that which may first and most easily be traced by exact investigation to its efficient causes ; and as it is beyond a doubt the subject around which, at the present moment, the strife of opinions is most violent, it is that which will be most likely to repay the trouble of closer research. I have endeavored to facilitate this task so far as in me lies."—*From the Preface.*

"This is in many respects one of the most interesting contributions to zoölogical literature which has appeared for some time."—*Nature.*

The Atomic Theory,

By AD. WURTZ, Membre de l'Institut; Doyen Honoraire de la Faculté de Médecine ; Professeur à la Faculté des Sciences de Paris. Translated by E. CLEMINSHAW, M. A., F. C. S., F. I. C., Assistant Master at Sherborne School. 12mo. Cloth, $1.50.

"There was need for a book like this, which discusses the atomic theory both in its historic evolution and in its present form. And perhaps no man of this age could have been selected so able to perform the task in a masterly way as the illustrious French chemist, Adolph Wurtz. It is impossible to convey to the reader, in a notice like this, any adequate idea of the scope, lucid instructiveness, and scientific interest of Professor Wurtz's book. The modern problems of chemistry, which are commonly so obscure from imperfect exposition, are here made wonderfully clear and attractive."—*The Popular Science Monthly.*

D. APPLETON & CO., Publishers,

1, 3, & 5 Bond Street, New York.

MISCELLANEOUS PUBLICATIONS.

The Power of Movement in Plants.

By CHARLES DARWIN, LL. D., F. R. S., assisted by FRANCIS DARWIN. With Illustrations. 12mo. Cloth, $2.00.

" **Mr.** Darwin's latest study of plant-life shows no abatement of his power of work or his habits of fresh and original observation."—*Saturday Review.*

The New Nobility.

A Story of Europe and America. By J. W. FORNEY, author of "Anecdotes of Public Men," etc. 12mo. Cloth, $1.50.

"Colonel Forney has written an exceedingly clever and entertaining story. The reader will have little difficulty in surmising the import of its title: he will hardly need to be told that the members of the new nobility are those able, energetic, dauntless, and self-made men who are the strength and glory of this Republic. The dialogue is particularly bright; the descriptions of European life are vivid and truthful, attesting the extensive acquaintance of the author with society and letters."—*Philadelphia North American.*

Lady Clara de Vere

A Novelette. From the German of FRIEDRICH SPIELHAGEN. Appletons' "New Handy-Volume Series." 18mo. Paper, 25 cents.

The story was undoubtedly suggested by Tennyson's famous poem, "Lady Clara Vere de Vere."

Mary Marston.

A Novel. By GEORGE MACDONALD, author of "Robert Falconer," "Annals of a Quiet Neighborhood," etc. 12mo. Cloth, $1.50.

"The merit of the book does not lie in the plot, but in its thoughtful observation of the world we live in—what it is, and what it might be. 'Mary Marston' is a fine work, which may be read and pondered over with a view as much to improvement as amusement. There is nothing careless or slovenly about the drawing of any character, nor yet about any other part of the book. The author is evidently too thorough to send his work forth to the world in a condition less good than the best he can make it."—*London Spectator.*

D. APPLETON & CO., Publishers,

1, 3, & 5 Bond Street, New York.

MISCELLANEOUS PUBLICATIONS.

A History of Greece.

From the Earliest Times to the Present. By T. T. TIMA-
YENIS. With Maps and Illustrations. 2 vols., 12mo.
Cloth, $3.50.

".... It seems to me to be an uncommonly successful Grecian history, condensed yet clear and lifelike, abridged yet sufficiently full
and fresh, at once scholarly and popular; suitable to be used in
schools, and at the same time instructive and attractive to that large
class of intelligent readers who have not the time to read the large
works of Curtius and Grote. You have done well to bring the history
down so as to include *modern Greece*, and you have made this not the
least valuable and interesting portion of your book."—*From* W. S.
TYLER, D. D., *Amherst College.*

History of Herodotus.

An English Version, edited, with Copious Notes and Appen-
dices, by GEORGE RAWLINSON, M. A. With Maps and
Illustrations. New edition. In four volumes, 8vo. Vel-
lum cloth, $8.00.

Luke, Gospel History, and Acts of the Apostles,

With Notes, Critical, Explanatory, and Practical. Designed for both Pastors and People. By the Rev. HENRY
COWLES, D. D. 12mo. Cloth, $2.00.

Longer Epistles of Paul:

Viz., ROMANS, CORINTHIANS I and II. With Notes, Critical,
Explanatory, and Practical. Designed for both Pastors
and People. By the Rev. HENRY COWLES, D. D. 12mo.
Cloth, $2.00.

Divine Guidance:

Memorial of Allen W. Dodge. By GAIL HAMILTON. With
Portrait. 12mo. Cloth, $1.50.

The Art of School Management.

A Text-book for Normal Schools and Normal Institutes,
and a Reference-book for Teachers, School-officers, and
Parents. By J. BALDWIN, President of the State Normal
School, Kirksville, Missouri. 12mo. Cloth, $1.50.

D. APPLETON & CO., Publishers,

1, 3, & 5 Bond Street, New York.

CLASSICAL WRITERS.

Edited by JOHN RICHARD GREEN.

16mo, Flexible Cloth . . . 60 cents each.

NOW READY.

MILTON. By STOPFORD A. BROOKE.

"The life is accompanied by careful synopses of Milton's prose and poetical works, and by scholarly estimates and criticisms of them. Arranged in brief paragraphs, and clothed in a simple and perspicuous style, the volume introduces the pupil directly to the author it describes, and not only familiarizes him with his method of composition, but with his exquisite fancies and lofty conceptions, and enables him to see practically and intelligently what an expressive and sonorous instrument our tongue is in the hands of one of its mightiest masters." —*Harper's Magazine.*

LIVY. By the Rev. W. W. CAPES, M. A.

"Well deserves attentive study on many accounts, especially for the variety of its theme and the concise perspicuity of its treatment." —*London Saturday Review.*

VERGIL. By Professor NETTLESHIP.

"The information is all sound and good, and no such hand-book has before been within the reach of the young student. Any one who wishes to read Vergil intelligently, and not merely to cram so many books of the ' Æneid ' for an examination, should buy Professor Nettleship's scholarly monograph."—*London Athenæum.*

EURIPIDES. By Professor MAHAFFY.

"A better book on the subject than has previously been written in English. He is scholarly and not pedantic, appreciative and yet just."—*London Academy.*

SOPHOCLES. By Professor L. CAMPBELL.

"We can not close without again recommending the little book to all lovers of Sophocles, as an able and eloquent picture of the life and work of one of the greatest dramatic writers the world has ever seen." —*London Athenæum.*

Other volumes to follow.

New York: D. APPLETON & CO., 1, 3, & 5 Bond Street.

WORKS OF ARABELLA B. BUCKLEY.

Uniform in size and price with "The Fairy-Land of Science."

Life and her Children.

Glimpses of Animal Life from the Amœba to the Insects. By ARABELLA B. BUCKLEY, author of "The Fairy-Land of Science," etc. With upward of One Hundred Illustrations. 12mo. Cloth. Price, $1.50.

CONTENTS: I. Life and her Children.—II. Life's Simplest Children: how they Live, and Move, and Build.—III. How Sponges Live. —IV. The Lasso-Throwers of the Ponds and Oceans.—V How Starfish Walk and Sea-Urchins Grow.—VI. The Mantle-Covered Animals, and how they Live with Heads and without them.—VII. The Outcasts of Animal Life; and the Elastic-ringed Animals by Sea and by Land. —VIII. The Mailed Warriors of the Sea, with Ringed Bodies and Jointed Feet.—IX. The Snare-Weavers and their Hunting Relations. —X. Insect Suckers and Biters, which Change their Coats, but not their Bodies.—XI. Insect Gnawers and Sippers, which Remodel their Bodies within their Coats.—XII. Intelligent Insects with Helpless Children, as illustrated by the Ants.

Fairy-Land of Science.

By ARABELLA B. BUCKLEY, author of "A Short History of Natural Science," etc. With numerous Illustrations. 12mo. Cloth. Price, $1.50.

"It deserves to take a permanent place in the literature of youth." —*London Times.*

"So interesting that, having once opened the book, we do not know how to leave off reading."—*Saturday Review.*

A Short History of Natural Science and the Progress of Discovery,

FROM THE TIME OF THE GREEKS TO THE PRESENT DAY. For Schools and Young Persons. By ARABELLA B. BUCKLEY. With Illustrations. 12mo. Cloth. Price, $2.00.

"A most admirable little volume. It is a classified *résumé* of the chief discoveries in physical science. To the young student it is a book to open up new worlds with every chapter."—*Graphic.*

"The book will be a valuable aid in the study of the elements of natural science."—*Journal of Education.*

D. APPLETON & CO., PUBLISHERS, 1, 3, & 5 BOND STREET, N. Y.